Homo Technica

This edition published in 2021 by Analytical Media
in conjunction with Amazon

Book cover design: by Viv Loves Film
Copyright Book cover image "AI (Artificial Intelligence) concept"
by metamorworks/Shutterstock

PROLOGUE

'**The only way** to experience reality,' Peter Walker explained, 'is directly, through meditation. We soon realise that our world is created by our minds and not the other way around.'

We were sitting in an Italian restaurant in London. It was the end of summer. He was interested in my studies, and in my experience working with the latest Bio-Aid devices. For me, it was a chance to catch up with an old friend.

'Our mind is part of that universe, of course, intimately involved in its creation,' he continued, pausing to look into my eyes.

I asked Peter to tell me his experiences of the previous two years, in becoming an advisor to two governments and of his impending marriage.

'We talk every day, and the reunions are a delight,' he told me of the latter, laughing.

Over dinner and over the course of the next few weeks he shared it all. This is the story of his journey.

'A very personal one,' he emphasised. 'One that harnesses the wisdom of generations, as well as the successors to these.'

Peter raised his arm to show he was wearing an older-generation AR. I nodded to show I understood.

'After all,' he went on, 'these show us why we must continue to adapt and grow.'

Peter and I were re-introduced by a mutual friend, a lady called Ceiridh. He treated her over several months. This is how she described to me their first session:

"'There's an estuary, a river estuary. Flat land on the opposite bank. I'm standing near a pub. It looks like the River Exe; I'm looking west,' said Peter, holding my hands. He told me he recognized the place; he had holidayed there a year earlier.

'Oh yes!' I exclaimed. *'That was where I rented a cottage five years before. I lived there for about eighteen months. I'd been severely depressed after my divorce and needed to get myself together.'*

'The other thing I see is a young girl, aged seven. I don't know why,' he added.

'Oh, that was me too!' I shouted.

I told him it was the last time I was ever really happy. My father deserted us on my eighth birthday. Simply by closing his eyes and touching my hands, Peter had immediately identified the two seminal moments in my life."

'Be careful how you write my story,' he cautioned. Raising his arm, he added 'We all have access to these gifts but if they are used with bad intent, they may harm more than heal.'

ONE

A lone pianist is playing easy-listening jazz to a half-full restaurant in Brighton. Seated near a window, Peter is staring outwards at passing clouds. Lost, as so often, in endless internal dialogue, he hears only Margaret's final words.

'…into trouble along with those people she's hanging around with?'

Peter knows his wife is referring to their daughter Lilian, so he tells the AR device on his wrist to show the current status of his daughter's friends. Within a second holograms of their current or latest images appear in sequence, before disappearing moments later. Then he repeats his reply of the day before.

'See, they're all doing normal things. And I've looked into their past records, Margaret. There's nothing criminal in any of their activities. So, can…'

'I know, but they seem so… I don't know… coloured,' is her interruption.

Peter chortles, then scolds. 'Margaret, you just can't say that sort of thing!'

Lowered chins and stolen glances follow. Peter's bloated fingers twitch and dance; a gold ring is gripped while a wrist turns. Beneath their table's calm surface, his feet move to a soundless, frenetic rhythm. While they tap up and down, he lapses into another daydream.

Margaret is leaning forward, elbows and forearms resting on napkin and cutlery. A small nose and large brown eyes stare from below her curls like a resting owl. A fatty lump bulges from the nape of a neck Peter once longed to kiss. The pink AR on her wrist is an older, projecting model. She ends their silence.

'I'll take the duck as a main course, and the paté to start.'

Peter sighs, a sound echoed and mocked by a swirling gust that blows apart restaurant doors and lifts tablecloths, heralding the approach of a summer storm. A waiter smooths a corner flat before lowering their drinks.

'Maybe I shouldn't have said anything about the colour of her friends, but she doesn't have a job,' intones Margaret.

'Lilian's a consultant. She works for lots of different companies,' Peter reminds her.

'But she's not employed by any, is she? So how does she earn any money?'

'Lilian has contacts who introduce her. She's always at lunch or breakfasting somewhere. It's how they do things in New York.'

Peter knows little of their daughter's activities but feels obliged to defend her. 'I'm sure it's all above-board, Margaret. I have to go visit Pop again soon. On the way over, I'll spend time with Lilian.'

'Well, make sure you do. I'm fed up worrying so.'

Peter's wife is placated. Then he says, 'You shouldn't worry, dear. She'll be fine.'

Margaret's reaction is explosive. 'Don't go patronising me! All you ever do is work. I can't remember the last time you supported me. It's as if our children don't exist.'

Peter's agape mouth utters no sound. Margaret's eruption continues. 'And you're the worrier, not me. I've never known such a timid man. I should have listened to my mother. "A small man with small ambitions," she said. And she was right!'

Emptying her glass in two large gulps, Margaret replaces it with a thud. Peter glances around. Other diners avoid his eyes. His response is spineless: 'I'll make sure I go see her.'

The couple fall silent until the waiter delivers their first course. Peter's AR buzzes. He looks down at his wrist and stops chewing to listen. The tiny speaker in his ear crackles once before repeating:

'Mister Walker? Mister Walker, is that you?'

The caller's hologram is familiar, but Peter frowns, unable to recall his name. A second later, the caller's name is displayed.

'Mister Walker, I have bad news about your father. He's taken a turn for the worse. You must come straight away.'

Peter coughs, spurting crayfish onto the table. Margaret's eyes follow their flight. She mouths an unspoken question. Peter holds up a finger and gazes at her, eyes wide.

'What's happened?'

The caller is a nurse. He relates more details. The conversation ends abruptly. When Peter's hand returns to the table, Margaret reaches across and holds it with both of hers. A waiter is summoned, and a bill is paid.

Outside the restaurant, a line of distant purple clouds slides behind rooftops and chimneys. It is a summer evening and there is a steady breeze. The fresh seaside air cools Peter's skin. His shoulders shiver while he holds open the Robo-taxi door for his wife. Once inside the vehicle, Peter looks forward and speaks the single word 'home'. The couple's journey passes in silence.

Recalling over cocoa how much as a child their daughter Lilian loved her grandfather, Peter calls her before retiring to bed. They arrange to meet at JFK so they can travel the rest of the way together.

'It's close now,' he tells her.

TWO

Sarah stands, pulling up her panties. She flicks their elastic top with her fingers to fit them around her waist. Pushing down the cistern handle, she opens the unlocked door and walks out of the brightly lit bathroom while the toilet flushes noisily behind.

Seated in the centre of a king-sized bed, Lilian hears the toilet flush and abruptly ends the call with her father before looking up. She watches Sarah walk towards her, the fabric of a T-shirt moving in harmony with breasts bouncing lightly beneath. Her voyeuristic moment goes unnoticed by Sarah, whose eyes are adjusting to the softer glow of a single lamp.

Stretching one leg over both of Lilian's before kissing her lips, Sarah tells her: 'That was lovely. Truly lovely. Thank you.'

She lies down, placing her head on the silk pillow next to Lilian, who says, 'Thanks, babe. You are *so* hot I can't even begin to tell you! I'm so glad you moved in.'

'God, are you kidding me? I love this city. I'm so happy being here with you.' With her right hand, Sarah grabs hold of Lilian's bicep. Squeezing, she adds: 'You groaned a lot this time!'

Sarah leans her head into Lilian's shoulder.

'What are you working on?'

Lilian's lips brush the top of Sarah's head. She answers: 'I'm looking at how much we earned today. We made around two thousand dollars while we were making love.'

Pushing lightly against Lilian's arm, Sarah sits upright.

'That's obscene! Not the amount. It's your calculating that's vulgar.'

Lilian tells her: 'They're all new sign-ups. Those profiles you made are working brilliantly. And those photos of you too! Phew, they seem to attract more men than anything.'

Sarah's eyes light briefly on her new Dior handbag before staring through their bedroom's floor-to-ceiling window. The Manhattan skyline is clearly visible beyond the distinctive pillars and cables of the Brooklyn Bridge. Her response is deadpan.

'They're not all of me. Some I just scraped from the web. The best ones are of my friend Julia, especially the racier ones.'

Her face lit by its glow, Lilian stares at the screen. Pointing, she continues: 'It was a great idea to hire a professional photographer. All these guys think they're in with a chance of dating a supermodel. They're falling over themselves to buy upgrades. It's a joke! I'll bet half of them are over fifty and gross.'

Sarah giggles as her gaze returns to her partner. 'Ha! Yes, or else they're spotty little boys who've stolen dad's AR.'

Lilian laughs. 'We should offer links to gambling sites. We'll get a cut for the intros. I'll look into it tomorrow.'

Sarah's eyes move to gaze at the view outside. 'Yes, do that in the morning. And look for an apartment in Manhattan too, like you promised.'

Laughing anew, Lilian asks: 'Are you sure you want to move again?'

Sarah pouts playfully. 'Yes, and why not? You can afford it… and me. Right now, though, I think you should give me some more loving.'

Lilian grins. 'What – *again*? Are you sure?'

The fingers of Sarah's right hand toss her hair. She lifts up the bedsheet with her other hand. 'I love this city,' she exclaims.

THREE

Next morning, a Robo-taxi delivers Peter from Waterloo to a grey house in Holborn, a former merchant's home converted long ago to office suites. Drowning momentarily in a swirl of street noise, calm returns to its entrance hall as soon as external doors close.

Peter manoeuvres his suitcase up the stairs and through an over-sprung door. He looks up to greet Janet, his smiling assistant. Peter has forgotten her recent illness. When he asks how she is feeling, her reply surprises.

'I'm feeling much better, thank you.'

'Oh, that's good!'

Peter settles into his small, second-floor office and sits behind a chaotic, cluttered desk. Paper notes, files and half-completed crossword puzzles are piled over its walnut and leather surface, spilling haphazardly onto a surrounding parquet floor.

Moving slowly to protect a sore hip, Janet stands still to deliver bad news as briskly as possible.

'I'm afraid the landlord has been on the phone again this morning. We're behind nearly three months now. I've already had a call from those bailiff people. And the cleaner's refusing to work unless I pay him something this week.'

Peter's response is crisp.

'They'll all have to wait. I've just heard my father's dying, so I'm off to California today. If I can get a flight. Use that as an excuse; it should keep them quiet for a bit.'

Janet's response is sympathetic. Peter then outlines his travel needs. 'I want to stop off *en route* in New York, to collect my daughter. She's coming to San Francisco too. There should be a flight at lunchtime.'

Peter enquires: 'No word from Alistair, I suppose?'

As though sipping on vinegar, Janet's lips purse.

'No, I've heard nothing from your partner.'

❧

Check-in at Heathrow is routine. Peter answers questions from an automated system about the purpose of his trip, where he will be staying, whom he will be meeting, and how long he will be away. The answers to most of these are checked against details provided and collated by his bank, which has for more than two years been required to pass details of all financial transactions to a Government monitoring system.

A secondary system reviews a summary from the trackers built into Peter's AR device and his car, which confirms he has visited no locations that are under active surveillance, nor has he attended any meetings deemed disruptive or 'potentially' so. A flashing-red warning alerts a supervisor that Peter came within twenty yards of a closely monitored climate regeneration activist only one day earlier, before displaying a brief video clip of their passing. He approves the system's suggestion for a resolution.

Peter is then asked if he has ever met the unidentified woman, whose passport picture is shown on the display in front of him. When he answers 'No', the video feed of his answer is analysed by a facial-reaction system, which confirms that Peter has answered the question truthfully. A second later the gates are opened, and Peter is allowed to pass through and into the departures lounge.

Settled on board the upper deck of his plane, Peter counts the number of rows to the emergency exit before sitting back to accept a pre-flight drink from a smiling stewardess. Cocooned and comfortable, he falls asleep before the plane leaves the ground.

❧

Peter arrives in New York tired and dehydrated. In the glass-panelled arrivals hall of JFK airport, his daughter Lilian is waiting. Dressed in faded-leather jacket and over-size, grubby black shoes, she is taller than her father, so bends her knees to greet him with a hug.

Flicking a loose strand of brown hair behind her ear, Lilian answers Peter's first question less than honestly.

'I'm well, thanks. Been really busy, setting up a new B2B bitcoin trading-site. Split up with Julie though. Yeah, a couple of weeks ago. No particular reason, just reached a natural end, I guess.'

Taking control of her father's suitcase, Lilian points towards the doorway behind them. Peter comments on the part of her answer that he understands.

'Sorry to hear about Julie. She seemed a nice girl. Pretty too.'

Lilian's response sounds both wistful and laconic, even though she has had more than one girlfriend since.

'Yeah, a rare combination, but life goes on.' She asks: 'Any more news on Pop?'

'He's stable, but it's only a matter of days.'

After only a second's thought, Lilian tells him: 'Listen, Dad. I'm not coming over with you. I just have too much to do. I'll come over in a couple of days, OK?'

Peter fails to hide his disappointment. Before he can say anything, Lilian adds: 'Come on, I'll walk you to your terminal. We can chat on the way. It's just as easy as taking the automated walkway, and I don't need to get back for an hour or two yet.'

After fruitless minutes spent trying to persuade his daughter to change her mind Peter acquiesces and they begin to walk. He is glad of the chance to stretch his legs but soon begins to perspire. Half-way to the terminal he persuades his daughter to stop for a coffee. Once seated he tells her: 'Mum's more worried about you, you know.'

'Why's she worried? I'm doing fine. I love it here,' is her only response.

'Maybe, but she worries about the kind of people you mix with,' Peter explains.

Lilian's reaction is immediate.

'My friends? Hell, Julie used to snort the odd line of coke, but that's about all. And the guys I know are as straight as they come: investment bankers or consultants, mostly.'

Raising palms in supplication, Peter softens his tone.

'I'm sure they're all fine young people, but she's your mom: she'll worry no matter what you do. I told her I'd find out more.'

'Okay Dad, sure!' Lilian frowns. 'Your flight leaves at three, right?'

Her father nods a response. Lilian spends the rest of their time describing her web portal as an online marketplace for buyers and sellers of rare commodities, transacted in many different types of online currency.

'It's nearly developed. We plan to launch in a couple of weeks. That's why I'm needed here.'

Satisfied that his daughter is working on a real project, Peter remains silent. By the time he boards his flight his thoughts have returned to the condition of his father.

&

When she returns to her apartment in Brooklyn, Lilian collects a beer from the fridge then goes straight into her tiny study. Overlooked by an apartment block opposite, little of the fading sunlight cheers the room.

She looks at her wrist, making the room's videowall glow. The wall shows her website's URL address in one corner, with the words

Hot Girls for Hot Guys at centre in large, lurid red typescript. Lilian speaks a password. She carries on talking, creating a new female member with the name babe69playgal and the tagline *Hey, I know loads of sxc games...x*

Lilian sips at her beer then continues dictating, watching as the words appear on her screen.

I know what a man likes... a woman who loves sex. I love to taste, smell, lick, touch, stroke, pinch and bite (gently). I love to listen when your breathing gets ragged and intense. I love to tease and be teased. Mirrors can be fun. Oh, and please leave the lights on...

Selecting a video of an attractive brown-haired girl, Lilian swirls her hand to paste it into her 'Member's Info' section. She dictates a message to non-paying male members.

I'm originally from Tampa, but in New York at the moment. I'm willing to travel and want to meet up with guys or girls. I'm after new experiences. Drop me a line and let's party...

The system converts her message into a different female voice with a Floridian accent, as if from the newly created babe69playgal. Once Lilian is satisfied, the message is delivered.

Lilian leans back in her seat and lights a cigarette. She has the same rounded eyes as her mother. They stare at the screen from between high, prominent cheekbones and a thin line of eyebrow hairs, edged in fashionable gold. After breathing in a few puffs Lilian speaks again, beginning with the name picco-gal and the tagline *I'm looking for a serious relationship.*

Her cigarette burns out in the ashtray, releasing a final burst of brown smoke as it expires. A half-hour later Lilian is interrupted when

Sarah arrives, excited after an afternoon's shopping in the city. Bags are emptied, boxes discarded, and shoes and clothing spread around the apartment.

FOUR

On a crystal-clear day, Peter's mood lifts while he savors the view below his flight from JFK across the breadth of mainland USA. Sights range from the multi-colored, multi-textured sprawl of New York, over countless miles of greenery bisected by lines of tarmac, and onward past farmed circles that fade into many more miles of pale, arid desert.

Three hours later the plane is cruising above spectacular volcanic peaks, whose imperious cones rise from a carpet of mist: vast white limpets peering from a rolling, pale sea. Approaching San Francisco, it passes the Golden Gate bridge, whose iconic beams and stanchions mark the end of his journey's pageant.

Peter sweats freely while striding along the moving walkway to the main terminal building. He passes speedily through immigration then collects his bag before riding the automated railway to the rental car lot. A few minutes later, he is being driven to a hospital downtown.

His father has chosen to die at St Luke's, the hospital on Cesar Chavez Street where both men were born. Peter takes a deep breath of city air before hastening in through the main doorway. He needs guidance from his AR to find his father's room. As he approaches a young, blond-haired woman passes by and smiles. A tiny tremor rumbles in his gut. Peter turns and watches from behind until she disappears from view.

The door to his father's room creaks as he pushes it ajar. Pop's head turns. A craggy, ashen face beams a broad smile at his only child.

'Hi, Son!'

Ignoring the stench of antiseptic, Peter bends forward to kiss Pop on his cheek. He stands back and remarks: 'But you look so well. Why on earth are you in here?'

Although the reply is somber, Pop responds in the same light-hearted tone of voice.

'Ha! If you'd seen me retching blood this morning, you wouldn't have said that.'

For a half-second, Pop stares into Peter's eyes. He notices his son's shortness of breath, as well as a faint, unhealthy tang of halitosis. Pop's eyes flicker for a moment, the only physical sign of his intuition at work. Peter asks: 'Have they told you how long you've got?'

His father issues an abrupt condemnation.

'No! Pile of bullshit from the doctors, as usual. Even the automated ones just talk crap. The nurse is a good lady though. She told me I should expect to live another two days at most. That's not too bad, and it's kind of what I already knew.'

'Are you in pain?'

Pop's face brightens.

'No, they've given me plenty of morphine. You're lucky I'm here. In a minute I may fly out the window and round the chimneypots again.'

Peter sits. Pop changes the subject.

'Tell me, how are your wife and kids?'

As he listens to Peter's rambling answer, Pop nods his head up and down before asking: 'And you?'

'I'm well. Working hard, as always.'

Pop has no wish to listen to palliatives.

'You're not well, son. I can see you work too hard and you're too stressed. It'll kill you if you're not careful.'

'I want to slow down but, how can I?' is Peter's rejoinder. 'I'm the breadwinner.'

So close to death, Pop has no wish to argue. When he speaks again, his tone is conciliatory.

'I guess so, Peter. But you can't bake bread if you're laid out flat in a wooden box.'

'I know, Pop. I *will* slow down, soon.'

Pop speaks in the softest tone his gravelly voice can manage.

'Hold my hand, son. Listen to me. In your whole life I've never seen you so tired and stressed as right now.'

'Look where I am, Pop.'

'There's no joy in your eyes, son. *None.*'

Father and son hold hands for a long while, neither man desiring to speak. Pop directs an unseen, unconditional love to his son.

'Life's too often about coping and enduring, unnecessarily so. Your wife and kids aren't your reason for living anymore, are they?'

'No, I guess not. I'm not sure what is.'

Pop is unimpressed.

'You should give up work and go find yourself. Your kids are grown up. Last time I met Margaret, I told her to stop sponging off you. She gives you nothing in return.'

'You're right, I don't love Margaret anymore. But I can't just leave her. And I won't abandon the kids.'

Pop's head returns to his pillow. He speaks calmly.

'Well, you have to find a way to live your own life, son. And you'll have a little money when I'm gone.'

The men return to their silence. Aside from an occasional hubbub in the corridor, a hiss of air-conditioning is all that can be heard. Eventually, Pop raises his hand, motioning for Peter to pull open a drawer. He asks for a key from inside, which Peter fetches for him.

Holding the key between thumb and forefinger, in a weakening voice Pop announces: 'Take this and go back to my house. When you get there, I want you to do something for me.'

He checks Peter is paying close attention.

'Up in the attic there's an old trunk. Wooden with leather straps. You can't miss it. Inside are all my papers, plus something I want you to read carefully and completely. My granddaddy passed it on to me.'

'What is it, a book?'

'A journal. A *special* journal,' Pop explains. 'It's near two hundred-years-old. It speaks to me still.' He adds a coda: 'It sure helped me to crystallize my life.'

'Okay, Pop. I'll fetch it out later. For now, though, I'll just stay right here, and you can tell me what you've been doing these last weeks.'

For the next half-hour, Pop talks of his recent paintings, pausing frequently to catch his breath, his eyes occasionally closing into a short doze. In return, Peter skips lightly over his financial problems and tells of his daughter's achievement in starting a commodities-trading website.

Pop is unsurprised by Peter's blindness to Lilian's real activities. He views the delinquent morality of his beloved

22

granddaughter as his life's greatest failure. He is also aware of Peter's own situation but declines to question him further, certain those problems will eventually work out. Growing tired, his attention wanders. No longer able to remember a sentence begun moments before, his eyes close.

Peter leans over and whispers 'Goodnight, Dad' into his ear. Feeling proud and pleased that his father has no self-pity, he closes the door silently behind.

☙

Less than a mile away, Angela returns to her apartment home. She knows her mentor is gravely ill and may not live through the night, so pours herself a glass of organic white wine. Consciously using the past tense, she reads the label and says aloud, 'This was one of his favorites too.'

In melancholic mood she settles onto the sofa where, remembering their visit to the winery, she recalls: *It was such a beautiful day. I wanted to kiss him.*

Angela stares at the wall. A half-glass is consumed before she picks up a folder to work on her assignment. A week earlier Maureen asked her to write down all the reasons why she wishes to join their Order. So far, there is only one line on the page.

After holding a pen in her hand for more than a minute, Angela tosses it lightly onto her coffee table.

'It's hopeless,' she says, 'How can I be expected to concentrate on anything while Jeff's…'

Her voice trails away. A tear forms, wiped away by slender fingers. She walks into the kitchen. Then, realizing she is standing there with no memory of why she entered, Angela returns to the lounge. Another large gulp of wine is taken before the glass is placed on an edge of the coffee table, adjacent to her AR. At the same instant, the device chirrups.

The surprise causes her hand to jerk, causing a few drops to spill. 'Bugger!' she exclaims before picking up and holding the device between two fingers. She looks at its glass face and speaks a single word: 'Hello.'

'Hello, Angela,' says Maureen. 'I hope you don't mind my calling you so late.'

Angela's back straightens. She clears her throat before responding.

'No, of course not Maureen. It's lovely to hear from you.'

'I have the feeling you are struggling with your assignment. It's understandable, given the situation with Jeff.'

'Yes,' admits Angela, 'I am finding it hard to concentrate.'

'Well, put that task on hold for the moment. There's no urgency. Its purpose is only to make you reflect on what you want to become.'

'Thank you, Maureen. I would prefer to return to it in a few days' time. Once Jeff…'

Angela's hand rises to her nose, stifling a sniffle.

'We're all upset,' Maureen tells her. 'It won't be long now.' A moment later she adds 'But he's led a wonderful, fulfilling life. Try to marvel at that.'

Angela's head nods up and down several times in rapid succession. Maureen waits for her movements to end.

'There's something else I'd like you to do for me instead, if that is okay?'

'Yes. Yes, of course,' Angela replies, still flustered.

'It's Jeff's son Peter. He's arriving today from England.'

'I saw him arrive at the hospital, just an hour ago,' Angela confirms. 'I'm sure it's him. Their faces are so similar.'

'Good,' Maureen responds. 'I would like you to get to know him too. Help him to settle in. He will be spending a lot of time here in the city, more than he knows. And of course, there's his grieving to overcome. I know it's a lot to ask of you, but it's most important that he feels at home.'

'I'll be happy to do it,' Angela replies. 'Honestly, I would.'

Maureen thanks her.

'And please, Angela. Feel free to call me at any time. It's wrong to struggle through grief alone.'

The two women exchange a few more words of comfort before ending their video call. A second later Angela hears Jeff's voice sound inside her head.

'He's so exhausted,' it tells her. 'World-weary, just as I feared.'

Her response is instant and sympathetic, felt a mile away by her dying mentor, an unconsummated love.

Hector Martinez brushes the hoodie away from his face, to focus on a list of names on the wall.

'Apartment seven-twelve,' he reads aloud. Hector sighs and presses the buzzer with his gloved hand.

Upstairs, Sarah looks at her wrist and answers: 'Walker residence.'

'Good evening, ma'am,' Hector says. 'I have your Chinese food.'

'Great, I'll buzz you in. We're on the seventh floor.'

A minute later, Hector emerges from the elevator. Wearing slacks and pullover, Sarah is already waiting at the open apartment door. He hands over the cardboard box. She points the AR on her wrist at him before turning away. His AR beeps an acknowledgment of payment and he turns to depart. The door closes behind her with a clunk.

Soon seated on the pale leather couch adjacent to Lilian, she swallows a piece of half-chewed chicken and crosses her legs.

'This was a great idea. But why don't they deliver by drone?'

Lilian lifts a bundle of noodles to her mouth. Chewing quickly, she swallows with a gulp.

'They're banned here.'

Sarah announces: 'I think I've found our new apartment. I've arranged a viewing for two o'clock tomorrow.'

'Okay, babe. That's great. Great. You're sure you want us to move?'

Sarah places her chopsticks together and looks up.

'I'm sure. It's nice here, but there's so much more for us to do in Manhattan.'

Lilian jabs her fork towards Sarah's plate. 'Okay. So, hurry up and eat! We promised to meet up with Larry and Tina in Meatpacking in about an hour.'

Sarah's jaw drops. 'I'll never make it. Better call and tell them we'll be late.'

Nonchalantly chewing, Lilian leans back. Her words are reassuring.

Later that evening, the couple arrive at the Skyline nightclub in Little West 12th Street. They are shown in without needing to queue and make their way to the bar. By this hour the DJ is working hard, and the club is bouncing. Larry and Tina order them all tequila shots. Their drinks are downed in a single gulp.

Within an hour, all four are stood outside on the covered terrace, laughing and high as kites. Larry walks off to order more drinks, prompting Sarah to visit the bathroom. Tina wastes no time.

'So, Lilian. You get my last message?'

'I sure did, babe. When're you thinkin'?'

Born of a black father and Latin mother, the girl's dark features draw inwards as she pouts.

'I'm free all day, tomorrow. Larry's staying at my place but he's out of town 'til late. Why don't you come by?'

Lilian lifts a near-empty glass to her lips and sips. She leans towards Tina.

'I'll be there around lunchtime. I have to go to a meeting in Midtown, but I won't be late. What you see in him anyway? He's way below your cut.'

Tina laughs as she answers: 'He makes me happy and he knows how to make a girl smile, if you know what I mean. Leastways he did. But he don't have no reason to be out of town. I think he's sniffing round some other chick.'

'I'm sorry, babe. Never mind, I'll make it up to you tomorrow, on his behalf.'

The pair smile at each other and, arrangements made, their bodies relax and separate. Tina asks: 'So, how's it all goin'? Your business, I mean.'

'It's going fantastic, absolutely fantastic! Everything's coming together; it's like a perfect storm. We're going to be so stinking rich I can't tell you.'

Recoiling from the gushing flow of words, Tina steps back and slides a finger across the side of her mouth. She speaks as her eyes flick sideways.

'That's great, babe. Now, watch up, here they come.'

Sarah and Larry return, carrying two drinks apiece and laughing each time the drinks spill over the glasses' edges. Larry remarks: 'That was fun. We had to drink some on the way back here. This place is buzzing. Let's drink these before bustin' some moves!'

Sarah is suspicious of the awkward body language between her friend and girlfriend.

'Are you two okay? When we left, you were both laughing your heads off.'

Lilian shrugs it off.

'Hey, we're great. Now hand me that drink.'

Sarah and Tina make momentary eye contact while Larry hands the glass to Lilian. A moment later, Lilian's AR buzzes. Peter's face appears.

'Hold up a minute everyone, I'll take this outside.'

Lilian answers as she arrives at the quiet smoking area on the terrace.

આ

Lying wide-awake in the spare bedroom of his father's house, Peter is summoned to the hospital but arrives too late. In the early hours of the morning, Pop passes away. Peter removes the cover from his father's face, then sits unmoving beside him for an hour before kissing a cool cheek and speaking a tearful goodbye.

Once outside, Peter takes a deep breath of the fresh morning air, then another. The sky is lightening over the hills to the east. He walks over and sits in the rental car to call his wife. Margaret's sympathetic but sleepy afternoon voice soon vexes. He ends their call with an excuse about needing to tell Lilian.

After being driven around for a few blank minutes, Peter tells the car to pull into an empty car park at East Beach. He is shocked by the height of the newly raised tidal barrier that now dominates the shore, the city's most visible response to increasingly turbulent, rising seas. He climbs to its top to stare at the Bay. He calls his daughter while strolling along its broad promenade in front of the redeveloped Ghirardelli's.

Lilian's tone is comforting.

'Dad, I'm so sorry. I didn't think Pop would just die like that.'

'It's okay; it happens,' replies Peter. 'How are you?'

Lilian's answer approaches genuine concern.

'I'm fine, Dad. Are you okay? And are you staying in SF?'

'Yes. There're all his affairs to sort out, people to notify and so on. I'll be here a few weeks at least.'

Lilian is impatient to return to her friends.

'I'll come over soon to help out. I have a couple of things here to sort first. I'll let you know when.'

After the call ends, Peter walks a disconsolate half-mile further along the shore before returning to his car, and then his father's house on Russian Hill.

FIVE

The guest bedroom is plainly decorated. White walls act as a backdrop to contemporary paintings and native-American sculptures, all dominated by a large bay window facing east. Its three lower panes reveal a lightening, panoramic view of water, islands, bridges, and shoreline.

Warm rays from a rising sun stir Peter from a fitful slumber. Eyes blink as his body eases upwards, surveying in a blur the scene across the bay. As if happening in some other place or to someone else, events of the previous day have passed in a dream.

A cold realization of loss strikes without warning. Tears stream onto Peter's cheeks before dropping onto a stuttering chest. The product of years of graft and disappointment, his stoic detachment is lost.

A half-hour later Peter walks into the hallway and lowers the loft hatch, scaling its extending ladder to reach the boarded floor. He is clutching a key. Brushing imagined dust from his clothes, Peter surveys the attic. There is only one trunk. Inside lies a file of papers resting atop a journal, just as his father described. Papers and journal are lifted out and carried with care down to the lounge, where he sits on the expansive sofa to read.

Documents read and for the moment discarded, Peter turns his attention to the journal. Inside its front cover is an inscription: *This book belongs to Wilhelm Scheffler, now knone as Jake Green.*

Behind the first page are three sheets of paper yellowed with age. On the first, the newest, Peter recognizes Pop's handwriting.

Son,

If you are reading this then I am either dead or close to it.

First of all, I must tell you I die a happy man, proud of you and the decent life you have led. I may not always have agreed with what you've done, but I know you always acted in the best interests of your family and I admire you for that. I guess I just want to repeat: I'm proud of you, son.

This journal is my most valuable bequest to you. I'm sure any money I bequeath will be helpful too, especially as I know more than you realize of the difficulties you face. But money has only a passing value. The words in this book are immortal, their wisdom invaluable. Fully absorb the message they impart, and your life will be transformed.

I hope you find it as useful and heartwarming as I have.

With love always

Pop

Peter's eyes well up once more. Instead of indulging the emotion, he sits bolt upright and places the page back inside the book. Peter discards the two other loose papers, anxious to open the journal. His heart sinks when on its inside he reads the poor spelling and grammar of a childish scrawl, which begins: *This is my journel my name is Jake an im now twelve. I cum from Hamberg tho I can hardly remember it.*

'Surely there must be more to it than this?' thinks Peter. An ill-educated child's observations would hardly have interested his father, no matter how long-ago written. He flicks over a single page. At the top, in a more legible scrawl he reads: *Don't believe what they tell, that my kin give me to them folks as is now my family…*

Although his interest is piqued by the hint of a kidnapping, Peter still does not believe such a story could be all the book contains.

He flicks over fifty pages, to the middle of the journal. Below a pencil sketch of a man and boy, in a fine scrawl that covers half a page he finds written there these words: *The old man's touch was light, barely even perceivable. Within an hour I began to see the world differently. I felt the energy that flows through us all, connects us all. Not only to other humans but to all life, sentient and non-sentient.*

I felt uplifted, as if a secret world had just been revealed. A world I always knew existed but that I had somehow forgotten. My belly felt its vibration, my ears heard its song, and my heart sang with joy!'

Reading those words, Peter feels his heart lift, although it is many weeks later before he realizes why. His heart-rate leaps. His breathing increases in frequency and his eyes flicker and search around, as if afraid he may be found out. His skeptical mind is soon telling Peter the passage is fanciful nonsense, but the warmth spreading through his body is undeniable.

As his breathing and heart slow, Peter's hands and arms lower. His head drops and he drifts into a brief meditation. He soon falls asleep. The face of a blond-haired woman appears in his dream, one he recognizes but is unable to name: a premonition, or ancient memory perhaps, but one he thinks no more of.

The journal falls from his lap onto the floor, waking him. After shaking his shoulders and lifting his head, Peter retrieves it. Satisfied it contains far more of interest than he feared he clutches the journal tight to his chest, wrapping both arms around it.

He does not open the journal again on this day. Such a book should be read slowly, with deliberation and with each page savored, so all its wisdom is absorbed, he decides.

SIX

In the kitchen of Tina's New York apartment, she and Lilian have finished their preliminaries and are standing toe to toe, lips touching. About to disrobe, both are flush with excitement at the prospect of imminent, illicit sex. As their lips part, Lilian steps one foot back and takes hold of both straps of Tina's dress.

'Here, let me lift that.'

Tina wriggles her hips, a more seductive movement than Lilian was expecting. Tina allows her dress to be pulled over her head, revealing new, red underwear. Resisting the urge to tear off her remaining clothes, Lilian pushes once more against her body. Her tongue darts across Tina's sweet lips.

'I love the feel of your skin. It's color too,' enthuses Lilian.

Losing themselves in shared passion, the two women make love for over an hour. After a loud, shivering orgasm Tina shouts: 'God! No man ever knows how to do that.'

For a minute after, neither wants to move. Conscious once more of the imminent return of her boyfriend, Tina says, 'That was fantastic, and you sure as hell are one lusty mother. But we should get dressed. I know he won't be long. He called to say he was returning early.'

Lilian rolls to one side, exhaling loudly. 'That was wild! And kind of exciting, knowing we might get caught.'

Tina laughs. Sitting up, they look into each other's eyes. Placing her right hand onto Lilian's cheek, Tina says, 'Yeah, edgy. But kinda foolish too.' Withdrawing her hand, Tina adds: 'Come on; my ass is gettin' cold. Let's get dressed and I'll make you a coffee. Or would you prefer somethin' stronger?'

Lilian sits upright, grabbing for her shorts and panties.

'Coffee's fine. Are you sure he won't guess?'

Tina fastens the buckle of her bra strap. Reaching for her panties, she stands.

'About us? If he walks in, we'll tell him you just dropped by to see us, and I made you a drink while you wait. So long as you don't look all guilty, he won't suspect.'

Lilian lies back while she pulls up her shorts. Fastening the buttons, she announces: 'That was fabulous. I'd love to do it again.'

Lips parting into a smile, Tina pushes a long index finger towards her.

'Okay stud, but not today.'

Within a minute, both are dressed. Tina stands in the kitchen while Lilian goes to the bathroom to pee. As Lilian closes the bathroom door, the front door of the apartment opens and in walks Larry, Tina's boyfriend of two years.

Larry is twenty-seven years of age and, conscious of his white-trash background, dresses to emulate the social-media heroes he follows daily. White and black sneakers stride across the apartment, feet splayed wide below long legs covered in shining, electric-blue trousers. A loose-fitting jacket sways from side-to-side as he walks, so wildly that the lower end of a zip-fastening snags on its fabric just below an elbow, creating a bat-like wing. Entering the kitchen, he walks up to Tina and kisses her on the cheek.

'Hey, babe. That's great, I'll take one of those.'

Tina air-kisses him in return but retrieves the cup from his hand.

'I'll make you another. Lilian just showed up looking for you. She's taking a leak.'

Larry's chin rises. At that moment, Lilian opens the bathroom door. As her head appears, Larry asks: 'Yo' man, what you doin' here?'

Lilian tries to hold her friend's gaze but fails. Her eyes drop to the floor for a fateful instant.

'Oh, I just came over to see you, talk some business. I thought you'd be home.'

Instinctive rather than expert at interpreting body language, Larry knows his friend is lying.

'So why didn't you jus' call me?'

Lilian shrugs.

'Surprise, I guess.'

Larry's eyes narrow, certain now that his friend's lie is not trivial. In as casual a tone as he can muster, he continues: 'You sure you ain't been up to no good with my girl here? I know what you's like!'

Desperate to recover the situation, Lilian forces a nervous smile and moves towards him.

'Hey, man, you can't be serious. Lighten up!'

Larry pushes her away.

'No Lilian, I ain't cool on this. That's what this is, ain't it? You two been humpin' behind my back!'

Lilian anxiously tries to reassure her friend.

'No! That's not true.'

Larry rarely carries his gun. Lain unused in the glove compartment of his car for weeks, it is only pressed into the rear of his belt on this day because he decided on an impulse to clean it. Pulling the .22 calibre revolver from his backside, his intent is only to look cool and in control, by scaring her for banging his girlfriend.

'Well hump on this, bitch!'

A second later, watching with a childish glee the look of shock on his friend's face, Larry's intent crosses a line. He swipes at her face, narrowly missing her left cheek. Lilian falls. Tina reacts by jumping onto his back, screaming while reaching to pull the gun from his hand. The instant before Tina's scream, a sickening crack sounds from below: the rear of Lilian's falling head strikes the edge of a chair, breaking her skull.

Lilian groans for a second with a mystified, far-away look in her eyes before lapsing into semi-consciousness. Tina knocks the gun from Larry's hand and drops to Lilian. Turning her head to Larry, sheshouts: 'You damn fool, you've killed her! Call an ambulance! Now, damnit!'

Larry looks at Tina, then at the gun lying on the floor. Angrily, he roars: 'I should shoot you both, bitch.'

He strikes her hard across the face with the back of his hand, then retrieves the gun before running out of the front door.

Holding Lilian's cheek in one hand, Tina lifts her arm and shouts, 'Emergency!' The automated operator answers at once. Tina speaks amid tears.

'I need an ambulance... Here, at...'

Tina confirms the address then tells the operator that Lilian is losing a lot of blood and they need to hurry. She returns to tending Lilian, trying to stem the loss of blood by pressing hard against the rear of her head. Lilian drifts in and out of consciousness, groaning while Tina labours crying over her.

As soon as the emergency team has stabilised her and stemmed the flow of blood, Lilian is taken to a hospital emergency room.

৵

Called from her home and comforted on arrival by Tina without explanation, Sarah is soon seated in the waiting room outside. Her gaze alternates between the floor and an absent-minded study of notices on the wall. Occasionally she stares for a moment at the nearby receptionist or at her friend. Tina's awkwardness under her gaze tells Sarah everything she needs to know about what has happened.

After a few minutes of silence, a nurse approaches the two women and asks: 'Which of you two is a relative?'

Sarah looks up at the standing nurse.

'I am, I guess. I live with her.'

'That's good enough. Would you sign for this? It's for her handbag and AR.'

Sarah reaches for the proffered papers. The nurse hands her a pen and explains while Sarah signs. It is the first time she has used such an old technology in months, so Sarah has to concentrate with effort to make her hand move. The nurse is reassuring.

'Don't worry, she's in good hands. The doctors are saying they expect her to survive, although it'll take a few months for her to fully recover. The new procedure they're using seems to be working well, but it's a good job you called in so quickly.'

Tina explains: 'Yes, I was there when it happened.'

The nurse looks across at Tina and adds: 'There's a policeman outside. I expect he will want to interview you both, but I'm sure that can wait.'

The nurse turns on her heels. Her shoes squeak as she walks back to her desk. Sarah places Lilian's AR device into the handbag then turns to Tina.

'Would you mind fetching me a coffee? I feel faint and I'm so thirsty.'

'Of course not,' Tina says. 'You should have asked before.'

As soon as Tina is out of sight, Sarah retrieves the purse from Lilian's handbag. Inside one section is the scrap of paper she seeks – written backwards the password numbers for Lilian's accounts. Sarah makes a careful note of the numbers by speaking them into her raised AR.

She returns the purse to the handbag just before hearing the click of Tina's returning heels. Unheard, Sarah mutters: 'That's your bank details, and I'll read your texts at home later.'

❦

Once Lilian is out of danger, Sarah returns to the apartment. Seated in the lounge, Sarah speaks to her AR. Before the connection is effected, she drops her hand to cancel the call. That is the closest Sarah comes for several days to telling Lilian's parents about their daughter's injuries. They are serious but probably not life-threatening. *So, they don't need to know yet*, she reasons.

Turning around, Sarah walks over to Lilian's workstation. Courtesy of her unexpected access to Lilian's passwords, she transfers all the money from Lilian's main business accounts into her own bank account. Within an hour Sarah has sent a message to all of Lilian's clients notifying them of a change of web address and offering them a reduced monthly price if they switch within forty-eight hours. The introductory offer of one free, live chat proves especially popular.

Within seventy-two hours, almost all of the clientele has switched to her newly registered website. While Lilian remains unconscious in hospital, Sarah changes all the passwords then deletes all her files.

SEVEN

Funeral arrangements and meetings fill Peter's next days. Dinner of a half-bottle of merlot and a tasteless, microwaved beef ragù is interrupted when his son arrives to stay for the single remaining night before Pop's funeral. They have barely spoken in months but, after a slow start father and son reminisce for an hour before retiring. His son tells him that Lilian won't be coming.

'She called to tell me, now she won't even answer my calls. What is it with her?'

Peter is disappointed but not surprised. He apologizes on her behalf.

'Don't worry, she'll come round. She loved him too. I expect she just wants a little quiet time.'

By the time his son rises the next morning, Peter is dressed in black and ready for the funeral. He spends a half-hour leafing through the journal while his son showers and breakfasts. Three pages in, Peter reads a margin note written by the author, clearly added well after the main text.

The overland trip was merciless. A plodding, endless trek for most, a harsh and painful experience for others, death for quite a few. For me it was a journey begun in unspeakable darkness that ended with light in my heart. And, ultimately, access to the universal goodness that pervades and connects all things.

Peter has pondered no more than a few moments upon any spiritual matters since leaving university over two decades before. He leans back, relaxing into a sofa cushion. Closing his eyes, Peter recalls how his father helped him to understand stories from the Bible as allegories, metaphors or hyperbole. Later dabbles with Zen Buddhism, Jainism and even Sufism during his degree studies, occasionally discussed with his father around a dinner table, he barely remembers.

Denied with vehemence at the time, Peter now finds it easy to admit he turned his back on a spiritual life from weakness; a need to feel secure, grounded in a material world he could touch and sense around him. That youthful fear of being different, of being 'found out' has since, he realizes, defined his entire life.

Interrupting his contemplation, Peter's AR buzzes. Margaret does not bother with a greeting.

'Why haven't you answered before? I've been calling for hours. There are letters here, threatening to throw us out of our home. One even mentions court action, and another tells us a date you're due in court! What's going on?'

Peter has received many warning letters but is surprised proceedings have reached court so soon. He feigns innocence.

'I don't know dear. I haven't seen them.'

'There must be some mistake, a stolen identity or whatever they call it'.

Five thousand miles away from her wrath, Peter decides now is a good time to tell Margaret the truth.

'There's no mistake, dear.'

Margaret begins a lengthy outburst, concluding: 'One of the letters from Barbells Bank says you owe them three hundred thousand pounds, and uses phrases like "Central London Bankruptcy Court". It looks pretty serious to me.'

Peter explains that his business is bankrupt, and the bank will likely demand the sale of their home.

'Last year, I had to give a personal guarantee to get a loan,' he says. 'It's how the banks get around limited-liability legislation.'

A tearful Margaret agrees to take no action until Peter returns home. No mention is made of the day's funeral.

'It will all be okay,' he assures her, before saying goodbye.

His son has overheard the conversation, but only asks: 'You're ready to go?'

They leave the house together. The service is being held at a church, a nineteenth-century stone edifice complete with steeple and slated roof. Gathered outside when they arrive is a large crowd of varying age, gender and origin. One group is standing in a circle with hands joined performing a near-silent ceremony; others talk quietly. Peter is annoyed: the funeral director made no mention of another service taking place at the same time as Pop's. As they approach the church door, a flustered director steps forward to meet them.

'Mr Walker, you should have told me you anticipated so many mourners. We will not easily fit them all in.'

Peter's eyes widen and lips part. Mystified, he struggles to find words.

'You... you mean... these people are all here for my father? I had no idea he was so popular. Who are they?'

The director shrugs.

'Oh! I assumed you would know. Well, there's no time to worry about that now, Mr Walker. We must get the service under way.'

The director raises his arm.

'Please, take the pew at the front on the left.'

A moment later, he addresses the crowd.

'Ladies and gentlemen, if you would kindly make your way into the church, the service is about to commence.'

Inside the church, a large photograph of a smiling Pop sits on a tripod stand, greeting mourners as they enter. The church is full to capacity, with many of them standing.

While people are still being squeezed in, Peter hears strange noises from behind: chanting in whispers and the sound of crystal bowls singing long, ethereal notes. Peter looks around, mystified. He requested only the usual hymns and psalms; no mention was made to him of any prelude. The sounds die away when the church organ pipes a loud, mournful tune. His son's attention diverts to a young woman in the row behind. At the end of each hymn and during each eulogy, he turns to smile.

At the end of the service, a brief outburst of wailing and chanting follows the priest's closing remarks. The congregation files into an adjacent church hall, where over a hundred mourners stay to chatter and console over prepared food and drink.

Peter mingles while his son singles-out the young woman, spending the next hour solely with her. The new couple leave quietly in her car a little after noon.

When the crowd in the hall begins to thin, a woman in her late twenties approaches Peter, holding out a slender hand. Slim and blonde, wearing a dress and color-matched shoes with low heels, her lips widen into a smile. *A little like Pac-Man*, is Peter's reaction *but attractive, with fine bone structure*. While he admires her rounded face and porcelain skin, Angela introduces herself.

'I knew your father very well. He was an inspiration to me,' she adds.

Peter's attention moves from the woman's long hair to her eyes. He is lost at once within their blue depths. A second later, Peter manages to ask how she knew him. Angela's reply is effusive.

'He was a great man, so professional, so aware of my feelings and so helpful to me, I can't even begin to tell you.'

Peter's expression turns to surprise.

'I'm sorry, I don't really know what you mean. I thought he just wrote for various magazines?'

'He's helped many of us here. Didn't you know? He was special. He *is* special. He told me he had a son.'

Angela's light-brown eyebrows narrow.

'He was very proud of you, although he worried you work too hard and don't have much of a life.'

An ironic laugh escapes Peter's lips.

'Well, that's true enough. But how did you meet him?'

'He was recommended to me by a friend,' says Angela with a warm smile. 'Most of us met him that way, leastways the ones I've spoken to.'

There is a brief pause while a caterer offers canapés. Peter asks: 'If you don't mind my asking, what do you do for a living?'

Angela's bright blue eyes focus on his, attempting to divine the level of kindness or concern they reveal. She answers with reluctance.

'Now? I'm a healer. Your father led me to it.'

The revelation surprises Peter, who has no idea Pop did more than dabble in counseling.

'He healed you and then taught you to heal, you mean?'

Angela decides Peter's eyes reveal a kind but troubled soul. Her shoulders relax. She is happy to do as Maureen asked.

'Yes. I was a sales rep before, a horrible job. I was miserable – beyond miserable – when I met him.'

By now the gathering has melted away. Caterers hover, waiting for them to depart. As they leave the hall, Peter asks: 'Would you mind if we meet again? I'd like to know all about what you do, and what Pop did.'

'Pop?' Angela looks confused. 'Oh, you mean Jeff. I'll be delighted. Here's my number; call me anytime.'

Angela first offers her card and her hand but then gives him a brief peck on the cheek. For a moment Peter imagines himself pulling Angela's body tight to his, pressing a desperate tongue deep into her opened mouth. He blushes. It is their first ever kiss, freely given within minutes of meeting.

They stride down the pathway to their respective cars while a cadre of Mexican caterers clears up behind.

EIGHT

His son departs the following morning. As soon as he is alone Peter summons the courage to call Angela. There is no answer. He leaves a message, explaining he would like to meet up with her. He passes the rest of the day in front of an unwatched television screen. Drowsy contemplations turn to his daughter, thence to the journal. He reads a short passage:

'Mona asked me about it only once. I told her how amung the chaos a man with scarf across his face aproached me. 'I think I saw your family at the end of this street,' he reassured me. So I followed the man there. Fine trails of smoke and burning ash blew past us as we walked. Then he pointed to an alley and shouted 'They must be down here.' I was scared by now. My lips trembelled when I spoke 'I.. I don't think I want to go down there.' I heard voices ahead. I cried out 'Papa, is that you?'

By the time he reaches that question a deep-seated unease, another premonition, has welled up inside Peter's belly. He decides to read no more until later in the day. While dozing, the premonition becomes a sullen foreboding. Images of bankers and creditors as vultures and jackals drift through his mind, waiting to pick clean the innards of his now minimal wealth.

The notion of disappearing enters Peter's head, of retreating to a quiet, hidden home in Oregon. Doubting he could afford to maintain

Pop's house he wonders if any legacy could stretch to a cabin in the wilderness. In contrast to his stressful situation in England, the idea of a quiet, remote life in his own Walden is immensely appealing. Peter soon decides he would be unable to disappear for long, but resolves to remain in California as long as possible, whatever his financial situation.

Margaret calls again and immediately begins firing her questions. Peter explains again that his business is bankrupt. She has already heard the words but hearing them confirmed anew Margaret is shocked.

'But how has it happened? It was making money not long ago.'

Calmer than he expected, Peter quietly explains all: the emergence of automated accounting and the closure of many accounting firms, his lack of drive, his partner's failure to bring new sales or investment, the bank's insistence on personal guarantees, and so on.

'My partner is taking specialist advice, but I'm pretty certain the bank will force us to sell our house,' he says.

Margaret holds back tears while Peter says he will update her within a day or two. She does not ask when he is returning home.

৵

At that same moment, lounging in Peter's office in London is the bow-legged, black-haired and brown-eyed figure of Alistair Bachelor, wearing a pale-grey suit and tie. His mouth opens to welcome his guest, revealing oversize white incisors. As soon as Janet leaves them alone Alistair explains: 'All the debts are in his name and all the cash is already in our account.'

His guest is Terry Payless, a tall, overweight insolvency advisor from Stevenage, who confirms: 'I've done the deal with the administrators. They're only interested in getting their fees. We'll have no problem.'

The two men have struck a deal that, by placing the company into the hands of a corrupt and co-operative administrator, eliminates Peter's shareholding by forming a new business. Five days later, Terry is seated in Peter's office, telling him by video: 'There's no place in the new company for you, unless you can provide at least some of the cash,' he says.

Shocked by this news, Peter's voice rises in pitch and volume.

'What! What do you mean? You mean you own my company, and I don't?'

'Only if you can't come up with the money. You need about fifty thousand pounds by tomorrow, I'm afraid.'

Peter is red-faced with anger.

'You *know* I have no money. You're supposed to be acting on my behalf, not stealing the company from me. You're just a damn carpetbagger.'

Terry responds coolly: 'Well, if you study my engagement letter carefully, I think you'll find that I've agreed to help the company, not you.'

Peter shouts: 'You scoundrel. How could I have trusted you? Your professional body will hear of this, and the press.'

Knowing it would emphasize Peter's powerlessness, Terry remains seated. Speaking in a low voice, he says, 'I would be very careful about making such threats if I were you.'

When Peter calls home, Margaret's reaction to the news is bitter.

'You useless man! My mother was right after all. If I'd known it would come to this, I wouldn't have put up with you all this time.' Her short diatribe ends with a command.

'Stay in America. Don't come back here, I can't stand you around me anymore.'

NINE

By early evening Peter is seated at a corner table in a dingy bar, miles away from the apartment, contemplating a taxi ride back to make a video plea of clemency to his wife. His AR chimes. The voice at the other end is faint, but recognizable.

'Peter, it's Angela. I hope you don't mind my calling you.'

His face brightens. Self-consciousness prevents a lapse into excited babble. He turns towards the wall and lowers his voice.

'No, no, of course not. I'm delighted. How are you?'

'I'm very well, thank you. But how about you? I have an uneasy feeling you're in trouble.'

'Well, yes, you're right! Things aren't going very well at the moment.'

Angela is sympathetic.

'I'm so sorry. That's what I sensed. Is there anything I can do?'

Turning towards the bar, Peter leans forward and fondles a glass with his free hand. Pensive, he answers: 'Not at the moment. Matters just have to take their course.'

Angela asks again, 'You're sure?'

Peter is desperate to give Angela a chance to help, to involve her in his life in some way. He starts speaking without knowing what words will ensue.

'No. Well, yes, actually, there is something you can do.'

'Yes?'

To his surprise and delight, words issue easily.

'Well, I could really do with some company right now.'

Angela answers: 'I'd love to meet with you,' then hesitates. 'But do you mean professionally, or socially?'

Confidence growing, Peter continues: 'Very much socially. I mean I'm interested in what you do, of course, but I need a friendly face. I'll buy you dinner.'

Assuming Peter has implied he wants a sexual relationship, Angela replies with care.

'Well, maybe just for a drink but, of course. Would you like me to come round now?'

Peter gladly accepts the offer. Angela's voice returns to its initial, business-like tone.

'Stay positive and I'll look forward to seeing you very soon. Let's say, in one hour.'

Peter stares at his AR, seeking to overcome a lingering doubt that he has dreamt their conversation. Eventually satisfied it was no dream, a smile spreads across his face.

'Sometimes,' he reflects, 'fate really does seem to lay its hand.'

Draining his glass, Peter stands up and leaves. After speaking into his AR, he is whisked to the apartment by cab within a few minutes.

Before he arrives a message from Margaret tells him she will be filing for divorce the following day. Peter wonders briefly if it would be better to postpone Angela's visit but decides to proceed. While he waits, he absent-mindedly fingers a crossword book then retrieves the journal from his briefcase and reads a few more pages, selected at random.

It proves to be the story of a trek westwards across America, written by one of the first to complete the Oregon Trail in a covered wagon. As Peter reads, he realizes there are two tales. One is the author's physical journey: a boyhood kidnapping and forced adoption, through hazard and wearied exhaustion into premature manhood. The other tale records the boy's internal journey, from wide-eyed innocence through love, acceptance and forgiveness and an ever-growing awareness, to eventual spiritual knowledge and healing powers.

One passage in particular catches Peter's attention. He reads the words aloud, over and over.

Weve reachd a huge grass plain they call Powder Valley. Smack in the middle is a single tree, felled but with leeves still on. It must of bin cut down only a day before. I want to cry out loud. It feels like the hole land for miles around is cryin out for its loss. As if its very heart lies broken.

Peter has no idea why, but the words make him gasp. Palpitating and short of breath, he feels as if he too has been sliced in half. Fainting into blackness, his internal world sinks as if falling into the same valley's soft, fertile earth. He drifts into a short sleep, disturbed by dreams of falling and tumbling. When he wakes, he stares at the ceiling in gloomy contemplation of the ending of a life so slavishly built over more than two decades. His AR buzzes to tell him that Angela is at the door.

They exchange air-kisses and are soon settled on the oversize sofa facing the window, enjoying the view over the darkening Bay: a clear blue eastern dusk, invaded by a slow-moving army of purple and russet-orange clouds dispatched by the setting sun. A shared moment is devoted to absorbing the majesty of the scene, which ends when Peter remarks: 'Beautiful, isn't it? I never tire of this view. I love it here, you know. I always have.'

Angela smiles.

'Then you should stay. There's nothing keeping you in England, is there?'

Peter admits there is not and tells her he intends to stay as long as possible. They are soon swapping memories of Pop. Angela says, 'He was such a good judge of character, you know. He could size people up in a moment, literally. I miss him.'

After a number of reflections are shared, Peter is keen to learn more about her. He asks: 'Tell me more about how you spend your time, Angela?'

'Just the usual. I go to my classes, I go to work, I spend my weekends shopping and cleaning. I don't seem to find the time to do much else.'

He asks about her clients.

'They come to my office,' she explains. 'They're all genuine people: seekers after truth, or looking to get well, or get over some trauma. It's a vocation: part counselling, part intuition and part psychotherapy. You are either drawn to it or not, but there are times it just feels like work.'

In return, Angela asks about his business, then adds: 'I know you've had a tough time. I can see it in your eyes.'

'Some parts of it are tough,' admits Peter. 'I've effectively lost my business, although it should be called legalized theft.'

Angela interjects.

'I have the feeling it will turn out to be a good thing. Your father told me only a week before he… He told me that he hoped you would get out of it.'

Peter raises his eyebrows and ponders his response for a moment.

'Well, I would certainly like to do something different. It's time, and my wife wants a divorce too. So it's probably now or never.'

Peter opens a bottle of wine and they settle closer. At Angela's urging, he continues talking about himself.

'I've had to face up to who or what I am: my failings I mean. The good news is, I think I may begin to like myself again, and I haven't felt like that for years. Not since I was an arrogant young man!'

A nervous half-laugh issues from Peter's mouth. Angela's quizzical, sympathetic expression reassures him.

'I had ideals and ambitions when younger, of course,' he continues. 'Over the years they just disappeared. One minute they were there; the next time I thought about them I was twenty years older and they'd gone. Poof!'

An experienced enough counsellor to know she is hearing only a partial truth, Angela's chin lowers. Her neck draws back and lengthens, then her eyes stare into the distance. Peter fails to notice how well-practiced are her next words.

'It's very easy to become alienated, distant I mean, to lose sight of who we are.'

Peter continues: 'I think my real disappointment is that I no longer have any clear ambition; no goal.'

Continuing her free consultation, Angela offers reassurance.

'You brought up a family. That's worthy, and challenging.'

'That's true, although I'm not sure how well I did,' acknowledges Peter. 'After all, my son is a mystery and my daughter… she rarely speaks to me in any depth. It must have been hard on them both. I'm sure they were aware years ago that Margaret and I had grown apart.'

Angela asks: 'Why did you stay with her?'

'In all honesty Angela, I don't really know. It was easier, I guess. The arguments, the blame, the divorce, it's all such a lot of hassle. I guess we both felt it was easier to just grin and bear it.'

'The effect on your children is just as bad, either way. In some ways you know Peter, it's better for them if you split. They will have known they were being brought up in a home without love. I know, it's what happened to me.'

Angela's hand rises to cover her mouth.

'Oh, I'm sorry Peter. That was thoughtless of me. I…'

'It's OK Angela, it's the conclusion I've reached too. It's why my daughter is as she is: utterly lacking in concern for others. It's because we never gave her the love she needed.'

Peter and Angela sit still, quiet for several minutes while they absorb the information about each other that has just been shared. Far from dissuading her, Angela's interest grows. She admires his ready admission and is attracted to the intimacy created by his honesty. For the first time she wonders what it would be like to make love with him. She decides to change the subject, to move their relationship forward.

'So, what next? Do you have any idea what you'd like to do?'

Peter's reply is plucky. 'I'd like to know more about what Pop did. And I'd like to get to know you better of course.'

Angela's response delights him.

'I'm sure we can manage both of those.'

Both laugh aloud. Peter is excited but perplexed. *Why is this young woman so interested in me? It can't be money, or is there something I don't know about her?*

The pair continue talking well into the night, jesting and toying, and opening a second bottle of wine. When their discussion moves to politics, Angela removes her shoes, lifts her bare feet onto the sofa and shifts them under her buttocks. She answers Peter's question about politicians.

'Yes, they're all soundbite-driven. It's how our media works, even with the extension of citizen participation and online assemblies. People are too busy; they don't pay attention for long enough. You can understand it, and we deserve it.'

Peter bends down to remove his shoes too. He moves on to tell Angela about the journal – without declaring its source.

'I've been reading a book about the Western pioneers and what they were seeking. I expected it to be freedom and adventure, but their aims were mundane: better land, escape from boredom, and so on. And America still looks makeshift. There's nothing permanent here: the houses are cheap and wooden. It's like nobody ever decided what this country is all about, nor believed they would remain.'

Angela's response is short and defensive.

'We call that freedom. You can build what you want, within reason.'

Influenced by alcohol, Peter says, 'A freedom that's become a license to be obese, lazy, over-bearing, and absorbed with the trivial, you mean?'

Angela's neck stiffens, but a smile soon parts her lips.

'Aren't we all? But I learned from your father that our inner self is where we need to explore – not the outside world.'

'That's what I mean,' says Peter, animated. 'I believed the myth. I was expecting the journey West to be allegorical, an exploration of import and meaning. Instead, they just wanted cheap land! It's as if America never had a soul, and still hasn't.'

Angela declares: 'Your father used to say that the spiritual nature of this country is changing, but slowly. And it's up to us to ensure its progression continues.'

'Progression to where?" shrugs Peter.

'Towards bliss, I hope.'

As a young man, Peter read many books on Buddhist and Hindu philosophy, both academic and populist, so he recognizes both the statements and principles Angela uses. For a moment, Peter feels disappointed that his father, whom he knows was a learned thinker, has only explained such shallow knowledge to this young woman who was obviously a pupil of his. He is relieved when he hears Angela's next words.

'We are here for a purpose, whether we choose to do anything about it or not. Your father, for example, was an amazing healer. A fully-realized human being.'

The previous day Peter had read an enlightening passage from a later page in the journal. It is still fresh in his mind.

I soon learnt we all have a direct connection to all other beings, and to everything in our universe. Not only human beings but animals too, even the trees we see and the grass we walk upon.

We access this connection by deep contemplation or meditation, perhaps even by devotion. We do so directly and with ease, as soon as we realize our world is created by our minds, not the other way around.

There is no need for ceremony, or initiations, or rites, or any other kind of dressing. And there is no single, personal God. The creation of one is a simple allegory, intended for those who cannot yet comprehend more.

Instead, there is a universal energy, a Love of which we are all an integral part. All our thoughts, emotions and even the physical bodies of everyone and everything are all linked, and a part of this, across space and across time. And we all share our Love through the bounteous, eternal vibration of this energy.

Prior to reading that passage, memories of his father's long-ago explanations of self-realization had remained suppressed, deliberately hidden and ignored. Reading that passage has begun the process of re-discovering all that knowledge. And now, hearing a young woman use those same words, he is at last willing and able to recall much more.

Angela continues to extol his father's virtues.

'He knew things about us, about our past and our previous lives. And he knew of our future lives too. He even told me that you and I would be together one day, as we are now!'

Wondering how much of the truth of that is driven by her knowledge of what his father predicted, Peter is doubtful. He returns to the obvious.

'But he's dead now.'

Angela's smile is indulgent.

'Yes, his body is dead. But his spirit lives on. And not only in you and me and our memories of him. In future, it will live on in another body. When he is ready to create another one.'

Peter has always known his father was a philosopher, someone who reads books to gain an intellectual understanding of concepts and ideas. He has read many of his father's published articles. Until his funeral he had no idea his father was also a healer, someone who learned from, shared and used his direct experience of the divine.

The deep theoretical knowledge of his father was a part of the reason why Peter rejected a spiritual life. Having meditated while so young and having no desire to become an academic, he realized that intellect without experience was useless to him. Hearing now of the extent of his father's abilities, Peter wonders how much of his own journey Pop knew all about in advance. Tears well up as Peter wishes he had spent more time with him.

Angela says, 'You know, Jeff could look at a person and know within an instant why they were suffering. Not just its physical manifestation; he could tell the underlying emotional and spiritual ailment, if there was one. Straight away, without even asking a question. That's what he did with me. Meeting him was a transformational moment in my life.'

Stroking both sides of his Adam's apple with his right hand, Peter ponders her words before saying, 'He always knew when I was unhappy. It was uncanny, as if he was reading my thoughts. But the rest of what you say – I thought people went to live in caves for years before they could do anything like that? Pop never did so.'

Excited by his son's recognition – albeit limited – of Pop's qualities, Angela rocks her weight forward onto her feet and then back onto her buttocks. She suppresses an urge to yell before speaking.

'He didn't need to. He was an *Intuitive*. He could listen to your unconscious thoughts, to everyone's. It was a gift he had from an early age. And he had other talents too: foresight and clairsentience, most strongly.'

'I never knew that.'

'He hid it from his family or at least from most of them,' Angela continues. 'I don't know why. Except he told me you would one day be the same, just like him. "Once you've completed your journey into darkness," he used to say.'

Mouth ajar, Peter stares vacantly into the distance. His thoughts travel to the hospital room where he last saw Pop.

'He knew I was tired the last time I saw him. So tired, I really mean world-weary! It felt pretty dark.'

Angela surprises Peter again.

'Yes, he told me so that same night. Not in words. He was a telepath too, even while asleep and close to death. He was overjoyed you were at the end of your journey downwards and ready to move on, even though he knew he would not live to see it.'

This last statement is a step too far for Peter, who has never experienced and therefore does not believe in telepathy. He changes the subject. The pair continue to talk long into the night, often of Peter's physical and existential ailments. In each case Angela offers her analysis, prefaced with the qualification that compared to his father, she is only a trainee.

Peter finds it difficult to accept what to Angela is second nature: that physical ailments and emotional stresses are linked to and derive from spiritual ills, and vice versa. During their conversation, he remembers his youthful knowledge that all three of our bodies – material, emotional and spiritual – interact. The memory, as well as memories of his father's explanations, is discovered with regret; a regret that stems from his lack of courage, his turning away from a spiritual life.

Reiterating that Pop knew Peter was on a divergent path, Angela explains that people spend their lives moving toward and away from their goals or purposes.

'It is part and parcel of being human,' she says. 'Pop believed everyone has access to his abilities, but unless you are one of a lucky few, it almost always requires diligent meditation and self-knowledge, and sometimes dedicated guidance.'

Peter is weary and yawns deeply; he struggles to follow her meaning. Angela registers his yawn. She stretches her arms wide.

'Oh, it's so late! I must be going.'

Peter persuades her to stay, by saying, 'Oh, please stay. There's a guest bedroom. You can't drive home now. Look at the time.'

Outside, the skies cloud over during the remainder of the night. By morning, both can see from their respective rooms that it is raining heavily.

TEN

Peter wakes to the sight and sound of rainwater washing against the bedroom window, and the repeated drip onto its ledge of an overflow from the gutter above. Staring for a moment out of the wide window, even Alcatraz Island is obscured from his sight by mist. He stands to adjust the striped pajamas twisting around his backside.

Once seated, Peter represses an urge to rise and wake Angela, who is asleep in the guest bedroom. *She must be tired after our talking until the small hours*, he reasons. Instead he leans over to the bedside table and retrieves the journal, placed there the previous day. Keen to know how the story progresses, he lifts the edge of his bookmark, opens the page and begins to read.

He is struck by the first passage.

Course I knew that Mona was still alive. But I knew too that she was in mortal peril. Thinking no more on why, I held the round stone given me by the old Injun. At once I saw clear as day he was on his way to render assistanse to her. He smiled an looked up when he saw me watching. There are times you just now something is true. This was my first time I felt it too.

By now accustomed to the author's gradually improving grammar and spelling, Peter focuses upon the content of the paragraph and its message. It is the first time in the journal there is any mention of clairvoyance.

It must be a new skill he has acquired, thinks Peter. *I wonder how?*

Confounded at first, a moment of illumination follows: the boy's words confirm what he heard with skepticism from Angela the evening before. Although he questioned their veracity when delivered by her, he instinctively trusts the words of this written source. For a split-second, Peter even suspects the confirmation is itself pre-destined, that the journal's words somehow follow his own life rather than pre-date it. As yet, Peter has no understanding of how the *Universe* manifests such incidents. But this inkling is the first sure sign of his rapid spiritual progression.

Peter's analytical, puzzle-solving persona soon takes over. His analysis is unspoken but clear.

The young man accepts that truth is absolute, that another person's welfare or danger may be known and seen in advance and remotely, and that one can telepathically communicate information, in this case a confirmation of assistance, over a great distance!

As usual, analysis promotes doubt. Peter decides that, except for the assurance of his father, he has no reason to either believe or to question the earnestness of the young man's written words. Thus, he suspends judgment about his certainty of only a few moments before. Peter fails to recognize this regression, the inevitable and first backward step of many during his forthcoming spiritual journey.

Peter rests the open journal across his legs and closes his eyes to contemplate. At that instant, Angela knocks on his bedroom door. She has been lying in bed awake for some minutes, feeling pleased that

66

their evening had gone so well. Peter places his journal under the bed then grunts a response. She opens the door and steps inside the room.

'I hope you don't mind. I was just wondering if you want some breakfast before I leave?'

Peter opens his eyes and smiles broadly.

'That would be lovely, thank you.'

While she stands by the door, Peter tells her how much he enjoyed their evening together, then asks the first question that comes to him.

'Angela, do you think we've all lost our way?'

Her quizzical, interested look shows him he has her attention. He elaborates: 'I mean, were people more spiritually aware a hundred years ago?'

Angela is unprepared for such a question so early in the morning. Her first reaction is to make light of it, but she changes her mind the instant before her mouth opens.

'I don't know. I've heard it said.'

Earnest and intense, Peter continues: 'It's just that, the book I'm reading… well, the author takes it for granted that the things you told me last night are true. About Pop I mean; his talents.'

Angela walks over to the bed and sits next to Peter. She leans over, touches the top of his receding hairline with her palm then draws her hand around the side of his face and under his chin, lifting it. Lowering her face towards him, Angela's lips brush softly against his before pulling back an inch.

'You are a sweet man. And you're the first one to truly listen to me, ever.'

For the first time in years, Peter is invigorated and assertive. He places his arms around her back and pulls her gently forwards. Their mouths open as they kiss, and their tongues meet as lovers for the first time. Breakfast is forgotten as Angela first disrobes then undoes the buttons of Peter's pajamas. She chuckles.

'These are not the sexiest garments I've ever seen. You'll have to let me take you shopping later, okay?'

Peter babbles, 'For pajamas?'

Angela pulls the jacket from his back then slides next to him, under the duvet. Their naked bodies touch.

'No! I don't think you should wear anything in bed from now on. Except me, of course.'

Cool as a wood-nymph, Angela makes tender love for an hour with Peter who, by contrast, pants and sweats. Following initial penetration, she remains awhile on top then lies submissive and beguiling beneath him. They achieve deep and genuine orgasms only a few moments apart.

After resting in each other's arms, Angela rises.

'I'd love to see you later, but I must go home. First though, what would you like for breakfast?'

Peter wants to say something witty, but nothing comes to mind. He asks for tea and toast, adding: 'And of course, you naked next to me once more.'

Angela laughs as she leans to place a finger on his chest.

'Ha! I'll cook you breakfast and watch you eat it, but I've no time for any more of that this morning. If you behave, though, we'll see what happens this evening.'

The tone of their relationship set Angela disappears to the kitchen.

Peter can soon smell vegibacon and eggs being cooked. Lying in bed, he stares at the ceiling. An anticipatory grin spreads across his face. The chirping of his AR interrupts his musings. He picks up the device from the floor and, seeing that the call is from his wife, answers it with reluctance.

'Hello, Walker here.'

Margaret sounds annoyed.

'Surely, Peter, you know it's me.'

Peter resumes his usual meek manner.

'Yes dear, I suppose so. I...'

'Well listen,' she interrupts. 'Presumably you're staying at your father's apartment?'

Peter confirms. She re-treads their last conversation: she wants a share of whatever wealth he inherits and will take legal action if necessary. He responds wearily: 'Perhaps we can discuss it when I return. I haven't decided what to do with the apartment yet.'

Margaret expresses surprise.

'Oh, I assumed you'd sell it.'

'No, I may decide to live here.'

'Well, you'd better keep me informed,' Margaret says impatiently. 'I want a share, and don't you forget it.'

Peter ends the call and drops his AR onto the floor. A second later, Angela returns.

'Here you are, breakfast in bed. Did I hear you talking to someone?'

Peter explains. Angela sighs.

'Well, that's hardly fair! Surely this apartment and the rest of your father's things – they're yours?'

Between mouthfuls, Peter says, 'I believe so. Maybe not. We'll see what transpires.'

Angela is perplexed. Turning away, over her shoulder she says, 'Enjoy your breakfast. I'll just fetch my coffee.'

After removing the tray to the kitchen, Angela returns to Peter's room to kiss goodbye. They arrange to meet during the afternoon.

Peter lies alone in bed reflecting on an eventful eighteen hours. At first enlivened by the afterglow of lovemaking, he later wonders why a younger woman like Angela would find such an older, overweight man attractive. *I'm neither handsome nor am I wealthy, and I'm so much older* is his last thought before rising.

ELEVEN

One week after Lilian's injury, Sarah celebrates the overnight success of her new, lone venture by going to a nightclub with her two new employees. Over drinks at the bar, Sarah laughs aloud as she recounts tales of Lilian's insensitive lovemaking.

'Thank God I won't have to fake any more orgasms for the bitch,' she shouts, to the amusement of everyone around.

By the end of the evening, Sarah has convinced her friends to spend the next few days recruiting more girls to work for her 'dating-and-sex' business.

'Listen,' she tells them, 'we can all work virtually on this. I'm going back home to Denver for a few weeks. I'm not sure when I'll be back.'

Early the following morning, Sarah gathers together her belongings and packs them into a large case. After sitting at the foot of their bed while taking one last look around, Sarah raises her AR and calls Lilian's mother.

Margaret answers within moments. Sarah feels barely a twinge of conscience as she belatedly informs the distraught woman of Lilian's condition.

&

While searching through his father's papers in hope of finding a will, Peter is interrupted by the *chirp-chirp* of his AR, followed by the anxious voice of his wife.

He takes the first available flight to New York, where he spends the next few days at the hospital bedside of his daughter. Lilian is seriously ill but already, one week after being admitted, is out of immediate danger and recovering well. Peter is told that the fragmented pieces of Lilian's skull were easily located and removed or refitted by the surgical robot, that a new procedure has been used and that her recovery is being aided by keeping her in a coma.

While Peter endures long, lonely hours of waiting at his daughter's bedside, his mind returns to Angela. He struggles to remember the softness and scent of her skin, and the way her mouth creases into a smile. *It's as if something wonderful and important has started and then been immediately interrupted*, he thinks, before muttering aloud: 'Like a false start at a racetrack.'

Peter stays at his daughter's now vacant apartment in Brooklyn, where he sleeps in the spare bedroom. Clean and devoid of discarded clothing or character, it feels antiseptic – an annex to the hospital he visits twice a day. Following each visit to his daughter, he calls Margaret with an update. The calls drag on as Peter attempts to answer her many questions with more than 'There's no change.'

Within two more weeks, Lilian recovers consciousness. Lilian has no memory of her fall and has to be told what happened. It is the following evening before she wonders why Sarah has not visited her, when the only person at her bedside is Tina.

'That bitch Sarah has blocked me from contact,' she tells a shaken Lilian. 'And she seems to have left New York. At least, no one I know has seen her for days – no, *two weeks* now! Almost the whole time you've been in here.'

Tina's subsequent attempt at light-heartedness falls flat.

'Jeez, maybe the cold bitch just don't like hospitals, 'n she'll show up again when you're home.'

Lilian manages a smile in response, the first since her fateful fall.

&

Margaret arrives in New York carrying a letter, which she hands to Peter without explanation. While they are together, a review meeting is held with Lilian's surgeon. During this, her mother and father learn for the first time that the new procedure involved fitting a tiny new nanobiotechnology AR device, a 'Bio-AID' as they term it, into Lilian's head and arm 'to more quickly repair any residual damage to her parietal lobe.'

At the time Peter has little understanding of what this statement means, and no knowledge whatever of its significance. Only after asking are they told that her partner Sarah authorised the procedure. Peter leaves that evening and returns to San Francisco.

TWELVE

Margaret spends most days and evenings at the hospital, reading magazines or a novel to her daughter. Peter has arranged to call them each evening for an update. On the few occasions when Lilian is awake and cogent, he also manages to exchange a few words with his daughter.

She is soon able to walk, initially with a supporting frame. After six weeks under hospital care, Lilian is discharged to continue her recovery at home, where she is cared for by her mother and a daily call-in nurse.

Lilian knows Sarah has left her, but another week passes before she realizes she has been locked out of all her systems. It takes a further two days of frustrating communication with suppliers before she is able to recover her accounts and discover that Sarah has stolen all her customers, and her money. Source and deliverer of all her recent wealth, the business has disappeared.

This second shock results in a relapse. Lilian stays in bed for a few days, feverish and incoherent, before recovering. Her mother remarks to Peter, 'She lies completely still for hours, eyes staring into space.' Once stable, Lilian has, in the words of her mother, 'A faraway look in her eyes, as if she has seen things no man or woman should see.'

During the nights, Lilian rises frequently from her bed to stare out of the window at the moon, sometimes for hours at a time. And during the day, she adopts a habit of sitting completely still for an hour or more, not moving and not communicating in any way.

Over the next few days, Margaret notices that Lilian has an increasing habit of finishing her mother's sentences, as if she already knows what is about to be said. More than once, Lilian even seems to know the next action or movement that her mother is about to make.

'When you come back from the bathroom,' Lilian says one morning, 'would you mind bringing me my rings? I left them on the shelf.'

Margaret had only just become aware that she needed to pee and had not yet consciously decided to do so. By listening with focused attention to her mother's subconscious thoughts, Lilian learns that Margaret had no sexual contact with her husband for several years before his departure. Lilian also learns details of the nurse's private life and sexual predilections, hitherto hidden.

During the subsequent week, Lilian discovers by accident that not only can she hear the conscious and subconscious thoughts of her mother and nurse, but she can plant ideas into their subconscious, the part of their minds that drives emotions and actions. Idly wondering if her mother could still get a ring off her chubby fingers, a moment later she is still looking at Margaret's hand when the fingers of her other hand twist and loosen her wedding ring but fail to remove it.

Lilian practices with trivial exercises, silently instructing her nurse: *My nose is itching. I'd better give it a scratch.* Only a couple of seconds later, Lilian is delighted to see the nurse's hand reach up to her face and twice rub up and down the outside of her right nostril.

She soon becomes adept at using her new abilities to manipulate both her mother and her nurse. She makes the nurse feel the need to scratch her back several times in a row and gets Margaret to make up her bed for a second time.

Neither Margaret nor the nurse suspect Lilian of manipulation, which as each day passes becomes easier for her to control and direct, and more reliable in its effect. Margaret does, however, notice changes in her daughter's personality: a growing irritability and impatience when she fails to have her own way, even over some trivial matter.

When Margaret first tells him of Lilian's changed behaviour, Peter worries that his daughter may have some form of brain damage. He tells Margaret that, as soon as he is able, he will fly to New York to see for himself. Later that day, Peter realises during a meditation that Margaret's descriptions of Lilian's behaviours are remarkably akin to his own. Some are also similar to those described in the journal, especially any relating to intuition. Following this insight, Peter considers there is no urgency in visiting. *In some ways*, he decides, *it sounds as though Lilian's recent experiences may be doing her some good!*

Having no understanding of its composition or function, her parents have no reason to suspect the Bio-AID device is the reason for the changes to Lilian's behaviour and attitudes. Trialled simultaneously in other patients, the device's intended medical purpose is to compensate for loss of brain function caused by minor damage – in Lilian's case, the bruising to her left parietal lobe. It achieves this by adding biologically based computer-processing and storage, compatible with and directly connected to her brain stem, with its external communications powered by a tiny additional unit embedded in her arm.

The fall crushed part of her skull, showering tiny fragments into her brain but leaving a relatively small wound below it. The damage is insignificant, and her brain has readily adapted to the small volume of cellular loss without requiring assistance from the new device. Instead, the Bio-AID quickly raises her level of intelligence and conscious awareness, in part because it is supplying her brain with vast new levels of data, as well as categorising and pre-analysing the resulting information. In effect, it has enlarged both her brain's capacity and capability. One of the unforeseen consequences of this is a greater awareness of her own subconscious thoughts, even without entering a meditative state.

Unexpected, unmonitored and thus unknown to her doctors, the Bio-AID also has a radical and unforeseen effect on her subconscious mind. A biological computer, the AR's soft-tissue connections establish quickly, then grow and evolve in function beyond the experts' predictions. The increase in her brain's capability not only enables Lilian's conscious mind to readily access her own subconscious, as often happens during a deep meditation, but it allows both her conscious and subconscious to extend in function. The immediate result is that Lilian becomes consciously aware of the subconscious connection shared by all sentient beings and is thus able to observe the thoughts of others nearby, both conscious and subconscious.

Bewildered at first by the incoherent sounds of multiple internal voices and afraid that she may be going mad, Lilian makes no mention to her nurse or a visiting doctor of the symptoms, which she fears may be some kind of aural hallucination.

Within a matter of days, Lilian realises what she is hearing and begins to practice focusing her attention on a single individual, her mother, by filtering out and disregarding the noise from any other minds nearby. Once she has mastered this, Lilian is able to 'listen in' at will on her mother's every thought.

Further extensions to Lilian's subconscious abilities soon manifest. She becomes capable of the same levels of intuition and clairvoyance that were routine to her grandfather, and which her father is beginning to achieve, but with an intensity and clarity that astonish her. They grow in capability at an accelerating rate.

One week after first experiencing these connections, Lilian is able to hear and see the subconscious thoughts of others to the same level of expertise as that displayed to Peter by Maureen. This is so even if her subjects are not in the same room but are merely nearby.

By continuously practising the filtering-out process, Lilian is able to select and listen to the thoughts and feelings of anyone within range. For the moment restricted by her lack of mobility, that range is limited to her apartment building.

Within another week, Lilian is astonished to realise she is able to telepathically implant ideas and images into the subconscious minds of anyone in the building, one idea or image at a time and to one person at a time. She practices with trivial examples, using very precise and easy-to-understand wording. Her first test begins by implanting the same idea in two different neighbours, each barely known to her.

It would be very kind if I bought a gift of flowers for that poor girl in the apartment upstairs. I should do that. I will do it now. And deliver them personally.

Within an hour, she has received two bouquets and a get-well card.

It takes only a few more days for Lilian to learn how to control more complicated instructions with precision, and to establish the self-control required to ensure she does not unintentionally transmit any of her own thoughts or betray her identity.

The temptation to use her new-found abilities is too great to resist. She soon uses them routinely, controlling everything from the choice of food to be purchased or cooked to the evening activities of her mother and nurse. Lilian finds it easy to have her mother select steak instead of chicken, or to have her decide to fetch some fresh yogurt, or to bring a gift back for her. And it is easy for Lilian to instruct her nurse to sweep her room for a second or third time, or to bring a cup of coffee.

At first overwhelmed by the pace of her mental development, Lilian soon adjusts and quickly experiences these new abilities as perfectly normal. Within only a few weeks from their initiation, her lengthy recuperation has allowed Lilian to use her new thinking and intuitive powers as readily as if she always possessed them.

An occasional sensing of thoughts or feelings that do not belong to anyone in her building leads Lilian to suspect that her abilities extend considerably further. However, physical weakness prevents her from leaving the apartment to conduct a test. For the moment, she remains unaware of the presence of the Bio-AID. Hence it does not occur to her that, since it is connected to the internet, the device could be used as a medium for her to connect to anyone, anywhere. The first hint occurs to Lilian after an unscheduled appearance of Tina, who embraces and tells her: 'I just felt you needed some company.'

Lilian is aware that her new abilities are well beyond those of ordinary people like her mother and her carers, and powerful enough to cause concern if anyone ever suspects their existence. She never mentions her new abilities to either her mother or her nurse. And Lilian is soon careful, whenever she accidentally displays any sign of prescience, to laugh each occurrence off as a wild or lucky guess.

THIRTEEN

The reunion with Angela is passionate: excited chatter all the way from airport to apartment, a hurried shower and an hour of passionate lovemaking that leaves Peter breathless but elated.

Post-coital, they talk for an hour before making love again. It is the first time Peter has ejaculated twice in one day since he was a student. They lay back breathless, watching through the window as a fog rolls in across the Bay until they both fall asleep.

It is late afternoon before they rouse. Angela wakes first, nudging Peter and telling him they should dine out. Knowing he is short of money she offers to pay. Even in summer a foggy day in San Francisco is cold, so they are shivering by the time they dash under a bright red awning and into a Spartan-but-hip corner restaurant.

Peter follows behind, watching Angela move in her feline way between the tables. The waitress touches into brightness a fake candle centred on their table, which is situated well away from the bar. Angela orders for them both before steering their conversation towards Peter's health.

'You remember what we talked about last time, how I would find a fitness coach and a yoga class for you? Well, I've found both! They're for beginners and the teachers are, well, used to helping people who haven't exercised for years.'

Peter's smile encourages Angela.

'The fitness coach will begin with walking, swimming and lifting a few weights. The yoga is not only about physical fitness, but about keeping healthy *up here*.'

Angela rests the point of an index finger against her temple. Peter nods. Moving her hand to the centre of her chest, Angela spreads her fingers wide and adds, 'And here too.'

After a pause while plates of food are delivered, Angela asks: 'You probably know all that already, don't you Peter?'

Peter's answer is vague.

'About the yoga? Urmm, well. Yes, I suppose.'

Angela leans across the table to rub his upper arm.

'Fitness of the body is part of it, but its real goal is to prepare your mind to accept higher levels of consciousness. The two are intimately related, of course.'

The words Peter has read in the journal he accepts without question as genuine and truthful. However, Angela's words sound false to him: not a lie and maybe true but repeated with no understanding of their meaning. Confused, he is as yet unable to determine that his sensing this falsity comes from the *sound* of her voice, rather than the words or phrases Angela uses. Although unaware of its source, Peter's increased sensitivity to sound is a sure early sign of spiritual progress.

Instead of trusting his feeling and forgiving her pretension, Peter reacts by finding it both humorous and naive. Attempting to stifle a snigger, he snorts. Wine enters his nasal cavity from within his mouth. He coughs twice, spluttering small gobs of wine over the palm of his covering hand.

Angela offers him a napkin amid sideways glances from other diners. When the bout ends, Angela asks: 'Are you okay? I've never seen you do that before.'

Peter reassures her and takes a large swig from the glass of water by his side.

'I'm sorry, Angela,' he says, returning to the subject with apparent enthusiasm. 'I don't really understand it all, but I am delighted to give it a go.'

He takes hold of Angela's hand.

'Anything that interests you is interesting to me too.'

Her lips part into a smile.

'We start tomorrow. And we'll look at buying you some new clothes and maybe even get you a haircut. It will all make you feel like you belong here. At the moment, you look so… English!'

Both laugh aloud when Angela adds, '*Shabby* English.'

Their first course seems to Peter an unrecognisable mass of nuts, vegetables, pulses and fruits, dressed in coconut yogurt. After a few mouthfuls, he asks: 'Angela, I've not visited your home and you've never mentioned it. Tell me, where do you live?'

Angela's eyes narrow for a split-second before her normal, relaxed face reappears. Peter fails to notice.

'It's no secret,' explains Angela. 'I live in Noe Valley, just off Dolores Street.'

A few seconds later, she adds: 'That's how I met your father. He used to hold a clinic there, just around the corner from my apartment.'

His father never mentioned a clinic, but for the moment Peter is more interested in Angela.

'Your home, it's an apartment?'

'Yes, it's only small though. You're welcome to visit, but that's why I prefer meeting at your fa… *your* place.'

The couple carry on eating and drinking, talking mostly about subjects raised by Angela. These include the benefits of organic and biodynamic food, meditation and Ayurvedic spa treatments. Later, Angela progresses to talking about Shamanism, the power of crystals, the importance of unadulterated water and even mentions the presence of angels and spirit animals. All these subjects are new to Peter although, readied by the journal, he is prepared to listen and experiment.

As they stand and prepare to leave, Peter tells her: 'You know, Angela, I could watch you and listen to you all day.'

Angela leans over to kiss his cheek. A trifle intoxicated, Peter continues: 'I can't tell you how big the contrast is between my life here and my life in England. It's like heaven and earth, or heaven and hell. There I was in the depths of despair; here I feel I am breathing fresh air for the first time.'

༉

The following morning, Peter wakes early. Propping up his head with a pillow, he lies next to Angela, feeling her warmth and listening to her breathe while staring at clearing skies outside. As the tall towers of the Bay Bridge emerge solid and upright from dispersing fog, he ponders their conversation of the previous evening.

Although parts of it seem unreal, Peter's memory of their conversation is good; as if their concepts and ideas are floating, difficult to touch and with no substance. Overnight, his analytical mind has categorized what he heard. His thoughts form a list.

Ayurvedic – useful for health but not enlightening.

Organic – useful for health and clearing our bodies of junk.

Crystals – possibly useful for storing memories or feelings.

Shamanism – sounds like it's just a ceremonial-based means of entering into a meditative trance.

Angels and spirits – not sure what they are all about, but I imagine they are useful visualizations for understanding a particular kind of energy, rather as we picture God as a being in human form, no matter how unlikely that may be.

Meditation – the best way to progress towards… towards…

As the roadway spanning the Bay between the city and Treasure Island climbs into view the clarity of Peter's thoughts tail off. He has no idea why or how he arrived at his analysis. One final complex of thoughts enters his mind.

Angela is a typical seeker after Truth. *Knowing the real world is different to its appearance, she inclines to believe everything alternative she hears. Unfortunately, she uses inadequate discrimination and non-intuitive judgments when determining what is true and what is false. She longs for the* Divine *but plainly has no direct experience of it.*

Without understanding the source of his certainty, Peter knows that Angela will help accelerate his spiritual progress, and that he must use and follow her for that purpose. But he also knows he will soon advance beyond Angela's comprehension, and that she will not accompany his growth. She will be left behind: another 'seeker' who holds on to her doubts as certainties and is thus unable to move forward, at least not during this lifetime.

The upper arc of a bright morning sun appears over the distant horizon. Peter touches Angela's arm, in part wishing to communicate how much he appreciates her help and her unknowing sacrifice, but also to reassure himself that she is solid and alive, and not some unknown, ethereal being. She stirs but does not wake.

Angela is now an intimate part of Peter's life and of his purpose in this life, but she is no guru. He knows her words are empty of experience so each one must be doubted and tested, even when they express her deepest, most cherished beliefs. Some may be true or contain a truth, but Peter knows he must use his own judgment, his intuition or feelings, to determine where within them lies their *Truth*.

Peter replays internally her words of the previous evening, personalizing them, as if trying on a new set of clothes. Some feel uncomfortable and their sound has a harsh edge that makes him uneasy, like a cloth that irritates the skin or the shiver one feels when putting on a poorly fitted suit. Other words sound mellow, and Peter's reaction is to feel as if he has always known they are true. He decides this combination of sound and feeling must be how he determines their truth, at least for now.

By contrast to his feelings about the worth of Angela's statements, the words written in the journal have an immediacy and impact, as if spoken directly from someone's heart to his own and thus from a great *Truth*. When he hears each sentence, Peter's belly draws reflexively inwards and his solar plexus moves upwards, closer to his heart. *Maybe I can use this physical reaction to judge truth too*, he thinks.

Peter picks up the journal and reads another passage, from its thirtieth page.

Twin ropes rose in majesty over the whole wide river. Drips from the underside shining brite. Thin and tight was the rope. Evryone yelling and hollering at the oxes, whipping and cursing. The North Platte river was in flood and deep. Water was cold too. People stumbled and fell but all rose shiverin. No one died, tho the river tried its darndest.

He spends a few moments admiring the grit and determination of the wagoners, working together with single-mindedness to reach their goal. He flicks over a few more pages and reads the following.

I reelised then that our life lies in our hearts and in our love not in our actions nor our thinking. What we think and our ideas n all determines who we are and whether grief or good comes to us. If we think on struggling and hardship then thats what we get. If we want something good then that comes too. But only if we feel strong enough about it. Theres a real world behind the one we see. Its that world hidden from our thoughts that drives this one. Our God must have made it so.

Peter spends some minutes trying to understand the words, analyzing Jake's statements and experiences, as told. He discounts the notion of a personal God as being simply a reflection of the Christian belief system prevalent at the time of writing.

Peter's logic tells him that he is reading of three different but related concepts: one is that our mind generates our world or at least our experience of it; a second that our mind is capable of manifesting whatever we need or desire; and a third that there is a real world beyond the visible one. His growing intuition tells Peter that all three statements are true and that they are somehow linked, but is unclear how this may be so.

Prompted by the journal, Peter is beginning to trust his feelings and his intuition as a source and guide, both of the journal's truths and of Angela's limitations. This intuition is already telling him that this trust will soon extend to all matters, and Peter's real spiritual progress will then have begun. He places the book down and closes his eyes.

'It all seems back-to-front,' Peter says aloud.

Angela stirs again but does not wake. His thoughts continue. *She is solid, present and beautiful, but her words feel like a sham. Meantime, the words of a young man long dead and whom I never knew seem wholly real.*

Even though Peter's thoughts remain in part befuddled, he has experienced for the first time how to tell *Truth* from falsity. It is only a matter of days before he fully trusts his intuition far more than his reasoning, and the process becomes routine.

Angela wakes. They rise and shower together. The intimacy of this act is a delight to him. Although enjoying his evident pleasure, hers is tempered by memories of helping his father into the same, spacious cubicle and seating him there on a chair.

Once dressed, Peter disposes of bills delivered in the mail by throwing them into the drawer of his father's desk, which he has yet to sort through. After a light breakfast, Peter and Angela dress in casual clothes and leave for the first of his yoga classes, each carrying one of her rolled-up mats and a bag full of loose clothing. They walk the short distance in silence, listening to the sounds of the city: battery-powered cars and trucks, snatches of conversation, the hum of air-conditioners, children playing and somewhere nearby, a dog barking.

Peter feels shyer and more nervous than he can ever recall. A hubbub of conversation and laughter rises from a cluster of women gathered at one end of the hall, amid broad smiles and hugs. There are two other men in the room, both much younger than Peter.

Peter is introduced to the teacher, a slender woman in her twenties whose movements are smooth and sleek as a panther's, in the same manner as Angela. Mats are laid out in lines three feet apart on the sprung wooden floor. The students stand barefoot on each one. He is near the front, with Angela to his side.

The teacher begins: 'Good morning, everyone. I see we have some new faces, so I'll come and ask each of you a few questions in a moment. In the meantime, everyone please lie down, close your eyes and take a long deep stretch from head to toe.'

The teacher asks Peter a few questions about his health, interrupting his answers every few seconds to issue some new instruction to the rest of the class. Having heard a brief description of his ailments and his lack of experience of yoga, her instructions to Peter are simple: 'Follow the movements I make as closely as possible. Don't try too hard, remember to relax and smile, breathe steadily and come out of any posture as soon as you need to.'

Peter tries to emulate the teacher's position and movement. Attempting to copy the slow, rhythmic movements and fine postures of a big cat, Peter is instead a jerky Pinocchio, unable to articulate any limb as desired. He sweats profusely and pants loudly during the Asanas, while the other pupils around him appear serene and comfortable. Peter is relieved when the session ends with a long lie-down – an opportunity to recover his breath.

After another shower, juices and a light lunch, Angela leads Peter around a range of shops and outlets. By the time they reach the City Lights bookstore at Columbus and Broadway, Peter's hair is shorter, his legs ache and he is porting a growing load of bags and clothes, all paid for by Angela. They have walked across Chinatown and much of downtown San Francisco. One of only a few remaining old-style retail towns, it has survived by catering for the bustle of wide-eyed tourists browsing happily under clear skies and warm sunshine.

The couple spend a while in the store looking for books on yoga and other spiritual subjects, which Angela tells Peter will help him to learn and understand the theoretical background behind his lessons. Peter's expects his legs to seize with cramp at any moment.

Their taxi back to his apartment is a blessed relief, followed by an inorganic coffee and an impromptu fashion show. The new style of clothing makes Peter look and feel younger, even though the tired, aching body beneath them belies it.

FOURTEEN

The couple spend many days wandering the streets and parks or along the shoreline, hand in hand, before or after various yoga or meditation classes; and between visits to mediums and teachers of one spiritual discipline or another, occasionally shopping. Angela also introduces Peter to her brother Dane, who lives in nearby Sausalito.

'We were very close as children,' is all her brother mentions of the difficulties of their upbringing.

During this period Peter remains in a state of adoration that borders on bliss. He is aware of Angela's intellectual and spiritual shortcomings but loves her as much because of her restless search as for what he feels certain is a kind soul. All the while Angela's constant and continuous physical movement mirrors her so far fruitless search for spiritual fulfilment.

Within a couple of weeks, Peter has adjusted to the perpetual motion of their lives. He cannot recall when they last sat still at home during the daytime for more than a few minutes, except for when Angela has a client.

Seated and resting in the course of a brief respite, he realizes it is her restlessness that is the primary obstacle to her gaining or receiving any substantive spiritual benefit. The whirling bustle of her routine is in stark contrast to the 'sitting quietly, doing nothing' direction from their Zen teacher, or the instruction of their meditation teacher to take a few quiet moments every day – neither of which feature at all in Angela's life outside of their classes.

Later that evening, Peter suggests a slower pace of activity. Angela listens but becomes upset, interpreting his concern as a supposed lack of commitment. He tries to explain that Angela is unwittingly addicted to compartmentalizing her life, which is a bustle and hurry between fixed beacons of calm and meditation. He suggests they learn from those beacons and try to integrate the sessions' calm into their lives. Angela agrees, but the following day continues their madcap lifestyle as if the discussion had never taken place.

Peter enjoys the classes, especially those that force him to sit and contemplate. He gains in fitness and loses weight. As a result their sex life gains in vigour and variety. With some reluctance, he agrees to Angela's offer to pay for a partial hair replacement. Within a few weeks, new hair replaces his comb-over and makes him look younger still.

In addition to the classes and workshops they attend, Angela introduces Peter to an array of mediums, palm-readers, astrologers, and spiritualists. Although he suspects one or two are charlatans, most are earnest enough to earn his respect and a few are surprisingly insightful, one lady in particular. A medium and *Intuitive*, this lady insists that she must come to his apartment rather than have Peter visit her office. She also insists that he is alone. Angela arranges to be out for her visit.

'It may be better anyway, if she doesn't realise how much time I spend here with you,' Angela tells him without explanation.

Thus, one afternoon, carrying an umbrella against a late-summer squall raging outside, the tall, slender and perfumed figure of

Maureen arrives at his door. Peter's eyes first fix on her long, narrow neck but are soon drawn upwards to her piercing brown eyes, framed by a shock of long, grey hair.

She accepts a cup of green tea before sitting upright on one of his chairs. Her session begins by telling Peter of his past life, while he lounges opposite trying to take it all in.

'In your most recent life you were a... let me be sure a moment... yes, a Cayouse or perhaps an Umatilla chieftain. You moved around but mostly stayed within Oregon, near where today we call...'

Whenever uncertain of a name or a place, Maureen closes her eyes and tilts her face towards the ceiling. A moment later, a smile spreads across her face. Her eyes open as her head lowers. With a serene visage, she continues.

'Yes, that's it, La Grande. Along with many other members of your tribe you were killed near there in… 1856. It was a massacre; your whole family was wiped out. Even now you blame yourself for being too trusting of the Whites, the soldiers who killed you all.'

Although the date is later than the events described in the journal, the coincidence of location is great. Peter recalls it mentioned within the journal as an area in eastern Oregon that the wagons passed through: a huge bowl-shaped, fertile valley with a hot spring near their point of entry. It was where they first glimpsed the distant, snow-capped Rocky Mountains all knew they would struggle to cross.

Maureen is both intuitive and clairvoyant. Hearing his thoughts, she tells him: 'Yes, it was near the spring that you were killed. The ground there is boggy, but there's a low rise just to the east.'

Peter is surprised that she seems to have heard his thoughts but decides it must be a coincidence. She pauses and gazes directly into his eyes, as if searching behind them for more information.

'You blame yourself. That is why you are now so timid and full of self-doubt. You are afraid to make real decisions, or to stand up for what you believe in. And you do not expect to have what you want. You carry all this doubt with you from that past life. You aren't even sure you are *ready* for this life.'

Peter has no idea what to make of these revelations. Maureen is credible in all other respects, accurate in her descriptions of his present life as well as of his character. Maureen senses his doubt.

'I know you question what I say, so let me tell you a few things about yourself that only *you* know.'

Proceeding to tell Peter all about his wife, his unhappy family life, his children, including a recent injury to his son and his failed business, Maureen then describes in detail the partners who stole his business. Each of her statements is far more accurate and penetrating than Peter expects. He asks her about his future, about which she is coy.

'That's up to you. There are possibilities, *great* possibilities, but you must first find the courage to meet them.'

Maureen explains that he carries the same gifts of intuition as his father, and that those gifts are the same he once had as the spiritual leader of a Native-American tribe. She adds: 'You ignored your intuition then and chose to trust the white eyes. That decision cost you your life. Don't make the same kind of mistake again.'

The session ends with Peter mired in perplexity, and tears welling in his eyes for a dead family he cannot recall. Before Maureen leaves, she tells him to practice a forgiveness meditation called *Ho' Opono Pono*.

When Peter asks her what it means, she tells him: 'Please Peter, research its meaning. There are plenty of explanations available on the Internet. It is the most simple and direct request for forgiveness. Because of that, it is also one of the most powerful. Do not make the mistake of taking it at face value. Be sure to study and reflect on its message of Love. For yourself as well as for others.'

Peter's eyes open wide. Seeing his face shows an utter lack of comprehension she adds: 'And remember to ask yourself for forgiveness. Your *higher self*, not just your dead family. We all make mistakes Peter. It's long past time to move on and you are needed now more than ever.'

Maureen promises to visit again if he ever requires her help. Her charge is minimal, barely enough to cover the cost of her transport, which Peter pays in cash from his pocket. Peter cannot understand how Maureen makes a living, but she waves away an offer of more money and walks out of the door, raising an umbrella against the storm.

Outside the door, Maureen lowers her umbrella, stands completely still and looks up through falling rain at the dark grey skies. Her broad smile bursts into a joyous laugh.

The words: 'Oh thank you, my Lady! Thank you,' are shouted out aloud. Maureen repeats her gratitude over and over while she walks and skips back to her apartment.

One hour later Angela returns, keen to know Peter's thoughts on his session with Maureen. He is enthusiastic.

'What a woman! It was the strangest thing. She knows all about me and my past, even how I feel. Have you told her about me?'

'No, only that you are your father's son,' Angela replies. 'Jeff may have told Maureen about you, of course. They knew each other quite well.'

Peter tells Angela about Maureen's explanation for his timidity, at which she laughs aloud and reaches across to hold his hand. She tells him: 'Maureen always says things like that. Don't take it too much to heart. You were brave enough to fly here to me.'

The couple kiss and hug for a moment before Peter continues his tale.

Although Maureen's words have struck Peter as being honest and truthful, the message they impart is so far removed from any previous experience of his that he struggles to accept her words. They feel and sound like *Truth*, but accepting their message requires a suspension of disbelief of which he is not yet capable. He did not tell Maureen about the journal.

Lying in bed that night next to Angela, Peter resolves to be bolder about his new life. Doubts surface when he realizes he remains uncertain of its direction, or at least of its destination and purpose.

'Surely there is one,' he mutters.

Peter finds the journal's tale of Jake's personal and spiritual awakening wholly appealing. He wishes to emulate the young boy's clear thinking, his depth of knowledge, his devotion to a cause and, like the young man, to experience love. Not in the traditional obsessive and lustful manner of 'falling in love', although he wonders whether that is where his infatuation with Angela will lead.

What Peter seeks is *love*, which he still views in personal terms as being borne of intimacy, respect and mutual understanding with a woman, rather than as a universal, all-embracing *Love*. That level of understanding remains far away, but his growing spiritual prowess is already working its magic, manifesting change in both his world and his perception of it.

The crux of the journal's appeal to him are its simple descriptions of developing spiritual capabilities and its acceptance of them as natural, something to be expected rather than marvelled at. The boy has absolutely no need to lie to his own journal and thus his descriptions, Peter decides, are wholly reliable.

Prior to his arrival in San Francisco, Peter has spent his adult life avoiding any contemplation of the kind he now indulges in during every quiet moment. It is only a matter of days before he realizes that internal deliberations are part of his essence, something core to him, no matter how long ignored.

Waking early, he picks up the journal with no particular intention except to scan through a few pages, this time in the middle pages. The first line he reads tells him:

I felt the vibration in and thru the centre of my heart. Either emanating from that very spot, or connecting me to the vibrations elsewhere, everywhere else. For the first time I felt truly connected to everything around me. I knew then that all things are possible.

The journal's effect is profound, disinterring the youthful conversations he shared with his father that he buried deep in his memory long ago. There is a related effect of the journal, one of which he is unaware: the re-awakening of his youthful optimism begins to generate a positive outlook, as Pop knew it would. The tangible results are his involvement and explorations with Angela, but it also begins to manifest a broader wealth. Initially indirect by increasing the number of Angela's clients and thus her ability to support them, it soon changes Peter's entire world.

FIFTEEN

Twenty years old, Ellen Carter answers the door as soon as she realizes it is her best friend holding on to the buzzer. Her one-bedroom apartment is on the edge of New York's Chinatown, within earshot of traffic approaching the Brooklyn Bridge. It's ten minutes after eleven at night: very late for personal callers.

On the video call-entry system she can see her friend is upset. The look on her face reminds Ellen of a friend who committed suicide only a few weeks earlier. She presses the button to allow access for her friend then, wearing only a thin top and an old pair of slacks, rushes at once to meet her in the hallway.

In the narrow entrance hall her friend Karen, still wearing the sparkly dress she was wearing when they spoke four hours earlier, bursts immediately into tears. Between sobs her friend says, 'I'm so sorry but you're the only one I can tell.'

'Oh my God, Karen! Come in. What the hell has happened? You look like you've been raped.'

It's a guess but an accurate one. Karen's head nods up and down, twice. Ellen's sharp intake of breath is audible.

They enter her apartment. Karen's sobs become loud, bawling cries accompanied by a flood of tears. Ellen does her best to comfort her friend, keeping both arms around her as she leads her into the lounge.

They sit next to each other on the sofa. Knees bent, Ellen keeps one arm around her friend; the other consoles a hand that clutches a tissue and is shaking on Karen's knee.

'I know you won't want to hear this, Karen. But you… we… we have to go to the cops.'

Her friend looks up, eyes reddened, pleading.

'I don't think I can, Ellen. All that pawing and swabs, and the endless questions. You remember what happened to Julie. In the end they dropped the case.'

'I remember,' says Ellen.

Until a minute earlier she'd not thought of her for weeks. The funeral was the saddest event of her young life. The two girls sit together close. For a long time, no words are spoken. The silence is broken by Ellen.

'We have to go to the cops, Karen. There are carers in the city now, specialists who'll come with us. I can look up their number first.'

Her friend says nothing. Ellen guesses that's a good sign. *At least she's thinking about it*, she reasons.

'Do you want to talk to me about it, Karen?'

A splutter of coughs, cries and tears erupt. When they cease Karen says, 'I need to, Ellen. I need to! It was all so strange. Like I didn't want to but that I did too. Like I was being told I had to.'

Ellen has no idea how to react to the words she has heard. She knows from the experience of their deceased friend that any expression of doubt or hesitation will be taken by an investigator as implied assent. Since there is no realistic prospect of a conviction, the guy will be interviewed but not charged.

'Tell me more,' she says. 'Explain exactly what happened.'

Karen's memory is good, and her tale is detailed but confusing. She begins: 'It was our first date. I'm sorry, of course you know that much already. He was nice enough. Sweet, actually. Charming in some ways but so full of himself. All he could talk about was him. By the time the main course arrived, I'd decided I wanted to go home.'

Both women exchange glances.

'Almost as soon as that thought entered my head, it was followed by another. "You should sleep with him first," it said. It didn't feel like my thought, it was more like an instruction. I even looked around to see if someone had said something. The next thing I know we're in his car and I'm feeling tired. So tired I fall asleep.'

'You were asleep while he drove you home?' asks Ellen.

'No, to his place. When I woke up, I'm in his flat. I've no idea how I got there. I'm taking off my dress, willingly. I unzip the back, slip it off along with everything else and leap onto him. All the time, he's staring at me from the bed. Like he's laughing inside.'

'I do all these things for him. Anything he wants. But the whole time I'm thinking: "I don't want this. What am I doing?" The next thing I know he's on top of me, grinding away. I ask him to stop. Then I tell him to carry on. It's the voice in my head again, telling me what to do. It's there the whole time.'

Ellen has no idea what all the symptoms mean. She tells her friend: 'Karen, it sounds like you've been drugged. Or hypnotized, somehow. We need to get you to the hospital. They'll take swabs and a blood test before you speak to the cops.'

Karen has not finished her exposition.

'There's one more thing, Ellen. After he's done, he drives me home. He doesn't know where I live. I mean, I've never told him. But he knows exactly where to go.'

A loud gasp escapes Ellen's lips. She cries: 'He must have been stalking you! Or maybe he went through your bag while you were asleep?'

'It's a lockable one, Ellen.'

Two hours later the girls are sitting together, holding hands in a bland, almost empty consulting room. A doctor tells them there is no trace of any drug in Karen's system.

'None whatever. Just a small amount of alcohol, that's all,' he says.

'Then how do you account for my friend's behavior?' asks Ellen.

'I can't,' is the doctor's reply.

The police interview fares no better. Ellen fumes, Karen is left in tears.

'They don't believe me,' she says between sobs.

The investigating detective reads a summary produced by their AI-based interrogation analysis system before reporting their findings to the two women. Keeping his eyes focused on Karen, he tells them the bad news.

'Based on what you've told me Miss, there's no reason to arrest this man. I'm sorry,' are the detective's penultimate words. As he leads them out, he tells them something that shocks them.

'The only thing I can tell you is that you're the third girl I've seen this week who's named the same guy. I don't know what that means but I'd sure like to know. I'll be in contact if I have any more questions for you.'

Both women look at him aghast. They realize the cop is a decent man, doing his job as best he can. In turn the two women thank him and leave. They never hear from him again. A week later the detective is found hanging from a support beam of the High Line, only a few hours after he's interviewed the alleged rapist. He is one of three suicides discovered in the area during the same night.

❧

Across the Hudson River, beyond the sea wall and gleaming towers of Jersey City, Enrico Giordano is sitting in his office in Newark becoming ever more frustrated with his new client. He's yet to earn a penny from the woman and she's already used up nearly an hour of his time. He wishes he'd never agreed to meet her. He could be working on the alimony case he's just been given. Or he could be playing golf. *Hell*, he thinks, *I'd prefer to be cleaning a toilet than listening to this horseshit.*

In all his years as a lawyer Giordano has never heard anyone say they signed away their house, but they didn't mean to. Now she wants it back. He tries again to explain, for the third time.

'But you signed the papers, Dolores. If you didn't want to give him the house, why did you sign?'

After she repeats that she does not know why, he asks another, pejorative question. The same question as before but phrased a little differently.

'Are you telling me you want I should go to Court and tell the judge you were happy to sign it before but now you think what you agreed to was unfair, so you'd like it to be changed. To be unsigned?'

Dolores is equally frustrated. Giordano is the third lawyer she's seen today. She answers his question while thinking a*t least not so facetious as the last one.*

'No, I'm saying I always knew it was unfair and that I never wanted to sign it. I just did. I can't tell you why. Maybe I just flipped.'

'Dolores,' he begins 'the law doesn't work that way. We sign things to show that we agree to them. I don't think the judge is going to take too kindly to you changing your mind.'

She tries to explain, again.

'I just told you, Mr Giordano. I didn't change my mind, sir. I never wanted to sign it. I just did.'

After a few more minutes of fruitless verbal ping-pong Dolores decides to give up. Giordano's is the third law firm she's been to already. Without money she knows there's little hope of finding a lawyer who'll listen long enough to understand.

'Damn,' she says aloud, 'And I don't know why the bank won't listen to me neither.'

Dolores is obese, many pounds overweight. Her AR has stopped working and the walking between buildings is taking its toll. As soon as she exits the front door, she rests her buttocks on a low brick wall.

'Damn!' she says again. 'Damn! There's gotta be a lawyer somewhere who'll listen to me. Otherwise me and the boys'll be homeless. An' that's jus' not right.'

After sitting on the wall for a few minutes sobbing and muttering about her 'useless, good-for-nothing, s-o-b husband', Dolores decides she has no option but to visit City Hall and to plead destitution.

The city of Newark has been transformed in recent years. The Mayor's office is in a gleaming, high-rise building that also acts as a hub for the many technology ventures now based there. A long-time resident of the city's rejuvenated center, through her office window on an upper floor the Mayor can see an extended line of complainants, queueing and being controlled amid multiple scenes of anger and confusion by a combination of automated-robot and human police.

'What the hell is going on?' the Mayor asks her assistant. 'This is the third day in a row it's been like this. Each day worse than before.'

The assistant's name is Gerald. He shrugs his shoulders while the Mayor continues to stare out the window. Mayor DeFiore does not notice Dolores approaching the end of the queue. There are so many men and women in the growing crowd her eyes have no reason to pick on any one in particular.

Her assistant tells her: 'I was speaking to one of the cops earlier. He told me the only consistent thing in their stories is they are all claiming they've done things they didn't mean to do.'

'That's hardly new, is it Gerald?'

'No, ma'am. The only thing new about it all is the sheer number of them. It's the same in every city in the US, ma'am.'

Gerald's comment is not entirely news to the Mayor. She has already received calls from the Mayors of several other boroughs in New York State.

'You mean it's nationwide, Gerald?'

'I'm afraid so, Ma'am.'

Gerald joins the Mayor at the window. His eyes focus on Dolores while he tells the Mayor that his brother in LA has told him the same is happening there, and elsewhere.

'It seems to be the case too Ma'am, that the onus falls especially hard on women. Particularly the vulnerable, old or colored. I've no idea why.'

'This is dreadful. You'd better get me Terri on the line, straightaway.'

'Yes, ma'am. You mean President Terri…'

'Yes.'

Mayor DeFiore's uncharacteristic, irritable interruption confirms to Gerald just how concerned she is. He leaves her staring out of the window to make the call.

SIXTEEN

Removing Peter's obsession with money and material gain is an accidental achievement of Angela. Peter is completely besotted with her, so cares little about anything else. Infatuated to the point where he is happy provided that they are together, his previous obsession with acquiring wealth has become irrelevant. Aglow inside his adoration, Peter does not realise that one obsession is simply replacing another. The intrinsic mental and spiritual sickness causing his addiction remains.

Peter has little money, only a few hundred dollars. He has collected utility bills and statements and placed them all, unopened and unpaid, in a drawer. He has thus delayed any decisions concerning the apartment, or the direction of his life. Debts have become a guilty secret he prefers to forget. The electrical power to his father's apartment is within days of disconnection, when Angela tells Peter she has tickets to the Burning Man festival.

Angela drives them to the festival, held in the Black Rock Desert of northern Nevada. Surrounded by SUVs and giant mobile homes, they pitch a modest tent next to her old Toyota. Inside, Angela makes camp-beds and thin blow-up mattresses seem as comfortable as possible, by adding thin cotton or lambswool blankets and scattering colourful cushions around.

Close by their small tent is a family's encampment of much larger, multi-room tents. A few more yards away rest large mobile homes and even a huge truck whose trailer comes complete with bedroom suite, bathroom and kitchen.

The couple spend the first day wandering around, taking in the various sights and sounds. Mainly the result of wealthy lost souls desperate to appear unique or individual, Peter soon decides that what they display is childish but occasionally original and humorous, and sometimes all three.

Angela knows a large number of attendees, who hug or embrace her freely with genuine affection. Peter finds the whole event earnest and entertaining, gay in the older sense of the word, but decides within an hour of arriving that the whole enterprise is a sham – *a misdirection by and of people who, with a little thought, should know better.* Whatever he chooses to become, he determines, it is not one of these frivolous people.

Communication coverage this far into the desert is normally non-existent but, for the duration of the event special mobile communication wagons with tall, extending masts and noisy power units have been set-up to enable everyone's AR devices to continue working.

Amid a hubbub of drinking, partying and tomfoolery, Peter falls asleep with comparative ease and wakes refreshed and content.

'It may all be a foolish waste of time,' he tells Angela before they rise 'but I like the atmosphere of this place. It's carefree.'

On their second day, Peter receives a call from his father's attorneys, telling him they are ready to read his father's Will. The call from the attorney's secretary is short.

'Mr Walker, is that you?'

Peter confirms his identity.

'We've sent a number of letters to your father's address hoping they would reach you. I'm afraid we had no address for you...'

He is about to say something similar when the young woman continues, 'I am pleased to say we have now located all the assets belonging to your father. I'm sorry, I should say that *belonged* to your father.'

After some discussion, an arrangement is made.

'You are the principal beneficiary, Mr Walker. Would Monday suit you, at our offices?'

Peter confirms he will attend and is given the address. He looks across at Angela, who has already guessed the reason for the call. She is inquisitive.

'Have you any idea how much is involved?'

'The lady didn't say, and I never thought to ask.'

Angela chuckles before asking: 'I mean, it's none of my business, but wouldn't it be fabulous if it solved your money problems, at least for now?'

Reminded of how much he missed Pop and of how little he saw of him over recent years, Peter's reaction is morose rather than excited or curious.

'It surely would. Pop was comfortable, but I don't believe he was rich. At least it should keep the wolves from my door.'

Guessing his sombre mood, the expression on Angela's face changes. Affecting unconcern, she takes his arm.

'Well, let's not worry about that now. Come on, there's lots more to see.'

Angela drags Peter by the hand, pulling him towards a group of male forty-year-old bikers attempting to ride along while standing on a single motorbike. The sight relieves his melancholy, but the call has affected them both. Unable to relax and enjoy the festivities, they leave the Burning Man event a day earlier than intended.

They spend the journey home with their conversation turning again and again to how much and how liquid Pop's assets are. Less than a half hour from its start, Angela has said: 'You know, I was thinking, if there's a little money. We could take a long vacation.'

After Peter replies with a grunt, her eyes leave the road when she turns to face him.

'Nowhere fancy. But it would be nice to go somewhere, don't you think? Maybe Mexico.'

Peter's head turns too. He smiles and says, 'A holiday together would be lovely. Let's see how much there is before we get too excited though.'

By the time they reach Peter's apartment both are desperate not to mention the elephant now standing in the centre of their room. They try but fail to find an alternative topic of conversation. It is the most uncomfortable Peter has ever been in Angela's company. They decide to spend the night apart, the first time he has slept alone in weeks, and agree to meet next in the city after he has visited the attorney's office.

❧

The law firm's offices are all that Peter expects: thickly carpeted floors, papered walls adorned with expensive-looking copies of works of art, sculptures in every corner, names on every door and all on a high floor overlooking the Bay. The anticipated shrinking of the need for lawyers following the development of cheap, AI-based online legal advice has not happened, overtaken by an ever-expanding growth in litigation services. *I should have become a lawyer, not an accountant*, muses Peter while he waits.

He is shown into an office where a suited and bespectacled lawyer in his fifties asks him to sit opposite. The man introduces himself: 'Bradley Williams the Third, Mr Walker. How do you do?'

They shake hands.

'Do you have some form of identification, Mr Walker? It's a simple matter of formality.'

Peter hands over both his British and American passports. Bradley writes the details onto his notepad, adjusts the gold-rimmed glasses that are drifting down his aquiline nose and confirms that all is in order.

He continues: 'Mr Walker. Firstly, let me say on behalf of our firm how sorry we were to hear of your father's passing. He was a customer of ours for many years and although I cannot say that we saw him frequently, on those occasions that he visited we were always most pleased to meet with him. I recall him as being a man of considerable charm and humour.'

Williams acknowledges Peter's thanks, then sniffs and picks up a sheaf of papers from which he reads.

'You are the sole heir to your father's estate. No other person has come forward with any reasonable claim to contest the Will nor, as I understand it, are they likely to do so. Therefore, it is my pleasure to inform you that net of fees and disbursements you will shortly be receiving a cheque in the sum of seven million, eight hundred thousand and twenty-two dollars, US. In addition, you will receive the title deeds to the two properties that your father owned, which have been independently valued as I understand it at some further four-point-eight million, or thereabouts. This latter includes his apartment, where I believe you are presently residing.'

Peter's mouth has fallen open in shock; his head is moving from side-to-side involuntarily. He hoped to receive the apartment plus a few thousand dollars on which to live, so the sums quoted are beyond his comprehension. The lawyer is still talking.

'This considerable sum is available to you at once since we have already liquidated the principal investments held by your father, save for the properties as he instructed us to do. There is also a hand-written letter, which your father requested that you read over the next few days.'

Williams lifts his head, hands over an envelope and adds: 'I am bound to offer you our assistance in any way you deem desirable, perhaps with introductions to investment advisors and so on. There is no hurry. Indeed, may I suggest that you take a week or two to consider the options for your future before contacting us to arrange such an appointment?'

As Peter begins to appreciate his good fortune, questions circle in his mind. He says: 'But Pop never kept any documents at his home. I had no idea.'

The lawyer runs a flat palm across the thinning hair atop his scalp. He explains: 'We acted in all matters for your father. He preferred not to bother himself with detail. If you would care to see all the records, I am sure...'

'Oh no, not at all!' Peter interrupts. 'I'm sure there's no impropriety. If Pop trusted you, then I'm sure *I* can.'

'Well, thank you, Mr Walker. Whenever you are ready to seek advice, please let me know. In the meantime, my very best wishes to you.'

Williams presses a buzzer to summon his secretary. The two men shake hands across the desk and agree to meet again in a week or two. When he reaches the lobby, Peter's hands and legs are shaking. His heart is beating so fast that he must sit and rest. After a minute of breathing deeply, his heart rate gradually slows. As he calms, he begins to take it all in. *It's more than enough but, thank God it's not so much that I'll be on some rich list*, he considers. The money arrives in his bank account later the same day.

Needing time to think over what to tell her, Peter chooses to walk the two miles to his downtown rendezvous with Angela. He decides not to tell her about the extent of his new wealth, in case that changes their relationship. *She either loves me for what I am, or not at all*, he reasons.

After making that decision, Peter's thoughts turn to his father:

Why didn't Pop tell me he was so wealthy? Where did he get the money? Then, selfishly: *All my striving and failure over the last two years could have been avoided.*

A brief resentment arises in Peter. A moment later, this is replaced by a deep guilt at having thought in such a way about his father, whom he knows cared deeply for him. *Pop knew I was in trouble so he must have had good reason not to help*, he concludes.

It takes several days for Peter to truly accept that Pop's decision was a wise one. He eventually realizes he would feel even more of a failure if dependent upon his father, and he would not have learnt or changed at all without the benefit of his recent experience. *I'd probably still be with Margaret, worried and miserable*, he reasons.

A new determination arises to use his inheritance wisely. Speaking its confirmation aloud in the shower one morning, he adds: 'I don't know what that means yet, but I will do it.' Then he resumes an amended rendition of the chorus from an old musical.

'I'm gonna wash that gal right out of my hair…'

ॐ

Life with Angela carries on as before. They attend classes, eat out, spend afternoons shopping or visit a beach. The only difference is that Peter now pays for meals and any other expenses.

'To pay you back for all the help you've given me,' is all he tells her, implying only that for now at least, he does not have to worry about money. When Angela seeks to share the cost of their celebratory dinner by telling him, 'At least let me pay half,' Peter is forced to admit his new wealth is large.

'There's more than enough. And for a holiday. We should go somewhere exotic I think, don't you?'

Angela smiles and rests the palm of her hand over his.

'That would be wonderful. I don't mind where we go. Anywhere you want.'

Affecting to be more concerned with his emotional and spiritual development, Angela tells him, 'You know, Peter, when we first met you never spoke about your feelings, at least not your deep, personal ones. You were open about your financial problems of course, but your feelings were pretty much an unknown, even to you!'

Knowing he spent most of his adult life cultivating detachment, Peter agrees.

'Yes! I don't think I ever relaxed until I met you.' Laughing, he adds: 'In fact, until I *slept* with you!'

'Peter, you should be proud of yourself. You fit into that new Armani shirt, your belly doesn't protrude, and you no longer perspire when we do anything active,' says Angela, reaching her hand across the table to his. 'Including our lovemaking.'

Both laugh. Peter tells her: 'You know, I'm as happy now as I've ever been. Having a little money again means life is easier but it makes no difference to that.'

Angela looks directly into his eyes. The right edge of her lip lifts into a tiny half-smile before she stands, leans close to his ear and whispers: 'After telling me that, you are going to have to take me straight home after dinner!'

Lying awake later that night in contemplative mood, Peter reconsiders their lifestyle. *I still feel that all this striving, all these classes, take us away from any genuine contemplation. We pass the day and we gain experience and experiences, but we are no closer to being enlightened, whatever that means.*

He then makes a resolution: *I'm going to tell Angela we have to change.* Knowing how difficult that conversation may be, he decides to graduate the change – *I'll suggest we begin with the vacation.*

Peter decides to seek guidance from his journal, which he now knows will always reward a consultation. While Angela sleeps, he opens the journal. A loose page falls into his hands, which turns out to be a letter written, he guesses from the date, by his great-great-grandfather. Peter's attention is immediately drawn to its third paragraph.

I realised my intentions were not of the best. My new-found abilities enabled me to gain at the expense of others. But each time this happened, I felt a gulf widen in my gut, like my soul was emptying out. I decided I had to change, not just my manner of making money but how I spent the whole of my life. I had no inclination or calling to become a priest, most of whom I have anyway found to be petty or mean-minded souls. I had no idea what this change meant, so I decided I had to go somewhere to find out.

The next paragraph describes how the writer boarded a ship bound for the Orient, and how he ended up in a Buddhist monastery somewhere in modern-day Indonesia. The following paragraph continues: *These people were all self-less in their devotion to each other and to their tasks. There were occasional petty acts of meanness but these were rare, very rare. Nearly everyone wore a smile. I had no desire to understand their religion or ceremonies, but its principles stuck with me: devotion and care will lead to greater love and awareness. I decided to take these principles back with me to the West and to set up there. After a few weeks spent in Hawaii, I arrived in San Francisco at the end of June, and never left there again.*

Peter knows the messages in each paragraph are significant, but they are also very different. He soon hears from his daughter, when he learns why both are important.

SEVENTEEN

Maureen flicks her long plait of grey hair behind her head, stands, then turns to stare out of the window. Behind her, a grey-tinted desk, slim desk-light, plain pink carpet, a pair of over-size, pale-white sofas, an armchair and a wall-length, coated-metal bookcase convey an atmosphere both peaceful and efficient.

Bathed in sunshine from a rising sun the mid-morning view across to Sausalito and Oakland lifts her heart, evoking feelings reminiscent of lazy days spent with her last love. *That was years ago,* she tells herself, *almost a lifetime.*

Already aware that Angela is approaching, Maureen has no need to look down to the street four storeys below but does so anyway. *Such graceful movements. To think I once looked so young!* Maureen shakes her head to dispel her mood. *I always feel like this when I see Angela,* she muses. *It must be because she reminds me too much of my own youthful vigour.*

A minute passes while Maureen stares out of the window. Returning to her seat just before there is a knock at her door, she shouts 'Come in!' A practiced raising of her voice, just loud enough to be heard in the anteroom outside.

Angela enters smiling.

'That's a lovely new skirt,' remarks Maureen. 'How are you?'

'It was a present from Peter,' is the answer. 'And I am very well, thank you. Busy of course, between giving and going to classes. And spending time with Peter, of course.'

The repetition tells Maureen that her client is nervous. She stands and points towards the sofas before saying, 'Come, sit down and relax. There's much you want to tell me.'

Angela sits and takes a sip from the glass of water earlier placed by Maureen on the coffee table beside her. The next five minutes are taken by an update on activities and places visited. Maureen listens attentively, making occasional movements with her hand to indicate that Angela should continue.

Unconcerned with the specifics of actions and places, Maureen's attention is neither on the words Angela uses nor their intended meaning. Instead, she listens to the *sound* they make.

'It's like listening to a symphony,' she once remarked to Angela, who is both her client and a pupil. 'We *feel* or sense the true meaning – what it tells us about a state of *Mind* – through losing ourselves in its ebb and flow,' she had added, even though she knew Angela would not understand her words.

Her update completed, Angela lowers her shoulders and eases back into her armchair, waiting for Maureen's questions to commence.

'You have been busy,' begins Maureen. 'Now tell me about your feelings for Peter.'

'I... I... don't know,' stutters Angela. Knowing that with this very first question Maureen is probing her integrity, her heart sinks.

After checking her adherence to the *yamas* and *niyamas* of her early training, Angela knows there will be a follow-up, which Maureen delivers moment later.

'So, tell me. How does it feel when you make love?'

'We have a very good, active sex life. He's…'

'That's not the question I asked,' interrupts Maureen.

'No, I… No, I guess not. Well, I love him. He's kind, caring. And I think he loves me. It's still early days, of course.'

Angela' s fingers have begun to twirl lengths of hair. Maureen asks: 'He knows about you and his father?'

'No, of course not! I doubt he's ready for that.'

'How do you think he will react when he finds out?'

'I've no idea. Really, I've no idea!'

'Don't you think you should tell him, before he finds out from someone else?'

Her persistence eventually pays off, when Angela reluctantly admits to having toyed with Peter.

'I like him. He's charming, and thoughtful. That may not have been my original reason for chasing him but it's true. And now he's lost some weight, I think he's rather handsome.'

The real payoff comes a few moments later, when Angela elaborates.

'I don't want to tell him because he will think I am only after his father's money. And yes, I was at first. I felt entitled. I may have slept with his father but that was more companionship than anything. We never made love. Yes, I would have, I admit, but by then he was no longer capable. But now… Now I know Peter's over ten years older than me, but I like being with him. He's different.'

'Good,' enthuses Maureen, 'now we're getting somewhere! It's always better to face the truth, isn't it, Angela?'

Maureen did not need reminding that it was at her request that Angela first approached him. The two women spend a few minutes discussing how and when Angela should tell Peter.

'Be honest, Angela. Tell him the truth, that you loved his father but that you were never *in love* with him, nor did you ever make love with him. He will be hurt but he will understand. He will eventually be grateful you took such good care of him. You should do it straightaway,' concludes Maureen.

'I will,' promises Angela, 'within a few days. A couple at most.'

'Angela, the path you are on dictates you must tell the truth. Not only to others but especially to yourself. And by not revealing a fact you know would affect others' behaviour, you are telling a lie.'

'I know. Truly, I know,' acknowledges Angela.

'Unless he asks you should not tell him that I asked you to care for him. Not yet at least. It's important that you never lie to him. Do you understand.'

Angela nods her head then, realizing that Maureen wants a more positive affirmation, she adds: 'Yes, Holy Mother. Oh, I'm sorry! Yes, Maureen.'

Maureen tuts. 'It's important to remember, Angela, that we are not a religious organisation. At least not in any conventional sense. We do not require anyone to believe in any particular God, nor even in a

God. What we pursue is a connection to the *Divine*. And any individual member may conceive and understand that in any way they wish. It was a central teaching of Mary and, we believe, of Jesus. You understand that don't you, Angela?'

'Yes, Maureen. I am very sorry.'

Forgiving of the young woman's slip, Maureen continues with her guidance.

'It's OK that you sleep with him, Angela. After all, our purpose is to spread Love and to bring reconciliation to men and women. You should also consider being blunt about why you were attracted to him. About your foreknowledge of his father's wealth and the appeal of his money.'

'I can't tell him just like that!' Angela shrieks. 'He'll never forgive me.'

'Angela,' begins Maureen, 'if you don't tell him and he later finds out then he will be justified in never forgiving you. If you tell him now then yes, he will be angry and upset but he will examine his heart and be able to forgive you. Completely.'

'I...I don't know,' is all Angela can reply.

'You must think hard on it,' Maureen tells her young student. A moment later she adds: 'You do realise who he is, don't you?'

Angela replies with an honest, 'Other than his father's son, no. I don't know what you mean.'

A few seconds later she is astonished when Maureen tells her, 'He is the one who will lead our Order.'

Angela remains quiet while she stares open-mouthed at her teacher and mentor's face. Seeing Maureen's slow, confirmatory nod, she is unsure how to respond. Angela shakes her head as, in a low voice, she admits: 'I had no idea. None.'

'He will soon be ready. Soon enough.'

When Angela begins her next sentence with the words 'But that means…' Maureen interrupts her by placing a finger over her own lips.

'Not yet, Angela. Not yet.'

Maureen reminds her to treat him with care and with kindness.

Their remaining time is consumed with discussing how much Angela has learnt from the various books Maureen has told her to read, and whether her practicing of the various tasks set for her has been sufficient or has progressed enough.

Concluding their hour-long session, Maureen hands to Angela a prepared page of follow-up instructions, telling her: 'He may have been in trouble when you first told me you'd met him, but Peter will soon become a savant, or intuitive if you prefer. When fully capable, he will be far more powerful even than me. You had best tell him what we discussed before he starts to work it out for himself.'

Angela promises to do so, thanks Maureen for the session then departs.

As soon as the door has closed, Maureen walks over to her desk, sits on its leather chair and stretches a hand across to pull her notepad closer. Words appear on its screen the instant her dictation commences

I doubt Angela will ever become what she aspires to be. There is too much activity in her head, too little diligence in her approach to practicing her meditation or remote viewing, and the low level of her vibration shows a lack of ..something.. perhaps self-belief. I believe it is

123

a fear, inadequacy certainly. I'd better keep probing: there's probably something in her childhood, or maybe even acquired from a past life, or from her parents.

Maureen takes a sip from a glass of water, her first of the day, before continuing:

Angela will enjoy and participate wholeheartedly in our ceremonies and celebrations, will enjoy being among her fellow travellers and will gain knowledge of our practices and abilities. But it will be several years before the next stage in her training is reached, and she may never attain that level.

Angela is another of those young women who know there is more to the world than they can see but prefer to hide behind the superficialities of our Order rather than truly join with us to see beyond the Veil. She must be more committed to self-knowledge if she is ever to join us on our journey. The desire presently displayed by her is insufficient.

Leaning back in her chair, Maureen swivels it around to stare awhile over the rooftops opposite. *It's a shame*, is her silent lament. Aloud, to her partial reflection she adds a plea: 'So many young women, but so few have the courage and confidence to proceed all the way. If only they would realize how simple it really is.'

Staring down to the ground outside, Maureen touches her heart as she watches Angela cross the road and disappear around a corner. She swivels back to her desk.

Maureen separates her feet, relaxes her shoulders, places one hand in her lap and lays the other against a round-ended, smoothed and polished grey stone that is resting on the corner of her desk. The foot-long object is shaped like a *shivalingam*. Seated in its marble base, it is lying sideways with the rounded end pointing away. Her breathing slows. Moments later, her eyes close.

Within an instant, Maureen is aware of leaving the confines of her body and her office. Sweeping skywards, her journey quickly reaches its zenith. Peering downwards, it takes only a second for her to reach into Peter's lounge. There she rests, observing.

His aura is already bright yellow. Only a few specks of red and green remain. His father was right: he surely is the one. It won't be long before he becomes wholly white. Then we will know for sure, she decides.

Peter is not consciously aware of Maureen's presence but there is a distinct effect. This time it is physical. He shivers, a slight motion visible to the naked eye but viewed by Maureen as a ripple in his aura. His hands then move in tandem, once up and down each arm, stroking the skin of his bare arms. She smiles. *It's no good trying to warm them*, she wants to say. *It's only me.*

Before leaving, Maureen raises her arms to each side and inverts her hands. Opening her palms, a silent prayer is spoken. Waves of bright yellow light pass unseen from the top of her head and hands towards Peter, who feels the result as a tingling across his scalp. His right hand moves to gently rub the top of his head and finishes its movement by twice stroking his chin. *Just like his father*, thinks Maureen, chuckling.

Her eyes close and within a moment awareness is returned to her waiting body.

'I must call the others,' she says aloud.

Angela turns the corner and exhales loudly. It's a beautiful, clear noon: a tingling caress of bright sunlight warms her arms and the crown of her head. Her legs move at an easy pace: the distance to Peter's apartment can be covered at a stroll in less than fifteen minutes. Two teenagers whistle past on scooters.

'That was easier than I expected,' she whispers. *Maybe Maureen's mellowing with age* is her last thought on their session, added as the two boys switch from the pathway to ride along an empty stretch of street.

Diverting into one of the many organic food shops that have sprung up in the city since the granting of tax rebates for local retailers, Angela selects a range of fresh fruit and vegetables. They are stuffed into an old, recycled jute bag with a worn, barely visible logo on one side, whose handles Angela places over a shoulder.

Exiting the shop, Angela raises her arm to signal approval of the amount displayed above the door and listens for the quiet 'ping' that signals the money has been debited from her account. Five minutes later she arrives at Peter's apartment.

He is preparing lunch. 'It won't be long,' he announces cheerily while Angela unloads her bag. Once completed she steps behind him, places her arms around his waist and kisses his cheek.

'What are you making?'

'Hmm, it's an experiment. I guess you'd have to call it a ratatouille, served on a roasted sliver of aubergine and oat flatbread.'

'It sounds lovely. I can't wait.'

Angela can see their meal is almost ready so moves away and sits down at the oak table, which is bare of napkins, condiments or cutlery.

'Don't worry, all is ready,' announces Peter, reaching into the drawer as if in response to her thoughts. Less than a minute later, lunch is served.

'How was your session with Maureen?'

'This is good, Peter. I had no idea you were a natural cook!'

Another forkful of food is nibbled before Angela answers.

'It went well. I'm not sure quite what I gain from her sessions, but she is surely one switched-on woman.'

Peter knows better than to ask questions about what was discussed. Instead, he says, 'I've been thinking. It's time we had our holiday.'

'Oh, Peter! That's a lovely idea. I thought you'd forgotten.'

'I was thinking Baja would be way too hot at this time of year. So, I thought we could visit Canada. Begin in Vancouver and see where we end up. It's beautiful there in the Summer. Or so the guidebooks say.'

Angela's hand reaches across to his.

'I'll be happy anywhere. Honestly, I would. Wherever you want to go.'

'I'm glad you said that, because I've booked it already,' Peter announces. Grinning broadly, he adds: 'We start in Vancouver, then stay a couple of days at a wilderness lodge somewhere unpronounceable, before we go whale-watching in Alaska. We leave in two days.'

Angela makes a loud exclamation. Both stand. Peter's chair falls over with a loud bang. Both laugh at his clumsiness then hug. Tenderly, Angela kisses Peter's mouth before leaning back to say, with complete honesty, 'I'm so happy, I can't even begin to tell you!'

EIGHTEEN

The following night, Peter tosses and turns. Sleeping fitfully, his legs straighten or bend so completely that his toes reach the base of the bed or his knees graze his chin. His belly is cramped and aching, as if from indigestion, but he is otherwise well. Entangled in swirled sheets, he knows some kind of anxiety is again whirling through his mind and affecting his body. The results are as stressful as the worst moments of his bankruptcy.

There is no obvious explanation. All aspects of Peter's life have improved beyond measure. He feels relaxed and at ease in California. His daughter is out of danger and rehabilitating well, he has more than enough money, his ex-wife has agreed a reasonable settlement, and his son has promised to visit San Francisco again during the approaching autumn. His relationship with Angela has become close and devoted, and his physical health and spiritual growth are both progressing well – *almost hand-in-hand*, he observes, as if surprised.

Peter rises while it is still dark. Trying not to wake Angela, he creeps out of the bedroom and into the kitchen. To avoid speaking aloud and waking Angela, he waves at the kettle to switch it on. He stands resting a hand on the counter while waiting for the water to boil. A minute later, he carries a large mug of tea into the lounge.

Seated on the sofa facing the window, Peter stares into the darkness of the Bay. Points of light from the harbor, the Bay Bridge and the distant city of Oakland prick through the black canvas, each showing tiny glimpses of not-so-distant life. The thought *'It's as if they're trying to tell me something,'* arrives amidst a chaotic jumble of others.

Well aware that precognition is dismissed by many as pseudo-science, Peter prefers not to dwell on his growing sense of unease. He tries for an hour to ignore the feeling. He retrieves his discarded puzzle book as an aid to distraction.

Peter knows the feeling is not indigestion, neither is it the symptom or the result of any physical cause. His intuition is telling him that something difficult to deal with and possibly deadly is about to engulf all he knows. Eventually, he mouths the words: 'I don't care if it violates the rule of causality,' quickly followed by speaking even louder the remainder of his thoughts – 'I cannot ignore these feelings any longer!'

Realizing how loud he has just spoken Peter stares towards the bedroom door, fearful he has woken Angela. There is no sound from inside the bedroom and the door remains closed. He exhales with a gasp.

Unable to identify why, he knows his foreboding is unrelated to Angela, which means its source is likely him or one of his children. For several minutes, he sits on the floor in contemplation, fearing that his daughter is about to suffer another relapse. By the end of that time, he is certain this is not true. However, he is left with an equal certainty that Lilian is somehow involved, or affected, or may even be a part of the problem.

It is four in the morning in San Francisco, which means it is seven AM in New York. Peter decides he will call to check on his daughter soon after nine. It is three months to the day since Lilian was fitted with the Bio-AID.

Acting on impulse, Peter re-reads the letter from his great-great-grandfather. He is again drawn to its third paragraph, which is a warning of the results of gaining at others' expense and a commitment to reform. In his great-great-grandfather's case by traveling until he finds his true, honest path. Two sentences in particular seem to echo his sense of foreboding.

My new-found abilities enabled me to gain at the expense of others. But each time this happened, I felt a gulf widen in my gut, like my soul was emptying out.

Less than an hour later, Peter feels a light touch on his left shoulder. He has drifted off to sleep so is not certain if he has imagined or dreamt the touch, or whether it really happened. When he turns his head around, no one is there.

He stands and walks over to the bedroom door. Carefully turning the handle, he opens it far enough to see that Angela is still asleep. He closes the door and returns to the sofa.

A moment later, he hears a voice inside his head, its words and diction as clear and distinct as if spoken from beside his ear.

'Dad,' his daughter's voice says. 'Dad, I can tell you want to speak with me. Just think clearly what you want to say. I will know straight away what it's about.'

Eight weeks after recovering consciousness, Lilian has learnt how to communicate over a great distance. At her instigation, Peter

131

sensed her presence as a light, indistinct touch. After he failed to respond, her voice then appears inside his head. It takes several minutes for a confused and disoriented Peter to realize the communication is telepathic.

At first believing Lilian has somehow flown over to surprise him, he wanders around the flat looking for her. He is still peering into cupboards when she admonishes him and repeats her request.

'Dad, what are you doing? Just think clearly and let me know what you want.'

At this point, Peter accepts that Lilian must be communicating by telepathy. He is not asleep, nor is he daydreaming. There is no other explanation. He closes his eyes to concentrate and within a few seconds listens while his internal voice tells Lilian that he is concerned about her. His subconscious mind is generating the content of his message, but its communication is controlled by his daughter.

Knowing she can trust her father, Lilian begins to implant within his mind some of her recent experiences, in the form of clearly articulated sentences and moving images, accompanied by an instruction to tell no one else. She ends the process light-heartedly.

'Come on, Dad, this is cool stuff! Now I can talk to you whenever I want. And show you what I've seen. It's amazing!'

Shocked by the clarity of both her voice and the images she projects, Peter is unsure how to react. Many questions arise simultaneously. *Are we the only ones? Who else knows? Is it because of the shock to your brain? Do we need to keep it secret? Is this something anyone can do? What are the consequences if everyone gains these abilities?*

Sensing her father's unease, she attempts to calm him.

'Listen, Dad. It's cool. I don't know how or why this is happening, but it's great fun. I know lots of things I never knew before, and I can access all kinds of information at will. I can hear anyone's thoughts. Anyone I want, not just yours.'

Lilian feels her father's shock at hearing the last sentence.

'Not all at once, of course. I have to focus. But I can tell what people are thinking and feeling, even before they say anything!'

Lilian does not specifically state that she is able to plant ideas into other's subconscious minds, although Peter has just experienced exactly this.

He recalls the warning about misusing abilities he has just read in his great-great-grandfather's letter. Having studied philosophy as a youth, he is also well aware of the temptations and dangers of excessive power.

'Darling, please be careful how you use these new skills of yours. It's wrong to invade someone else's privacy. Or to take advantage of them. That's all too easy, once you know what they are thinking.'

He avoids using the word 'powers', although that is how he categorises her new abilities. He is deeply worried, a feeling instantly shared with his daughter. Continuing to talk as if all is light-hearted fun, Lilian does not mention that, as well as hearing others' present unconscious thoughts, she is now capable of hearing and seeing the past and future thoughts and experiences of others, sometimes from years ahead or behind.

'No one can keep any secrets from me. My mind is reeling with the implications of it all, Dad,' she longs to say, but fears that may be a step too far. *Even Dad won't accept that future stuff,* she reasons.

After their conversation, Lilian concludes *I doubt that even my own father fully believes me. We will see. I expect him to call me back by telephone, once he's got his head around what's just happened.*

Aloud but only to the room around her, she adds: 'At least I know it's all true, and that's enough for now!'

Her new intuition is already telling Lilian that she is not the only person able to manipulate minds, nor to comprehend and use the true, perpetual and simultaneous nature of time. At this moment, she has not realised just how many others there are.

NINETEEN

After their telepathic conversation ends, Peter's mind and heart are racing. Attempting to calm himself, he breathes deep and long for several minutes. His heart rate slows but thought after thought continue to arise and to churn. Question after question poses itself. Most go unanswered.

Turning on the lamp beside his sofa, Peter opens the journal at a bookmarked page. He re-reads those words, penned by Jake so many years before, where he outlines how thoughts determine our circumstances rather than vice versa.

What we think and our ideas n all determines who we are and whether grief or good comes to us. If we think on struggling and hardship then thats wat we get. If we want something good then that comes too. But only if we feel strong enough about it.

The handwritten words echo many of the teachings Peter has heard in various classes over the previous months. In class and in spite of the obvious earnestness of the presenters or teachers, Peter has always felt their words sounded hollow; empty, as if they may be true but are being spoken by someone with no direct knowledge of their *Truth*.

Like a yoga teacher who tells people how to perform asanas but never practices them herself, the teachers are merely repeating what they have read or heard, he muses. And, remembering the exception he

135

has met: *With the sole exception of Maureen, they have never visited the place where resides the wisdom behind those words.*

They may be written by a young, uneducated hand but Jake's words are very different: precise, succinct and spoken straight from the heart. They sound and feel wholly true. Peter finishes reading the passage and closes his eyes. In the presence of *Truth*, he feels immediately uplifted. He basks in its glow for a whole minute before his rational mind intervenes.

We accept without question that physical events affect our mental state, so surely the reverse may be true, it tells him. *That's plainly true, witness the effects of stress.*

Peter's logic continues: *If our mental state affects our bodies then maybe it affects our physical surroundings too.*

A freight train of thoughts rushes headlong through Peter's mind. *The hardships and pain I have suffered, the long unhappiness of an empty marriage and the decline of my business. Have I somehow brought all these upon myself?*

The thought of manifestation being driven and controlled by his own mind is so alien, so different to his everyday perception of physical reality that Peter's logic rejects them. However, the accompanying feeling of surprise is soon replaced with a certitude that he has stumbled upon a great *Truth*.

Wanting to hear the words to test their truth or falsity, Peter says aloud: 'Our minds create our universe, not the reverse!'

He knows from the sound created by the words that they are true, no matter how unbelievable they may be to his logical mind. He repeats the sentence and receives the same answer.

Peter's logical thoughts continue their attempt at distraction, identifying the source as being elsewhere. *No individual other than me can be blamed for all those events, nor thanked for the subsequent repairs and my recent acquisition of material and emotional wealth. One could blame external factors, like "my business collapsed because the need for professional accountants reduced following the development of automated accounting". But the more I think on it, those events have led from one to another in a chain of inevitability. They all started the day I decided to turn my back on what I knew of spirituality, and the true nature of the universe. And the repairs started soon after all of that life disappeared.*

Maybe, Peter concludes, *Maybe, there is no free will. These are trials we must simply endure.*

Unsettled by the memory of his lack of will, Peter moves to shift his weight then coughs, interrupting his train of thought.

And is all this, Peter's thoughts persist, *really the result of a slaughter ending my previous life? That was Maureen's explanation. Whether or not that is the source of my faintheartedness, it's undeniable it's led me into a mess. Perhaps that's what my father meant: I had to experience darkness to appreciate light. Perhaps we all do?*

Peter shakes his head, scattering his thoughts. He stands and enters the kitchen where he speaks the words, 'Kettle on', aloud. Resting on the edge of the table he waits for the kettle to fill and then boil. While perched there, his thoughts turn to Jake.

The old Native Chief must have recognized Jake for the savant that he already was. Throughout Jake's writing there is a spirit of

137

curiosity and generosity, as well as an obvious taste for wisdom and revealed truth, even before they meet. He was a wholly exceptional young man, stronger of character than I will ever be. The journal records his development, but the consistency and universality of his writings are clear from the opening paragraphs.

These are uplifting thoughts, accompanied by a rising of Peter's ribcage and a feeling of pride that Jake is his ancestor. Eyes stare unfocused into an unseen distance, where Peter glimpses something bright and eternal as his eyelids close.

Peter is now deep in meditation, connected to the universal energy that pervades all things. His train of thoughts are first replaced with swirls and patterns, then followed by an awareness of white light, which washes all around and through his body as if entering and leaving simultaneously from every direction.

Peter feels for the second time a presence on his shoulder. This time it is not his daughter but his *Higher Self*, wordlessly assuring of its power and presence and telling him that he is now, at last, traveling along his true path. Recognizing and acknowledging its presence for the first time since a child, his heart lifts. For a moment he remembers the term used by the eastern Orthodox church to describe it, best translated as *Divine Archetype,* before surrendering entirely to its embrace.

With eyes closed, Peter's conscious mind is guided upwards by and in the presence of his *Higher Self*, through layer upon layer of light and semi-darkness until it comes to rest in an expanse of pure white light. This, Peter instinctively knows, is where he comes from and to where he will return when this life ends, and where he will stay until he commences another life, whether on Earth or on some other planet, and in whatever form he desires.

While in the light, Peter knows and will later remember that it is he and his *Higher Self* who control the journal and are the source of its messages and its wisdom. The journal contains great *Truths* but is not magic. It is a mere mechanism, one used and controlled by his *Higher Self* to advise and guide him. He realizes for the first time that he acts in concert with his *Higher Self* to drive the content and events of all aspects of his life, as well as all of its surroundings and all of its manifestations.

The profound revelation ends by returning Peter through the multitude of layers and back into his body. The entire journey has taken only moments. He remains in blissful mood and his eyes stay closed, until an instinct tells him to open them. He finds Angela standing over him, staring at his face.

'I'm sorry,' she says. 'I didn't mean to disturb you. You seemed a long way away, somewhere happy. You were smiling. Were you meditating or daydreaming?'

Peter's throat contracts after his habitual embarrassed cough. When his throat clears, he replies: 'Yes! Yes, I was. Meditating, I mean. And deeper – or *higher* – than ever before.'

Peter has no idea what else to say. His first great experience of the *Divine* is impossible to describe with mere words. Angela's physical presence is in such stark contrast to the enlightened experience of only a few seconds before that Peter is certain he must look like a startled deer.

Angela asks: 'Would you like me to make you some breakfast?'

His positive answer sounds to Peter as though it emerges from somewhere other than him, but Angela is satisfied and walks into the kitchen.

A few minutes later, Angela and Peter are sitting opposite each other at the kitchen table. A mug full of steaming coffee is cupped in her hands and a half-empty dish of porridge sits in front of him. Excited and intense, for the first time Peter is ready to tell Angela more about the journal. He begins calmly.

'You know that book I've been reading?'

Inching her palms back and forth, Angela is twirling her coffee mug, first left, then right. She looks up.

'Well, the young boy who wrote it, he was an ancestor of mine. The young man, that's what he was by the end of the journey, endured amazing things but most remarkable of all is what he learnt from an Indian.'

Angela corrects him: 'You mean a Native American?'

'Yes. One who introduced Jake to his spiritual powers, powers that seemingly passed on to Pop. Jake wrote that we can all access them if we are prepared to have faith in ourselves.'

A frown appears on Angela's face.

'That's what your father always said.'

Peter continues: 'Jake, the young man, explains in the clearest, simplest terms what he perceives and experiences. He learns how to tell what others are thinking and feeling and knows how we affect and are affected by our surroundings.'

Angela's chin retreats. A signal, he is certain, of her disbelief. Peter persists.

'Take a look at me. All that unhappiness locked for so long inside me: penned in by my unhappy marriage, doubts about my self-worth, all those negative thoughts and emotions. It's no wonder that the end result was complete failure.'

Angela begins, 'I don't...'

Stretching one hand across the table to touch both of hers, Peter interrupts: 'My point is that I became positive and happy before things worked out well, rather than the other way around. My intrinsic hope and belief that somehow things would work out – a feeling imbued in me by Pop as a boy – caused my present circumstances to occur, in exactly the same way as my earlier unhappiness caused the financial and marital disasters. It was the very strength of my relief that the trials were over as well as my belief in some kind of serendipity or providence that made them all work out. We attract positive events by positive thoughts, rather than vice versa. That's what I mean.'

Peter's monologue has confused and discomfited Angela who, while professing interest and understanding, has only a superficial comprehension of his words. Her hands fidget with the mug once more. The wooden chair beneath her creaks when Angela shifts her weight from one buttock to another.

For the first time since meeting her, Peter recognizes his thoughts are sharper, better focused and more attuned than hers. Rather than learning from her, his intuition and understanding are now greater than hers. Both of them realize that the intellectual and spiritual balance between them has shifted, and the manner of their interaction will never be the same again. No longer is it Angela explaining experiences to Peter; it is now the other way around.

To ease the transition, Peter makes light of their conversation.

'I'm sorry. That was all very self-absorbed of me, wasn't it?'

Angela hides her true feelings.

'No, really, it's fascinating. *Truly.*'

Peter senses her disingenuity and begins reflecting on their relationship. With no clear idea of where their conversation will lead, he says, 'Jake, the young man in the journal, met a young woman. They lived as if brother and sister, but there was no blood relationship between them. He was kidnapped.'

Confused, Angela asks: 'They were lovers, but they were brother and sister?'

'It's a complicated story. But they loved each other, and they should have run away together. And no, he was kidnapped by her parents when he was a boy and they brought him to America and raised him as if he was their own, that's all.'

'That's terrible!' exclaims Angela. 'The kidnapping, I mean.'

'Jake is only fourteen or so when he eventually leaves. The young woman he loves refuses to go with him. I was so disappointed when I read that, although I've not reached the end yet. I hope they meet up again, like in a Hollywood movie. It doesn't seem right they should part. Or maybe I'm just a hopeless romantic.'

Angela laughs, loudly.

'I've never thought of you as one. You're far too analytical for that!'

'I guess you're right but well… who can judge?'

Angela asks: 'They loved each other?'

'Oh yes, they were devoted.'

With finality, Angela judges, 'Then it is sad.'

Angela yawns aloud and stretches her long arms wide. Ignoring her body language, Peter continues his tale.

'There was an evil character on the journey with them, one who stalks Mona, the young girl. Jake realized it and made sure they kept their distance.'

Angela walks over to the coffee machine. Peter continues as she pours.

'I think he knew that if you get too close to people like that, then you risk being infected by their negativity, or their evil. It's better to keep away. That man Payless I told you about, for example. He makes money by screwing people over, like he did with me. And he's defended by the bloody system!'

Angela turns her head, looking over her shoulders and directly into his eyes.

'There's not always justice in the world.'

Cradling her mug, Angela walks across the kitchen, past Peter and into the lounge. She does not hear Peter murmur, 'No, but there should be. I hope to God I never meet anyone else like him.'

Peter also reflects that he has taken advantage of Janet's kindness. *I must make it up to her somehow,* he decides.

Left alone with his coffee, the next thought that arrives in Peter's mind is a shock, delivered from somewhere or someone else.

'The real reason for the attention Angela lavishes upon you is because she has always known you will inherit Pop's wealth.'

TWENTY

Having sent the warning to her father, Lilian turns her attention to her former partner Sarah. Within a few minutes of implanting the idea of apologizing, Sarah calls her for the first time since leaving.

Lilian closes her eyes and her Bio-AID immediately shows a detailed picture of Sarah and her new apartment in Denver. Its precise location is shown on a map at the lower-left corner of her vision.

'I'm so sorry! I hope you understand,' Sarah begins.

After a few minutes of sobbing and craven apologies, Sarah recovers enough to tell a lie.

'I was scared and thought you were going to die! The doctors only gave you a fifty-fifty chance. I was distraught!'

Lilian has no need for her new intuitive abilities to recognize the lie: it is so far removed from Sarah's usurious character it would be unbelievable to anyone who knows her. Nonetheless, Sarah persists.

'I miss you, you know. We had such good times together!'

Lilian's response is cool.

'Where are you living now?'

Sarah tells of her return to Denver and the running of her new business from there. Within a few minutes of manipulation, Sarah has agreed to return control of the business to her. Passwords and full details of how to override the iris- and voice-recognition protections are handed over. In a final act of meekness, Sarah even offers to become Lilian's junior partner once more.

'It's too late for that,' Lilian responds coolly.

Lilian places another idea in Sarah's head, then has to stifle a giggle when she hears Sarah announce: 'Lilian, I am so sorry, but I must go. I really need a break from all this pressure. I'm just going to pack and then go to the airport. I think Hawaii or Bali sound great. I'll call you when I come back, if that's okay?'

Lilian ends the call gracefully. Then, delighted with the result of this first great test of her abilities, she transmits one last idea into Sarah's subconscious mind; one that ensures Sarah will never return.

Cold and calculating, Lilian decides without qualms that she has the right to be vengeful. Less than one hour later she deals in the same way with the man who caused her fall, with equally deadly result.

❧

Hector Martinez picks up his young son. Four-years-old, the boy's playful punches strike Hector's shoulders with no effect. Hector pretends otherwise. He drops to the floor, holding his son in the air with both hands at arms' length. He rolls from side to side, shouting and laughing.

'Ho, son! You're killing me! You're killing me!'

Within a few moments the boy is hugged to Hector's broad chest, where a kiss is planted on his forehead. He moans a disapproval

145

when his father announces: 'Hey, Santi. Daddy has to go. I'll just be a few hours though, okay?'

Hector tousles his son's dark brown hair.

'Then I'll read you a story before bedtime. You think about which story you'd like me to read and tell me when I get back.'

'I know now,' the young boy shouts back. Still shouting, he adds, 'I want you to make one up. About knights and dragons, and horses and pigs.'

'Pigs?' exclaims Hector. 'What on earth makes you think of pigs?'

'I like pigs.'

Hector kisses his pregnant girlfriend, Lisa, before leaving.

A half-hour later, Hector has picked up his load of pizzas and is about to deliver the first, to a flophouse in Brownsville. The bike's stand is broken, so he leans his aging motorbike against the nearest wall before removing its key. He walks up the short flight of stairs to the front door, where he mutters the single word 'pigs'. He laughs aloud as his finger presses a buzzer.

Standing a minute later at a third-floor doorway marked with a chalked '32', Hector opens the warming bag and pulls out a large, flat box. He is about to say 'large pepperoni' when the door opens, and the snub nose of a handgun is pushed into his face. The bag is dropped as Hector shouts a panicked: 'Whoa man, it's just a pizza!'

Hector is still holding the pizza box when he is shot in the chest. Lying dazed and bleeding on the floor, he is shot again in the side of the head.

Accustomed to violence and with no desire to become involved, no neighbors' doors open, and no witnesses appear. Larry turns and grabs his jacket from the hook beside the door, before reaching down while the world around him drifts slowly and colorfully downwards a split-second after.

Moving within a dream, he picks up the pizza box with a single hand. With his pistol in the other, he flees down the corridor, followed by a trail of lights and colors. He flies through a glass-paneled door at its end. Leaping each flight of stairs in three bounds, he reaches the front door in a matter of seconds. Undoing the latch with an elbow, he pulls open the door and pushes it wide with his left foot.

Alerted in advance to the crime, the first of four patrol cars arrives outside the front door of the building just as Larry emerges. Stunned by the sight of the police cruiser waiting for him, a second passes before he tries to conceal the gun. Simultaneously, both policemen retrieve Glock 17 handguns from their holsters and open their car doors. By the time their guns are pointed at Larry, the pizza box is dropped, and his arms are raised.

Larry shouts: 'Don't shoot, man! Don't shoot! It was only some kind of accident. I never meant to shoot him. He's just a pizza guy!'

The cops cannot discern his mumbled words. Seeing his arms raised, they approach and push him to the ground. As they cuff him, Larry continues babbling incoherently. Still high, the only words the cops can discern is 'told me to do it'.

After reading their prisoner his rights, one of the policemen remarks: 'Man, you gotta be quicker 'n that to get away with a killin' in this town! We got this call at least five minutes ago. What the hell was you doin'? Wiping yo' ass or somethin'?'

Larry has no answer.

The second policeman says, 'Jeez. It's like an epidemic in this town. Every one of the killings we've been to this week, some guy or gal is claiming it happened in a dream!'

TWENTY-ONE

After a day of agonising over how to deal with Lilian's warning about Angela, Peter decides to take a week-long break. He tells Angela a half-truth: he must return to the UK to sign various papers and tie up loose ends relating to his divorce. The following afternoon she drives him to the airport.

Unaccustomed to his new-found wealth, Peter has found a cheap hotel in Bayswater. Less than an hour after checking-in he has called his friend Raymond and arranged to meet him in a bar close to Oxford Street.

Once inside the bar, it takes a few seconds for Peter's eyes to adjust to the dark interior. By this time Raymond has walked over, right hand extended in welcome. The two men greet each other with handshakes and smiles.

'I hope you don't mind meeting here,' Raymond says, 'only we're having the house redecorated. It's a mess of pipework, plasterboard, workmen, and robotic sprayers.'

While they wait for Peter's drink to pour, both men share stories of recent events. Raymond holds up his hand to pay for the drinks as Peter explains about Lilian's injury, and then about Margaret.

'Yes, suffering from high blood pressure and depression I understand. She's looking after Lilian for the moment but she's planning to live with her sister in Scarborough. If you call that living, of course.'

'Ha!' Raymond grins. 'I went there once, a long time ago. That was enough. They speak funny and it's so damn cold!'

His intended joke falls flat. Within another minute he has asked about Peter's bankruptcy.

'The house was repossessed within a week. As soon as I notified them that I had no means of payment, they issued a writ. The automated Court doesn't give a damn.'

'Bloody AI systems! They have no heart,' his friend sympathizes before adroitly changing tack. 'It's been hard, I'm sure. But I'm jealous of you, you know, living alone. My wife's been driving me insane for years.'

This second attempt at humour fails completely. His former world having been stripped bare, Peter no longer feels obliged to think or communicate in such terms. With a serious expression, he says, 'You surely don't mean that.'

Disconcerted by his friend's rapid change of tone, Raymond blusters.

'I don't know. We've been married a long time. I suppose not.'

An uncomfortable minute's silence follows as the men sup twice at their beers. Peter breaks the silence.

'That's a very pleasant beer. How are things with you otherwise?'

'The job, you mean?' Raymond shrugs. 'Times are tough for accountants like you and me, but we'll pull through. With a little adjustment and belt-tightening.'

Both men move towards a vacant table near the window frontage. After they share family news, Raymond asks: 'And how are you coping?'

Peter explains: 'My inheritance means I don't need to work.' The rest of his assessment is brutally honest. 'I'm getting too old to retrain and change careers.'

Grateful his friend is so blunt, Raymond asks: 'You'll try get a job, though. Or will you just hang about?'

Peter elaborates: 'Yes, I suppose so. I've no idea what. I can't stand the idea of working for someone else, or even consulting to them. All those spotty twenty-somethings, jumped-up and talking about "focus groups" or "service mentality" or some other thing they've heard from a bloody online magazine. I don't understand half the words they use, and God knows what they talk about when they get home.'

Catching a change in mood, Raymond adds: 'They drive *me* insane too. Better when they're protesting about the lack of jobs or inaction on climate change. Were we as obnoxious when we were younger?'

'I don't think we spouted trite and pretentious business-school bullshit, did we? At least, not dressed up in over-long, meaningless, jargon-ridden sentences like this one.'

Raymond laughs. 'I guess you're right.'

At that instant a young Asian woman enters, picks up an empty glass and throws it at a young man standing in a group at the bar. It misses, strikes a wall and shatters. She shouts: 'You bastard!' then rushes forward and begins beating his head and shoulders with raised fists, still shouting.

'You raped me! And I trusted you. What did you put in my drink? I'm going to the police.'

The young man raises both hands to fend her off. Taking hold of her wrists, he says, 'Go ahead, luv. I've got you on tape beggin' for it.'

'Don't be so bloody ridiculous! And even if I did, you must have given me something.'

The young man turns to his friends and says, 'Like I told you, piece of cake.'

Everyone in the pub is watching. The woman wrestles her hands free, shouts a final insult then slams the door as she departs. The group of men laugh together and resume their conversation, more animated than before.

Peter coughs into a raised hand. He and Raymond look at each other and shrug. Raymond tells him: 'You know, there's lately been a lot of peculiar "goings-on". Nothing quite like that, but ordinary people committing crimes or complaining about things like rape, theft, and so on. It's as if there's something in the air.'

With no available explanation, the two men resort to traditional male interaction, mixing current affairs with populist xenophobia. Although Peter is still able to express these opinions, the sound of their words feels alien and discordant as if spoken from outside his body. Increasingly uncertain of any opinion, Peter knows his whole world view has changed within just a few weeks. He briefly wonders whether its source is the death of his father, the drastically changed nature of his new life, or even the journal and its relationship to him.

His friend observes only a changed personality and lack of confidence, but Peter knows far more fundamental changes are under way. The emergence of his readiness to accept non-material views of the world has already begun, affecting all of his beliefs, desires and ambitions. After sitting in silent contemplation for some time, Peter apologizes and attempts to explain.

'I'm sorry, Raymond. You know, I often find myself disappearing into these reveries now. I guess its delayed shock or something. Or maybe my inept attempt to use this slow and aging brain to cope with change.'

Raymond appreciates his friend's honesty. Although irritated by the inward-looking silence, he feels more kinship with Peter than he can remember. His response is gracious, and heartfelt.

'It's okay, Peter. We're old friends, aren't we? And but for the grace of God, there goes my business too.' He pauses, then adds: 'It'll all work out in the end, I'm sure. At least you've no money worries now, unlike the rest of us.'

Peter lets out a deep sigh.

'I hope so. For years I've had to put up with bankers and lawyers who twist every word I say to their own ends. They care nothing about right and wrong and are only interested in their fees. I sat among them and felt physically sick. Mind you, it won't be long before they're all automated too!'

An exclamation of support from Raymond is followed by: 'Yes, I was reading that most of the trading and market manipulation that made them so rich is now pretty much all done by machine. I...'

He is interrupted when Peter continues his tirade.

'The older ones are so cynical you can see it in their eyes: pain and self-loathing blunted by port and the best wines. And the younger ones, the juniors, they're well down that line too. I doubt their wives still want to make love to them. I'm sure they just lie there and let themselves be shagged, grateful for the money that frees their time for primping and pilates.'

Raymond laughs and places his hand on Peter's arm in a rare physical gesture between the two.

'Bankers and lawyers, eh? Best you have another drink.'

Raymond's wristband AR chirps. He knows who it is before answering. Fearful his meeting with Peter would become quickly embarrassing, he earlier arranged for his wife to call and provide an excuse for departing. He speaks to the device.

'Yes, dear. Oh, I see. Well, okay, I'll be home shortly.'

Having just experienced the only sincere, personal interaction he can remember, Raymond now has no desire to leave. Nevertheless, he turns towards Peter and frowns.

'Sorry, domestic crisis.'

Peter has used the same ploy in the past but is magnanimous.

'It's okay, Raymond. I have some things to do this evening.'

While the two men are putting on their coats a newsflash appears on the TV above the bar. The barman increases the volume so all can hear. The news anchor is reporting one of the first major plane crashes in almost a decade.

'…Aided by his co-pilot, it's now clear that the captain deliberately switched off the engines at a height of over thirty-thousand feet. Then the cockpit voice-recording shows that the two men calmly discussed golf until the plane nosedived into the ground at over five hundred miles per hour. Our aviation correspondent, Humphrey Gillespie reports from Bangkok on this second crash in as many weeks...'

The two men shake hands at the door and walk away in different directions. Raymond returns home to dinner and an evening of bored TV and politesse, rueing his snap decision to leave.

Emboldened by alcohol, Peter decides on an impulse to visit the home of his former assistant, Janet. He has never visited her home but knows Janet is single and that her home is less than two miles away. He decides to walk. Out of breath, he arrives thirty minutes later at her tiny red brick and slate-roofed terraced home. Peter presses the circular button of her doorbell and steps back to wait for an answer.

The door remains unopened and there is no sign of life from inside. Peter is surprised the entry system is not linked to an AR. Disappointed, he turns from the door. Opening the low gate behind and looking at Peter with a surprised smile stands Janet.

'Mr Walker. What a lovely surprise! Won't you come in?'

Janet bustles past and opens her front door. Once inside, she greets Peter by leaning her right cheek inwards to touch his face. Janet beckons him onwards.

'I'll make us a nice pot of tea.'

The lounge is as he expected: spotlessly clean and dominated by trinkets and mementoes dotted across the mantelpiece, a cupboard and a low mahogany coffee table. The glass front of the corner cupboard shows it is full of china and crystal. *This room has chosen to remain in the nineteen seventies*, he muses.

By the time Janet returns from the kitchen carrying a tray of tea and biscuits, Peter's breathing has slowed to normal and the perspiration under his arms has dried. Janet serves while Peter tells her of his time in California.

'I'm here for a week. I've not been looking for jobs, or anything. I know I should find some way of starting again, but I can't stand doing the same thing all over.'

He does not mention Angela, nor does her tell her of Lilian's injury. Instead, he begins by telling her of his 'horrible hotel.' Holding the handle of her cup between index and middle finger and with her little finger crooked, Janet sips tea in genteel fashion before delivering her news.

'I've been laid off, you know.'

Peter is aghast.

'No, surely not! Why would they?'

Janet takes another sip of her tea.

'They're closing the office and moving the business elsewhere. At least that's what they say. They wouldn't tell me anymore. And they're refusing to pay me any redundancy money.'

Indignant, Peter tells her: 'They can't do that, Janet. We must fight them!'

Janet is pleased to see him so animated on her behalf but lowers her head as she expresses caution.

'I don't know about that, Mr Walker. I'd prefer to simply find another position somewhere. They've promised me a good reference.'

After exchanging polite conversation for a few minutes, Janet enquires, 'Could I ask you to do something for me, Mr Walker? Only my sink is blocked, and I can't find a plumber.'

Peter agrees. They finish their tea. He follows Janet into the kitchen. As he walks, her tells her: 'It's so good to see you again, Janet. Most of my old friends haven't even called me. And you were always so loyal, and cheery!'

Lips purse and her nose wrinkles as Janet exclaims, 'I've tried calling you a few times, Mr Walker, but you never answer!'

'Oh, I know Janet. And I'm sorry. I wasn't ready to talk to anyone until now.' He adds: 'And thank you.'

Peter peers at the sink. 'It's probably just a small blockage. Do you have a plunger?'

Janet answers and fetches one. Peter pushes the plunger into inches of murky water before pumping up and down. Relaxing and less inhibited while he works, Peter tells of his earlier rendezvous.

'I just met with an old friend, the first and only such meeting since I left. He's very understanding, but we have nothing in common anymore, except our history. I've changed. What's happened has changed *me*, I mean. I don't yet know what it means, but I know I want something different.'

Janet is supportive, as always.

'You always were one for fine ideas. I'm sure you'll find something soon.'

A loud gurgling sound escapes from the sink as the trapped water swirls and subsides. Peter looks up with a satisfied grin.

'What about you, Janet? What will you do?'

'Oh, I don't know. I was never ambitious. I'm happy here in my little house, as long as there's food on my table and I don't have to worry about anything else.'

Peter returns the plunger to the draining board. A moment later, Janet adds: 'You know, Mr Walker, you could stay here for the week if you like. As a lodger, I mean.'

Peter twists his body around.

'Why, Janet, that would be lovely. Really, it would. But I wouldn't want to be…'

Janet's interruption is forceful.

'You'll not be any kind of imposition, if that's what you're about to say. I wouldn't ask you if I didn't mean it.'

Peter spreads his arms wide and gives Janet a bear-hug.

'Oh, Janet, you're a God-send. I hate all the noise and people in that place. It's awful, an endurance test suited to someone more sociable than me. But you're… *sure*?'

They separate as Janet's face breaks into a broad smile.

'I'm sure, Mr Walker. *Very* sure.'

TWENTY-TWO

Peter's breath escapes in a loud, vaporous stream, cooling as soon as it leaves his mouth. Placing both hands onto the mattress, he levers himself to a seated position on the single divan bed. Tired springs creak and groan, straining beneath him into a collective parabola. Janet's spare bedroom is small but comfortable. He has now been her guest for three days.

His right hand reaches over to switch on a lamp. He stares blankly at his glowing AR, but darkness has already told him it is early.

Really! he thinks. *Who would call me at this hour?*

He ignores it until it darkens. Peter has a message from Angela. He looks at his wrist as the AR projects a hologram that speaks: *Hi, Peter. I hope things are going well. I miss you. Give me a call when you have a moment x.*

Peter's mood brightens. His head rises. 'Eight hours' time-difference,' he mutters. 'That means she's thinking about me last thing before bed.'

His face breaks into a grin. *I'm a fool worrying over whether she knew of Pop's money. Who cares?* Peter decides not to reply until he can think of a witty response: *I'll call her this evening, while Janet's out at her class.* He links hands around his shins and rocks slowly back and forth.

Choosing to read more of the journal, Peter reaches into his briefcase and fetches it onto his lap. The first page he opens is around one-third of the way through the book.

The old Indian told me I was very brave comin so far without my kin. When I said I felt it was destine he laughed and said your destine is all round and in here. He held his left breast. Then he touched mine. I felt a tingling. It spread thru me. He asked "I have heard your God sent his son to you and that you beat him and tied him to a stake until he died. Is it true?" I ansered him its what our holy book says. He gave me a gift then told me "Young warrior, you must be carefull among such people. It is your fate to be with white men but you have the soul of a human being. If they see you talk with spirits they may persecute you too." He smiled at me like he was my oldest friend then tutched my forehead.

Peter closes his eyes and tries to picture the scene described by Jake: Native-American Shaman and young white boy, conversing on the prairie. Within a few moments, patterns swirl behind his closed eyelids and his body begins to feel light, as if floating over the bed. His arms and legs tingle, vibrating in tune with some ethereal, unheard song.

Remembering Pop's lessons from his youth, Peter knows he is meditating deeply and at the same time learning a great truth. His body convulses, for a moment fearful as it again experiences those sensations he so strongly rejected as a young man. Peter takes a deep breath and opens his eyes. His heart is beating fast and loud in a heaving chest. He lies down. It takes several minutes for his heart to slow.

He pulls back the curtains a few inches and stares out into darkness. His eyes pick out a few drops of cold rain, backlit by a streetlight opposite his bedroom window. He says aloud: 'All this must be why Pop gave me the journal.'

Leaning back, Peter recalls more of his father's lessons: the need to breathe deeply and steadily, to trust your feelings, to meditate regularly, and to keep your heart open. Fearful but knowing the depth of his father's love, he resolves to practice regularly.

'Perhaps when I return to the US,' he mouths in near silence.

Hungry for Janet's promised cooked breakfast, Peter heads downstairs. Hearing his footsteps on the stairway, Janet is pouring tea into a mug when he enters the kitchen.

There has been no suggestion, no comment, no question, no sideways glance, no winsome smile, no attempt to dress differently or to wear any special make-up. Peter of course knows that Janet adores him but, were he to speculate, he would describe her feelings towards him as motherly or sisterly. Even so, he makes no mention of Angela or her message. Keen to talk, he tells her of the journal.

'You know, Janet, I've been reading a book about the pioneers who crossed America to found the West.'

Janet expresses interest, so Peter continues: 'Yes, they set off in wagons smaller than this room and lived in them for six months while they crossed the plains, mountains and rivers. The hardships they suffered were incredible.'

Janet finishes chewing before responding: 'It's difficult to comprehend now, isn't it?'

Leaning forward, Peter enthuses: 'Yes, it is. And the most amazing thing is, they were ordinary people like you and me. They weren't explorers or missionaries. They just wanted a better life, so they set off into the unknown to find it. It's inspirational!'

Janet's lips spread into a small smile. She asks: 'Surely we all want that?'

Peter jabs at the air with his fork.

'Some more than others. I'm not sure I'd ever take that kind of risk. There'd been explorers and frontiersmen before them of course, but there was no real trail for them to follow.'

Janet's next question is one Peter has not yet considered.

'And did they find what they wanted?'

'I don't know yet, Janet,' he says. 'I haven't finished the story.'

Sprinkling salt on her eggs, Janet expresses a common wisdom.

'Well, I only ask because my mother was fond of saying that the grass is always greener on the other side.'

Peter is taken aback. Janet has never before expressed an opinion, nor shown any sign of being more than a shy, mousey woman. This time his response is more considered.

'Maybe so. Some died on the way, of course.'

Picking up his knife and fork, Peter asks: 'Have you ever been to America, Janet?'

Surprised by his sudden interest in her, she answers: 'When I was younger, yes, Mr Walker.'

Peter was expecting a negative answer, so answers only, 'Oh, I had no idea.'

Memories flood back as Janet explains.

'Yes, I worked there for a while. But then my mother was very ill, so I came home.'

Peter dutifully attended her funeral several years earlier. Sensing there is more to learn, he asks: 'And you never married?'

Over the years all memory of her past, failed love has faded to a less pained, deeper place. Janet has no desire to dredge it for examination, so she lies.

'No, I never met anyone that made me feel that way.'

Reverting to his earlier politesse he says, 'I'm sure someone's missed out as a result.'

Janet's eyes flash a long-hidden, impish smile, missed by the renewed self-absorption of her lodger.

'You know, Janet,' Peter continues, 'I spent years regretting what I've become, and never had the courage to change. Now change is forced upon me, I'm no longer sure of what I want!'

Janet's face is cast downwards until Peter asks: 'Do you know what my biggest failure is? It's my daughter. She has no morals. I failed to instil in her any concern for others. Her only goal is to make money for herself.'

'We all look after ourselves first, don't we, Peter? It's human nature.'

'Maybe. I still love her, of course. She's my daughter, after all.' Peter sighs. 'But what kind of aim or ambition is that? It's neither noble, nor challenging, nor is its achievement anything to be proud of. In fact, come to think of it, all the really rich people I've ever met were obnoxious. Every one of them.'

Peter's expression turns to a mild frown.

'I now realise I've spent my whole life doing just the same as her. It's my example she's following; chase the money and don't worry about anything or anyone else except your own family. It's not a creed I'm proud of. My father must have been disappointed in me.'

'You shouldn't be so hard on yourself,' Janet says. 'You're no different to anyone else, including me.'

'That may be, Janet. That may be. But the thought of it makes me feel hollow. I'm not even sure why I wanted money in the first place. I'm happy now, happier than I ever was at home with my wife, or with my clients. I don't think I could ever go back to that.'

Janet's heart leaps. She longs to sing out her next words but, as always, her galloping emotions are restrained. Lowering her head to avoid any expression, Janet says only, 'Well, you don't need to, Peter. Not if you're happy here.'

Missing all of the signals in Janet's body language and expression, Peter continues to talk of himself.

'I may take up evening classes, or get a job in a bar, or both. I want to do something completely different. Something inspirational, if I can. And if I can't find it, something I at least enjoy, or that stretches me. Does that sound pretentious?'

Peter's imperfections, his self-absorption and his ignorance of other people's emotions are part of what Janet loves about him. Peter does not admit, and Janet does not know that the source of his newfound motivation is sexual attraction to another woman. Unseen by him, a winsome smile lifts the corners of her mouth.

'Not in the least, Mr Walker.'

'Well, that's what I'm going to do, something different and special,' adds Peter, banging his fist on the table.

A startled Janet has never seen such resolve in him. Her mouth opens and her body jolts in response to the sudden noise. Embarrassed by what he fears has been an unseemly display, Peter sits still and silent, his face reddening. Sensing his discomfort, Janet asks: 'Tell me, Mr Walker. Those pioneers – were they any different to us?'

Peter is grateful for the chance to return to his normal anodyne manner.

'No, Janet. They were exactly the same. They cooperated when they had to, but when things got really tough, they looked after their own selves. But it's the exceptions that are the most interesting: I'm looking forward to reading how they ended up.'

'It sounds like a good read, and I can *see* it's inspired you.'

Peter nods. 'Yes, Janet, it is an inspiration. And now I have some big decisions to make. After all, I can't impose myself on you forever. And my new home is in California.'

On hearing those words, Janet feels her hopes gasp and subside. She falls into dismay. While rinsing dishes, a tear rolls down her left cheek.

Behind her, Peter's eyes cast around the tiny kitchen. Their gaze alights briefly on the folds of the skirt covering Janet's backside before moving onwards to stare awhile past her, through and beyond the glass of the window.

During the late afternoon a storm blows through trees and hedges, loosening poorly crafted masonry, wrecking recklessly erected umbrellas, lifting skirts and the edges of greatcoats and mackintoshes, and destroying the homes of birds and insects inhabiting the urban landscape around Janet's home.

During a fitful nap disturbed by snorts from his nose and gasps from his mouth, Peter hears within a dream the sound of the roaring storm outside: wind and rain and a cold brutal sea whose white waves break over sand and rock, rushing and whooshing, embracing a brave, beaten shore before a hurried, rolling retreat.

Propped at one end of the sofa with knees bent and head lolling, Peter is asleep. Janet watches the rise and fall of his chest, noting each breath as it enters or leaves his lungs with a tiny stutter. Her observant eyes watch the shudder of a leg and the flicker of an eyelid, dual signals he is waking. Shaken from her reveries by his spluttering cough and confronted by suddenly wide-open eyes, she strains to speak.

'Mi… ahem… Mr Walker, would you care for some tea? You've been sleeping. It must be your cold.'

While the kettle rumbles, Janet places her hands onto the draining board and looks at her reflection in the window, searching for some clue in the faint image. 'Chronic anxiety', her doctor says, causing her to stay close to home and to be in bed every night before nine. Her emotions climb. She silently mouths, 'I am not going through that again,' while the teaspoon in her hand stirs and stirs.

Bearing a tray of tea and biscuits, Janet returns to the lounge. She hands a mug to Peter. Punctuated by the violent storm outside, a long period of silence passes. It is Janet who speaks first.

'Well, I suppose I should be getting ready. My evening class starts at six.'

She rises to kiss Peter on his left cheek. Surprised by her approach, his face turns just as her lips touch his skin. His lips brush for an instant against hers. Their eyes meet. For a moment both feel an impulse to move forward and complete a clinch. Neither is certain whose eyes first move but both pairs look downwards, away from the other.

'Oh! I'm sorry, Janet,' says Peter.

'There's no need to apologise, Mr Walker. There's…'

Peter leans forward and rises, interrupting her. 'Well, I suppose I had better get changed too.'

As Peter climbs the stairs, Janet carries the tray into the kitchen.

After Janet leaves the house, Peter calls Angela. She describes in detail her last few days. Eventually he hears, '…talked on for too long. So, tell me Peter, what have you been up to?'

Peter at first manages only a stuttering reply.

'Huh... well... I... er... I...' but he soon recovers.

They talk at length, but their conversation is stilted, with many periods of silence. Before they say goodbye, Peter remembers to tell Angela he misses her and promises to let her know his arrival time.

'I'll pick you up,' she offers.

Using the large screen in the lounge, Peter begins his online search for flights. He is still comparing times and prices when Janet returns. He stands to greet her and removes her coat.

Janet asks: 'What were you searching for? I saw you through the window. Not porn, I hope!'

Peter has never before heard Janet utter any suggestive comment. Taken aback, his neck jerks as he turns to face her.

'For a moment there I thought you were being serious, Janet! I was just searching for flights to the US. I need to go back, the day after tomorrow.'

Janet's expression turns to concern. 'Can you afford it, Peter? Only if you need…''

'Oh, Janet. I've not told you! That is very kind but there's no need. I've inherited much more than I thought from Pop.'

Janet laughs out loud; too loud.

'Why, that's wonderful news. I'm so happy for you.' Her head lowers. 'I'm sorry of course, that he…'

'It's okay, Janet. And thank you.'

After a few moments she adds, in a quiet voice: 'It's a long time since I last went there. I could come wi…'

Peter reacts at once, interrupting: 'Oh Janet, not this time! This journey I need to do alone. Perhaps in the future, you could come and visit? I'll show you around.'

Janet tries not to show her hurt feelings.

'Very well, Mr Walker.'

Two days later he boards a flight that returns him to California. By the time he lands in San Francisco, he has confirmed his decision to forgive Angela. *Whatever her original motivation she is loving, we are happy, and I know she cares about me.*

TWENTY-THREE

During the drive to Los Angeles, Maureen uses her free time to reflect, to plan, and to communicate with some of her closest associates. Hanging next to her is the black dress with mock-feather collar that she will wear while delivering her speech. More than once while talking, her hand stretches out to touch the soft fabric. *It seems such a long time since there's been an occasion for you*, she wordlessly tells it. *And never one quite like this*.

A desk and workstation long ago replaced the two front seats in her oversize Tesla, so she spends most of the journey either dictating or on multi-person video calls. Only her closest Sisters know the purpose of the event. Those in the most distant locations are especially keen to meet with Peter in person. She consistently needs to lower their expectations of when that may happen. At this time Peter remains wholly unaware of the existence of their organization. While she is sure he will agree with its aims and will wish to join their quest, Maureen is by no means so certain of the *degree* of that commitment.

The Griffith Observatory is a landmark building well-known to any tourist to the city, as well as to anyone living there. Set on a promontory on the southern slope of Mount Hollywood, it has a winged dome on each side of a larger central dome. From a distance it looks like a twentieth-century version of a maharajah's palace.

Its position overlooking the Los Angeles Basin and downtown LA is second to none, and it's also within a short distance of the famous 'Hollywood' sign. The two sites are often visited together by tourists, in spite of the restrictions and problems with access and parking. Not that Maureen has any intention of indulging in anything so vulgar as tourism.

Her original instinct was to hold their gathering outdoors, on Alcatraz Island. The powerful, nascent symbolism of imprisoned, subservient women releasing themselves appealed to her, until the practical realities hit home of an outdoor meeting in unpredictable weather. And the problem of embarking and disembarking so many over choppy waters.

Located in the central dome, the Planetarium is normally only rentable by organizations whose goals are entirely consistent with the charter of the Observatory, which are educational and astronomical. It has taken Maureen considerable time and effort to convince their management that the goals of the Sisters of Mary Magdalene fitted within their criteria. The combination of being a minority, non-mainstream, secular (as defined by the Observatory and as declared in the Order's articles), diverse and female-dominated society with an almost two-thousand-year history, swung the assessment. Especially after it was mentioned that the new, female President of the United States was a long-time member and may even be persuaded to attend in person.

As a result of the ultimate in name-dropping, Maureen is able to use the enclosed, spectacular setting of the Planetarium for her announcement to the membership. It is ideal for her purpose.

Almost three hundred women attend in person, mostly from mainland USA, filling the circular hall to capacity. Another two-and-a-half thousand from all walks of life and from all around the world join by video conference. Only four attendees are male, all of whom attend online.

Although formed by Mary Magdalene, the organization is not Christian in the conventional sense. The attendees are of all skin colors, faiths and cultures, and speak many different languages. Since the eighteenth century their agreed common language has been English, one all Members must speak fluently before admission. That decision is reviewed every decade and has been changed only three times in sixteen hundred recorded years.

The round hall is darkened while everyone is seated so that the image of stars projected onto its surrounds are visible to all, whether online or present in person. It makes for an unusual but effective backdrop. The tiny objects are much less visible after a spotlight is turned on to highlight the speaker.

As their Honorary Leader, often referred to informally but misleadingly as Holy Mother, Maureen is used to addressing the membership at their biennial gatherings. However, this is a special event, set up at short notice. Her excitement over the news she must impart has spilled over into an unaccustomed nervousness.

For five minutes before beginning to speak, Maureen feels as if she may vomit. Her hands shake continuously. The symptoms continue even after she is fitted with her microphone and earpiece, and its battery unit is affixed to the rear of her black dress. They only cease at the moment she starts to speak.

'Sisters, I am so pleased to be here this evening,' begins Maureen. 'Beyond pleased, for it is my duty and privilege to be able to tell you that we have at last identified our Master.'

The dramatic announcement causes a collective gasp among the audience. Many of the women look around at their neighbors, seeking confirmation of what they heard. When the ensuing chatter dies down, Maureen continues.

'As you all know, our beloved prophet and founder foretold in her Gospel that she would be castigated and painted as a whore, that men would take over our Church and that we would be forbidden from holding any significant office for two-thousand years.'

Overcome by emotion, Maureen has to pause for several seconds. None of her audience notices and assume she is simply pausing for dramatic effect.

'Mary also wrote that we must form a secret society – ours – and that one day… one day we would be led back to our rightful place, not only in our Church but within a global society, of which our Order will remain a tiny but vital, guiding part. More precisely, in the fourteenth verse she instructed that we must first and forever worship God in our hearts and not in any physical building. "Our hearts," by which she meant our emotions, "are our link to God," she wrote, and "No work of man must ever seek to replace it."

That line in her gospel, along with the jealousy of male followers of Jesus was, I have always been certain, the reason why Mary was belittled and excluded after His death. She knew that such symbols of supposed power and permanence have no place in a world created by our Universal Spirit. Ironically…'

Again, Maureen needs to pause.

'Ironically,' she resumes 'Mary also foretold in the very next verse that we would be led back from this gross, subservient state not by a woman but by a singular man. One who shares our intuitive abilities and in whom is present in abundance the Divine Feminine.'

'It is therefore my great… my *divine* pleasure and duty to tell you that our long wait is over, that the mis-directions and blasphemies of the Church and all its derivatives will within our lifetime be no more, that this man is now among us and that he will soon, within a matter of weeks, be ready and known to us all here.'

There are gasps and shrieks of delight. Raising her voice above the persistent hubbub, Maureen declares: 'We must all prepare for the great changes that are coming. We must do so together, as Sisters. The world faces many perils, but the true nature of mankind will now be revealed, the dominance of men will be ended, the suppression of women will be overcome, and a new, loving and equal world order will be shared by all.'

Loud cheering erupts within moments. Women throughout the hall turn to each other, hugging and crying together. When the noise quietens sufficiently, Maureen tells them: 'It may take a generation or more to complete our task, but we will be forever changed. The differences between men and women will be made small and, after great difficulties and struggle, truly *human,* loving beings will evolve and shall prevail.'

Maureen next uses an ancient allegorical image. One used by Mary Magdalene in her 'lost' Gospel, and well-known to her Sisters.

'The Divine Feminine shall be restored to her rightful place at the left-hand of God. And we will join with men in celebrating together on Earth our new union and our shared Glory.'

Spontaneous applause bursts out. Those in attendance stand and begin to sing. Not in English, but in Latin. The singing continues until their ancient anthem's entire four verses are completed. After hugs and celebrations have followed the impromptu chorus, Maureen goes on to tell the assemblage: 'It is my great honor to instruct you now that when you leave here today, we must commence our work together, diligently and in concert, to prepare for and to ensure these historic, epoch-making changes now come to pass.'

Gifted with an exceptional degree of clairvoyance, Maureen is well aware of the future problems they will encounter, the resistance they will meet and the fortitude that will be required of them all. But today, she knows, is a day for goodwill, expectation and celebration.

The main message of her speech delivered, both tone and timbre of Maureen's voice change.

'For those of you here, there is food and drink which we may share while we talk through the plans that each of our Sisters has made. We must also agree how to welcome both this coming day, and this man. Those of you watching and listening from elsewhere, please feel free to continue to do so. We will return to a structured meeting within the hour. In the meantime, our camerawoman will be wandering around, recording this event and conducting brief interviews with some of those present. If you wish to address us through the main screen, please let the adjudicator know in the usual manner.'

Before ending her talk, Maureen issues a stern warning.

'Let me finally remind you all of our sacred oath. Now more than ever, it is vital that our secret remains so. We have waited too long… far too long… to be thwarted by careless talk. All over the world there remain those in power who are devoted to ensuring our rightful place is never regained. We must not let our excitement lead us to break that oath.'

Watching the speech on a computer screen from within the Oval Office is President Whitmore. As with nearly all watching proceedings on the call, Terri Whitmore is ecstatic.

'I never for a moment thought I would see this in my lifetime,' she says out loud to the famous room, for the moment empty of souls other than her own.

TWENTY-FOUR

The Panic arrives from nowhere. During September, Bio-AIDs receive no mention in the popular press and are barely a subject of note in medical journals. By the end of October, the airwaves are full of little else.

Sensationalist coverage in the online and broadcast media becomes a daily occurrence, ranging from the routine stuff of tabloids – *Your neighbor's spying on your lovemaking* – to the ridiculous – *Are aliens using our minds to control Climate Change?*

Unregulated online rumor websites especially prosper, generating endless conspiracy theories and huge extra revenues by speculating on the 'hidden' and 'limitless' power of the implanted devices' users.

Manufacturers issue outright denials, backed up by ever more aggressive lobbying. Within the learned establishment there remains for months total skepticism about any non-physical claims for the devices. The first commentaries from government scientists are absolute denials, labeling the claims as 'pseudo-science of the worst kind' and 'the stuff of pulp fiction'. In such an environment, no academic risks their reputation by publishing support for the 'theories'.

Peter is among the first to know about the extent of the crisis, weeks before the story reaches the press. The source of information is his daughter. Two weeks after issuing her warning about Angela and just a day after his return from the UK, Lilian uses ordinary, non-telepathic communication to tell her father: 'There are many more like me, Dad. *Thousands*!'

Her words instill in Peter a gnawing, primal fear that never leaves him. Lilian's elaboration only serves to worsen his fears.

'Dad, there are all these people. I can hear them, in my head. They're all over the city, and in other countries too. It's scary, the kind of things they're saying.'

'I was afraid of that,' Peter says. 'You're not the only person who's ever had a head injury.'

Lilian asks: 'They're saying there's some device planted in us that gives us these powers. Is it true?'

'I don't know if that is the cause, darling, but there is definitely something inside you. They told me it works by repairing or replacing small amounts of damaged brain. Sarah authorized it, before we even knew you'd been hurt. From what you say, I suspect it's all true.'

His daughter's next statement comes as a shock.

'But Dad, some of these people have never been injured. They've bought the gear on the black market and had someone implant it. They manipulate their bosses, their neighbors, women they find attractive, anyone! There are all sorts of crimes being committed. People don't even know they've happened.'

She makes no mention of her own manipulations. Peter asks if Lilian can block other people affecting her.

'I know if anyone is trying to enter my head, instantly. It's like a silent alarm.'

Peter warns his daughter against being tempted to use her powers in the same way. Lilian reassures him, before adding: 'But Dad, these people. It's unbelievable what they're doing. Some of them are conspiring together. It's not just things like having sex with whoever they want. They're getting people to give up their life savings or telling them to commit suicide! I suspect that plane crash was directed by one. They have no qualms, some of them at least.'

ॐ

Unrelated to the Bio-AIDs, Peter is discovering new and extended intuitive abilities of his own every day, paralleling those of his daughter. Once again, the coincidence of abilities and timing is great.

Unlike his daughter, Peter's advancements are the fruits of assiduous meditation and training including regular use of the Ho' Opono Pono prayer given him by Maureen, whose inner meaning he now understands. His vibrations have risen in pitch and volume, his outlook has brightened, and Peter is also by now fully aware that his journey began when he was still a boy being guided by his late father.

That evening after dinner, Peter tries to explain his development to Angela.

'I've learnt to focus my conscious attention while remaining in a meditative state. I never knew this was possible,' he says. 'And my intuition has reached the point where I can quickly discern the original cause of mine and other people's problems.'

Angela is doubtful about his first claim, especially when he outlines how it makes it much easier to manifest but she is delighted to hear about his intuition.

'You mean you *sense* their issues, or their pain? That's exactly how Jeff, I mean your father, worked. He could just look into your eyes and he knew everything about you, your history of pain. *Clairsentienc*e is the term I think he used. He used to say it was like looking at moving pictures, more of a montage than a sequence of events.'

'Yes, that's precisely it.' Peter says, 'It requires a little interpretation.'

Unlike his daughter, Peter's abilities never involve manipulation, or implanting ideas directly into others' subconscious. They instead take a different direction. By communicating directly with universal energy, Peter receives guidance and wisdom in the form of messages, and insights. The bursts of insight happen so quickly – instantly – and contain so much information that at first Peter misses almost all of their content. It takes a few days for him to realize that he can store and replay them in his mind more slowly. By the time of his explanation to Angela, he is able to understand them in full.

The guidance obtained is invaluable, not only for his own use but for determining the truth about others. It enables him to know the true, underlying cause of any sickness he perceives in others' physical, mental or spiritual body.

Peter has not yet realized the full extent of his healing abilities, but he is well on the way to becoming an advanced healer, just like his father. He is already capable of manifesting positive outcomes but is only just beginning to realize he too is destined to become a healer. Bewildered and distracted by the news from Lilian, he is not yet using his new power in any methodical way.

In spite of his new intuitive abilities, Peter has no clear idea what to do about his daughter, or about all the others who have gained these powers of intuition and telepathy.

'And more, for all I know,' he mutters while Angela places dishes into the washer.

His few words are spoken too quietly for her to hear. She asks Peter to repeat what he said.

'Oh, it was nothing,' he says. 'I was just wondering what you are planning to do tomorrow.'

From what his daughter has told him, Peter knows most of those fitted with the Bio-AIDs have no qualms about using their powers for immediate, self-interested gain.

'Which means,' he reasons, mumbling, 'their abilities do not originate from universal energy.'

Peter's mind reels, full of thoughts and visualizations of wrongdoing, from sexual favors to monetary advantage to murder to jury-rigging. It is not long before he realizes the misdeeds are far more than mere invasions of privacy. Their harm is potentially devastating to any civilized society, and endless. Without privacy of thought and with large numbers of people able to control the mass of humanity without recourse, civilization will collapse. He knows he must somehow alert the authorities, but how, and who would believe him?

He settles onto the floor in his lounge. He meditates for an hour, continuing undisturbed while Angela enters and moves around him to the couch, where she sits reading. Peter emerges with the conclusion that he is witnessing the next stage of human evolution; an evolution brought dramatically and cataclysmically forward by the revolutionary expedient of extra biological computing power and telecommunications being implanted into human brains.

'We're moving from *homo sapiens* to *homo technica*,' he muses.

Peter needs a sounding board – someone more capable than Angela of understanding both his abilities and his dilemma; someone who has a strong moral compass.

Only I must not tell her my daughter's name, he decides.

As this thought enters his head, a single image joins it. 'Of course!' he says aloud, prompting Angela to ask what he means.

'Oh, it's nothing,' he says. 'Just an idea I had.'

As soon as he is alone Peter calls Maureen, who answers using an old-fashioned telephone, one whose external shape was designed in the analog era.

'I was expecting your call,' she says, then instructs him: 'Since it is important, you may come here at ten.'

The following morning, Peter arrives and is shown into Maureen's office. The interior is the opposite of what he expected. Large and modern with sleek furnishing, there is expensive, stylish artwork on the walls and minimal clutter. He is asked to sit in the middle of a large, white leather sofa, while Maureen sits on its twin, several feet away. Feeling nervous, Peter's first statement is not tactful.

'I expected your home to be dark and mysterious.'

'Don't be foolish!' Maureen says tersely. 'Now, get on with it. What do you want to know?'

Peter takes a few minutes to tell Maureen what he knows.

'Theirs are in no way spiritual abilities,' he explains. 'For people with these devices, there is no connection to anything beyond or above other human beings. No higher levels of consciousness or awareness. The devices simply extend brain function. Perhaps their interconnectedness derives from the telecom networks. Whatever their mechanism, they allow their owners to tap into and manipulate the subconscious minds of others, presumably at some kind of quantum level.'

'Don't talk drivel about things you don't understand,' she says.

Aside from his insight about rapid evolution, Peter is able to shed little light on the operation of the devices.

'Tell me what worries you,' Maureen says.

Peter explains that he fears mass anarchy, persecution and enslavement, and that he must somehow warn the authorities.

'Once they believe me, there should be a democratic choice as to whether everyone is given these abilities – or no one.'

'Isn't it obvious what they would decide? No one is going to vote against gaining extra powers, especially if there are fortunes to be made,' Maureen says.

'On the matter of politics,' she adds, 'there's always the risk that someone – or some other country – will develop and install them illicitly and use them to their advantage. There's never any going back on evolution, especially when it's generated unnaturally by technology rather than through natural selection. We've known that since the Iron Age!'

Peter knows Maureen's conclusion is true. 'Well, at least it may help us deal with all the problems caused by climate change. Save San Francisco from the sea. Among other things, of course.'

'You're either making an inane comment because you're nervous, or you think these devices are the universe's way of helping us to deal with our planetary, environmental crisis,' Maureen says curtly. 'Which is it?'

'I... I'm not sure.'

Maureen rises. 'I'll make some tea while you decide. The choice you make will determine how you must act.'

Peter is left to his thoughts while Maureen walks past him and along a wide hallway into the kitchen. He soon hears a kettle boiling.

His only thought is *I have absolutely no idea what to say next.*

Peter sips tea while Maureen stares and remains silent. His hand reaches into a pocket, unconsciously seeking out his old crossword book. The action is noted by Maureen's keen, brown eyes. She waits for him to finish his search.

'There's no need to be nervous of me. I know who you are and what you're capable of. I also know we could communicate all of our conversation in moments, telepathically.'

Maureen lifts her cup and sips at her *lapsang souchong*, then continues: 'You're afraid these devices will give others our abilities. Unlike you and me, they will misuse them because they do not communicate with the *Divine*. Surely then, all the devices are doing is allowing them to do what we are all capable of anyway. If we were to use our full brain function, that is.'

Peter takes a moment before replying, 'I'm sure what you say is true. But it's the inequality that's the problem. Those with devices will manipulate and destroy all others. At least, those who are not in any way either enlightened or connected.'

Maureen replaces her cup.

'Our evolution is inevitable. But you must warn the authorities because of the consequences of there being an unforeseen, unequal *revolution*, rather than our advance being gradual and manageable. What you risk with that approach is, of course, institutionalized chaos, with those in power manipulating everyone else.'

Peter nods in agreement. Maureen continues: 'If you allow the inequality to continue, the ability to manipulate the unconscious minds of others will inevitably result in two classes of human being. Those disadvantaged will be enslaved and eventually become extinct. This is what you fear most.'

Peter has read enough history to know how brutish and bloody the process of evolution can be.

'I must do something. And do it now, before it all gets out of hand!'

'Then you know what you must do,' concludes Maureen.

Peter stands to leave. Their goodbyes are friendly and, for the first time in his presence, Maureen's mouth widens into a smile as she offers her hand.

'You're doing the right thing,' she says, before adding: 'You might also consider that now is the time to start your own healing practice.'

'I... I hadn't thought of that at all, Maureen. Do you think I'm ready?'

'There's nothing quite so effective as a desperate face sitting in front of you to sharpen one's intuition,' is her reply.

The door is opened. Before Peter turns away, Maureen says, 'It pleases me to know your father's abilities have passed on to you. You may call me again.'

After Peter leaves, Maureen turns and leans back against the closed door. Her hands are placed together at her heart. Her knees bend while she sinks to the floor. Her face turns upwards and a wide, beaming smile lights up her whole face.

'Thank you! Thank you!' she whispers, again and again.

Peter returns to his apartment. Angela is out, working. He sits on the sofa and admires the view before looking at the AR on his wrist, then instructs it to call his daughter. Lilian answers at once.

'Dad, what's wrong?'

'Darling, I think we must go to the authorities. We should do it together or they won't believe me.'

Lilian is not pleased.

'What? You must be joking, Dad! They'll lock me up in Area 51 or somewhere. And everyone else too.'

Her selection of location later turns out to be prescient. Peter does his best to explain the likely outcome of doing nothing. Lilian is worried too but concludes their discussion

'I don't know, Dad. What makes you think they'll believe us? And I'm really scared they'll find some excuse to lock me up.'

Peter agrees to give her a few days to think it over.

TWENTY-FIVE

Two days later, his daughter is no longer able to answer Peter's call. Lilian is arrested, sedated and imprisoned in a remote army facility on the edge of the Mojave Desert. She tries but is unable to influence her captors.

They must have a device implanted too. Perhaps one that can somehow be controlled. Mouthing an expletive before speaking, she exclaims: 'That's even more worrying!'

In the moments before the sedative takes effect, Lilian alerts her father.

A day after her arrival, Lilian's Bio-AID is one of the first to be surgically removed. Twelve thousand more are removed over subsequent days, in the USA and elsewhere. None of the internees in the USA is allowed to leave, or to communicate with the outside world.

Tranquilizers are administered every three hours, preventing Lilian from using her augmentation device until her jailers are able to remove its core from her head and arm. A brain scan confirms there is no apparent, lasting effect on her brain's activity. Her days pass in a blur.

෴

While Lilian is interned, Peter seeks information from the authorities but is refused any explanation for her disappearance. Her incarceration is denied, and he is repeatedly warned against continuing to ask questions.

'I just know she's been taken, by some kind of army unit. That's all she told me,' he repeats more than once.

With no record of a telephone message or call from her as corroboration, Lilian's disappearance is registered as a missing person case. In the face of official denials, Peter feels compelled to alert the press. Citing the lack of corroborating evidence, they fail to act.

He enlists Angela's help in searching the web. Together they look for others in the US with relatives who have mysteriously disappeared after arrest. They soon find several hundred.

Within a week their online group has over one thousand members. Each person tells a similar story of strange behavior followed by a sudden disappearance or arrest. They agree to form a protest movement. Peter soon finds he is their de facto leader.

Small demonstrations are held in Washington and outside State Capitols, to no avail. Against the advice of Bradley Williams and on the day after three of their group's members are arrested in Ohio, Peter begins a legal action on their behalf. The suit is filed in a Federal court and names all those who have disappeared as well as those known to have been arrested. The uncensored, alternative press suddenly becomes interested in their plight, especially after they see their early stories being shared many millions of times. Even the controlled, international press begins to show interest. Within days, reporters arrive *en masse* outside Peter's home.

'I warned you,' is Bradley William's unhelpful initial response to Peter's call. A moment later he advises Peter to use the publicity to their advantage.

'The smart thing to do Peter, is to stand on your doorstep and talk to them all at once. They will all claim an exclusive and you may end up on the front pages of their websites. Everyone loves a hint of conspiracy.'

Peter does as he suggests. Outside his apartment, he reads aloud a prepared statement that begins: 'More than a thousand of our fellow citizens, some of them known to be unwell, have disappeared or been removed from their homes without adequate explanation by the authorities. Reminiscent of the worst excesses of dictatorships around the world, these illegal actions have been denied...'

Peter answers questions from reporters for nearly an hour, many of which are about his own daughter. Some of the questioners ask about whether his daughter is a terrorist. Many more of the questions refer to rumors of 'supernatural abilities,' about which Peter decides to say he has only limited experience. Fearing the public may not believe his daughter has gained telepathic abilities, he admits only to her being able to read other people's thoughts.

'Does that mean she can read your mind, Mister Walker?' is the first response to this admission. Followed by many others that ask him to elaborate. Peter's calm, measured replies win him the confidence of the millions who view his interview online. He becomes the face of the protest movement and his views are aired on screens across the country.

Both the movement and their legal action are stopped in their tracks when the President declares martial law the following day. The Presidential decree cites an 'unprecedented number' of foreign terrorists who have arrived on American soil and an assertion that 'it is my solemn duty to ensure the safety of all Americans.'

Similar pronouncements are made simultaneously in China, Russia, India and the major European countries, all of which have experimented with or installed Bio-AID devices.

ॐ

While Peter is answering the reporters' questions, Senator Francis Jackson is led by an aide along the carpeted corridors of the White House towards the Oval Office. It is late in the extended Summer. Outside, the sun is lightening the sky but is not yet visible.

It's more than three years since I was last here, he reflects. A*nd we had a different, male President then.*

His hips ache by the time he enters the celebrated room, but he manages a smile for the President, who rises from her chair and walks around the desk to greet him.

'Good morning, Francis! It's been too long.'

He kisses her proffered cheek, an honour reserved for a select few close friends.

'Good morning, Terri. I am delighted as ever to see you. This room suits you too: powerful and iconic!'

'Oh, you old charmer! You haven't changed a bit.'

The President waves away her aides and takes hold of Senator Jackson's arm.

'Come, sit over here next to me. What I want to ask of you is a favour. A big one. I need you to save my bacon.'

The senator's open mouth and startled face express his shock, but he lets himself be led to a chair before he voices his question.

'Terri, you know you only have to ask. But what on earth could be so bad?'

'Well, Francis, last week I issued an Executive Order to arrest and incarcerate over five thousand US citizens. There's a banning order in place but the media is already all over it. We will have to go public within the next few hours.'

'Terri! What have they done? Are they spies?'
President Whitmore's ironic laugh is loud.

'If only! No, Francis. It's much worse than that. Some of them have done nothing wrong at all. Well, so far as we can tell anyway.'

The President tells him what she knows.

'There are these devices, medical devices. Developed for helping brain-damaged patients. Not only here. They've been developed and sold all over the world. Some kind of merger of biotech and AI. It seems they give people unusual abilities, exceptional abilities. Ones we never thought possible, or at least not likely. They can read other people's minds. Worse still, it seems they are able to control or at least influence those minds. And to do so remotely.'

'And there are five thousand of these people in the US?'

'Approximately, yes. It seems likely that more have been imported and bought on the black market. They're almost impossible to detect.'

'You've done the right thing, Terri. Decisive action, it's the only way.'

'I believe so. Thank you, Francis.'

The President reaches her arm towards the Senator. Her fingers touch the back of his hand, resting on his knee. Leaning back, she tells him 'There was no choice. Jim was adamant.'

'Our National Security Advisor Jim, you mean?'

'Yes, Jim Beaumont. He's afraid the Chinese and the Russians are already using the devices to influence our military. And the Chinese are way ahead of us on this one.'

'Gosh, Terri! What does he recommend?'

'I don't know yet. I've asked for a detailed plan. I meet with him later today. With the whole NSC, in fact.'

The President reaches her hand over to touch the back of the Senator's hand once more. She continues: 'I consulted with the Leaders and the Speaker of course. All three concurred. The devices are being removed from those in custody as we speak.'

'How can I help, Terri?'

'I need someone to find a way forward, to lead us out of this mess. There's no going back, you know. Even if we banned them, there's no guarantee that other countries would abide by any ban. The consequences of other countries exerting mind-control over our military are beyond imagining.'

'It's unbelievable. You're sure this is real, and not some kind of scare-mongering?'

'Oh, it's real alright. I have personal experience of some of them trying to influence me. On the lawn outside are devices that transmit multi-frequency waves of some kind. A little like giant microwaves, I'm told. The cover-story is that they're being tested as a cheaper means of jamming drones. But they're really there to protect me from these people. They're installed at the Pentagon, NSA, CIA, NORAD. You name it!'

The senator realizes from the timescales involved that the military must have been experimenting with these devices for months, and probably years. He can sense the strain on his old friend and mentee.

'Terri, I…'

'I know, Francis, I know. And thank you for flying up from Dallas straightaway. I need you to form a new Committee, and to lead an all-party Hearing. As past Chairman of the Senate's Ethics Committee, and a co-sponsor of the National Artificial Intelligence Initiative, your appointment is beyond reproach. I'll be speaking to the nation this afternoon. We're going to use a cover story about active terrorist gangs. We will use 'operational security' as an excuse for not admitting how many have been arrested. I'd like to announce your appointment then. It will be billed as overseeing all the Federal investigations. But what you will really be doing is finding us a way out of this mess.'

'Of course, whatever you need. I'm honoured you ask.'

The President thanks him then tells him 'I have one more favour to ask of you.'

'Of course, Terri. Whatever you want.'

'There's one person I'd like you to include as an advisor, and a witness. You may have seen him in the news. His daughter's been incarcerated already. Her device was fitted after a fall, without her knowledge.'

He assures her that will not be a problem. She provides a card with Peter's name and contact details, then adds that the Senator may benefit by having a separate, private session with him.

'He's a quite exceptional man,' she tells him.

Her old friend and mentor remains sceptical of that but agrees to give it a try. They chat about family and friends for the ten minutes until she has to leave to prepare for her speech. Her last words to him are: 'You'll start today, won't you Francis?'

He replies 'I already have, Terri. I already have. And don't worry, we'll find a way out. And turn it to your advantage too.'

TWENTY-SIX

An emergency meeting of the United States National Security Council is no ordinary event. Established by the National Security Act of 1947 and chaired by the President, the Council provides advice on all domestic, foreign and military policies that relate to US national security. Its statutory attendees include the Vice-President, the Secretary of State and the Secretary of Defense and its advisors include the chairman of the Joint Chiefs of Staff and the Director of the CIA.

The room is sealed and protected from interference or eavesdropping by an array of security systems, supplemented by the temporary expedient of a microwave-based system such as at the White House. Automated recording machines are set in motion, monitored from outside the room by the FBI senior agent in charge of security for the meeting, a former special-forces major and Presidential bodyguard.

President Whitmore opens the meeting in the customary manner.

'I know some of you were involved in authoring the documents but, in order to expedite today's meeting, would everyone here present please confirm you have received, read and understood the electronic briefing documents that were prepared overnight by the Principals Committee.'

The other eight attendees who are present give affirmative indications. They are all well-known to each other so, no introductions are required.

'Thank you, gentlemen and lady. Duly noted.'

In that case,' the President continues, 'let me briefly summarize the purpose of this meeting, and the issues before us, as I see them.'

President Whitmore casts a long look around at each of the faces around the conference table. She begins with a dramatic statement of concern.

'It is my belief that we face the gravest crisis of this Presidency and, to my knowledge the gravest crisis our country has faced since 1962.'

None demur, several nod in agreement.

'Our information is disturbingly limited. We do not know the full capability of these devices, we are unsure of their precise method of operation, nor are we certain of the full extent of their present use and deployment.'

A competent public speaker, the President cannot resist pausing for effect. Her delay serves the purpose of emphasizing just how little anyone in the room knows. She resumes.

'What is so far clear however, is that they have the potential to disrupt our military, to influence our critical and political decision-making, to manipulate our economy and our financial system, and potentially to destroy many other aspects of our lives, personal and professional.'

The AI-based computer she is using to drive her prompter recognizes she has reached the end of her first page of notes. The screen refreshes in time for her to continue without pause.

'There is clear evidence that the devices have been and are being used to direct and control the minds of strangers over distances of more than 3,000 miles, and possibly worldwide. This means that external, foreign influence may be exerted over those of us who remain unprotected. By this, I mean the thoughts, desires, actions and opinions of virtually everyone in this country. It is likely many are being deliberately manipulated. The scale of the existing problem is considerable. We estimate approximately 12,000 devices are presently in the US but there may well be substantially more.'

The final section of her summary covers the emergency powers granted or being granted to the Committee.

'The Leaders of both Houses have agreed to an immediate repeal of the War Powers act of 1973, which means we have far greater freedom under law to interrogate and intercept persons here in the US, as well as to take appropriate action abroad, the necessity for which we alone may determine.

They are also considering my request that the repeal should be applied retrospectively, thus ending any debate about the legality or otherwise of the recent and ongoing incarceration of thousands of our citizens without due process, many of whom may be wholly innocent. As you know, we were previously operating under executive order 13224, the powers granted to President Bush after 9/11, which remain in effect.'

The screen in front of her again refreshes, in time for her to move on to outlining the purpose of the meeting.

'This situation cannot and will not be allowed to endure. The purpose of today's meeting is therefore to determine what remedial actions we must take, what communications we should release, and to set ourselves achievable targets and timescales to bring the entire matter to a satisfactory resolution.'

President Whitmore looks up from her screen to survey the room. All eyes are on her as she asks the members of the committee: 'Are we clear on these points?'

All eight members mouth a 'Yes, ma'am.'

'In that case, I will hand over now to our National Security Advisor, who will explain further our risks and our proposed plans.'

Paul O'Donnell thanks her then leans forward to rest his hands on the conference table. In his characteristic, Southern twang he begins to speak.

'We have classified our risks into the following categories, presented on the main screen in front of you in order of priority.'

All heads turn towards the large display screen at one end of the room. It shows:

Military – to our facilities or to unauthorized weapon use

Political – to our decision-making capability

Economic – to our industrial and financial prosperity

Domestic – to the health and welfare of our citizens

Foreign – to our standing in the international community.

He continues, 'In line with our standard procedure for dealing with threat level 4 and above, we are taking the following steps immediately.'

The screen changes to show four different steps, which Advisor O'Donnell speaks to in turn:

Step One – damage limitation.

All devices known or suspected are being removed.

Being conducted at special facilities in Nevada (Area 51).

Interrogations to follow.

Status: 80% complete.

Step Two – limit extension.

Imports of new devices have been halted.

All known shipments are being collected and stored.

All shipping records are being checked.

All ports and importers are being actively monitored.

Status: 70% complete.

Step Three – investigation.

Sample devices being studied under controlled conditions.

Sample volunteers being assessed in Area 51, Hawaii and Alaska.

Access to all manufacturing locations requested.

Access granted, except those in China and Russia.

Status: 50% complete

Step Four – development of countermeasures.

Development of our equivalent devices.

Psychological assessment and training methods.

Evaluation and monitoring of key personnel (susceptibility, adherence).

Logistical plan.

Status: 20% complete

Step Five – long term resolution.

None known.

Status: investigation 20% complete.

When he reaches the slide covering step five, Advisor O'Donnell explains: 'We are talking about reacting to an evolutionary level event, comprising capabilities barely imagined only weeks ago becoming available worldwide within two years at most. It is unlikely in my view, that countermeasures will succeed, even if draconian measures are introduced.'

His words generate a considerable amount of shuffling and expressions of shock around him.

'It is already clear from our initial testing,' he continues, 'that the effect of these devices may be neutralized only by others using the same or similar devices. Exposure to the present microwave-based protective devices provides only localized protection and may anyway only be temporary. Long-term exposure may well prove fatal.

The only feasible solution we are presently exploring is ensuring ubiquitous availability of these devices. In plain words, we will never be able to guarantee that no one in the world has one, therefore we must all have one.'

Sharp intakes of breath, exchanges of glances and worried looks accompany his final words. President Whitmore resumes control of the meeting.

'Thank you, Paul. Before we consider the implications of what we are hearing, let us please complete our briefing. Henry, would you kindly give us your updated report?'

Director of the CIA Henry Adams thanks the President then tells the Committee: 'Madam, and Members, we have clear evidence that devices manufactured in China are being sold here on the black market. There are also indications that this is being done with the active connivance of the Chinese government.'

Expressions of shock endure while he continues, 'If they are not already included within existing designs, we fully anticipate that these devices will in future contain modified chips that will allow the Chinese to control the minds of our citizens.'

Outrage accompanies the final words of this briefest of briefings. 'I don't need to tell you that such control imperils the physical survival of our country, let alone the entire basis of our democracy and our way of life.'

President Whitmore's heart is beating as fast as anyone's in the room. She waits until the individual conversations that have erupted subside.

'Let's keep order here, please,' she commands.

All members fall silent. Their President asks: 'Harold, would you kindly give us your briefing. Then we may discuss our proposed actions and conclusions.'

Secretary of Defense Harold Crabtree begins: 'In our opinion these devices represent an immediate and material threat to our military capability. As matters presently stand, we cannot protect all our military installations and facilities from these 'mind control' devices.'

Secretary Crabtree can sense the palpable, rising concern around him when he tells them, 'It will be at least a year before we have enough equipment to do so. Furthermore, we have so far performed only limited testing so, we are far less than one hundred percent certain that our present defenses will ever be entirely secure.

We have used the state of emergency to confine all our military personnel to their bases. This reduces but does not eliminate the risk of external interference, especially while they are outside the perimeter of protection for any reason. This situation cannot continue indefinitely. We may never be able to guarantee that our personnel have not been unduly influenced while away from the base, on leave or on duty.

We see no option but to ban these devices from our shores until such time as we are able to develop and manufacture these devices within the US, where development must be closely monitored before their use is authorized.'

Argument and debate ensue that last several hours. It is managed in a masterful, mature manner by President Whitmore. More than one member of the committee is privately grateful they have such a competent leader in charge.

The conclusions of the meeting are decisive. Its principal outcome is a vastly increased budget for research and development of American Bio-Aid devices, both for defensive 'denial of attack' purposes and for offensive use against 'enemies of the State'. The number of potential enemies is noted as considerable, including rogue states and especially the US's larger, non-democratic trading partners and rivals.

A new research center is set up in Area 51, where internet access is limited and strictly controlled, with remote offshoots for testing purposes as far away as Alaska and Hawaii.

The standardized search terms used in surveillance of worldwide telecommunications and social media networks are expanded, eventually by an extra four thousand words and phrases. Additional money for this purpose is given to the NSA, doubling the size of computing resources and manpower required.

The fourth major area granted increased expenditure is internal security, especially for additional equipment and resourcing for rapid troop deployment in major US cities and around government installations. A vast new Internal Security Directorate is created under the umbrella of Homeland Security, responsible for development, training and deployment of new electronic and psychological methods of control and countermeasures.

After the meeting, Secretary of Defense Harold Crabtree invites the Chairman of the Joint Chiefs to join him in his limousine for the journey to the Pentagon, where they have called a 'crisis review' meeting with senior military staff. Once sealed inside their transport, the Chairman turns to Secretary Crabtree. The two men maintain eye contact while they speak.

'You know we, the Chinese and the Russians have been experimenting with these for years, don't you?

Secretary Crabtree nods and says, 'And God knows who else.'

'I realize now our focus was far too narrow,' adds the Chairman. 'We saw them as an improved means of battlefield communication and coordination. But the real game all along was to exert mind control over the enemy.'

'Yes, Don. And worse, we're now way behind the Chinese. If they find out just how far, the results could be catastrophic.'

The two men discuss possible countermeasures and disinformation strategies as they are driven along I-395. Their conversation ceases as soon as the limousine doors are opened. They make a point of chatting jovially about their families while they are led through the building, and do not resume serious discussion until they are seated in the Secretary's office at the Pentagon's heart.

৵

Although he is not invited to attend, Senator Jackson is aware of the NSC meeting. He is personally briefed on its outcome by the President during their secure call of the following day. The senator in turn briefs the President on the arrangements he has already made to secure the necessary political backing.

'The Leaders are onside, even with the need for retrospective repeal. I've also invited that gentleman you mentioned to speak at the first session,' he tells her.

An experienced Washington insider, the senator ensures there are no dissenting voices within the federal government, at least none that will be taken seriously. A Senate investigative committee is set up and its members appointed, with the first hearings scheduled to be held within two weeks.

The bi-partisan Investigative Committee becomes the subject of intense speculation but as expected, is successful at relieving the political and public pressure on President Whitmore. She expresses her personal thanks to Senator Jackson, who fully understands the value of such a debt of gratitude.

TWENTY-SEVEN

When her first interview commences, Lilian has no idea where she is or how long she has been sedated.

'Lilian,' the female interviewer begins. 'How are you doing?'

Her eyebrows rise while Lilian stares at her questioner, but she offers no reply.

'Lilian, my name is Carmel, like the place. Would you please state for the record your full name, date of birth and your address?'

She complies. The interview commences.

'Lilian, the purpose of this interview is to ascertain the details of your experiences with the Bio-AID device, serial number US-472-17413, which was surgically implanted into you on June thirteenth this year. Would you begin by telling us exactly what happened immediately you recovered consciousness after that operation?'

Her reply is succinct: 'I woke in a hospital bed, confused. I had to be told what happened to me, as I had no memory of being injured. No one told me anything about a device being implanted, and at the time I had no awareness or knowledge of any special abilities.'

Carmel has been trained to use Lilian's name frequently, as an easy means of establishing empathy. It is her only means of doing so.

'Lilian, could you tell me when you first became aware of what you just termed your "special abilities"?'

'It was more than two months later. I was recovering at home, cared for by my mother and a day nurse. I realized that I knew what they were going to say before they spoke. At first, I thought nothing of it: it just seemed perfectly natural. Like something we all do with people we know well.'

Her interviewer's head inclines, and her eyebrows rise.

'Like you just did,' Lilian continues. 'We pick up cues from eye movements and gestures. Then I realized I knew what they were going to say even when they were out of the room. And then, a few days later I realized I could plant ideas in their heads.'

Carmel resolves to keep her movements to a minimum. She leans forward.

'Tell me more about that, Lilian. How did you realize it, and what limits were there on your ability?'

Lilian chooses her words carefully.

'Well, I don't recall ever actually *realizing*. It was just when I wanted them to do something, they would almost immediately begin to do it. I only ever used it for fun. Like when I wanted some chocolate. Although I did test it a couple of times. For example, by asking my mother to clean my room, even though she'd only just finished doing it!'

Lilian laughs, attempting to pass the whole experience off as something light-hearted, a kind of prank.

'And what did you think about that, Lilian?'

'Was it the wrong thing to do, you mean? Yes, of course, but it was only a little fun. I meant no harm, and it made no difference to them.'

'And what about later? Were you tempted to do the same with your neighbors? Or other people you met in the street?'

Lilian takes a long pause.

'Yes, I confess I did. But only to get them to do things like turn their TV volume down, if it was on too loud.'

Lilian is one of her first interviewees. This is the first time Carmel hears just how precise such a telepathic instruction may be. Her eyebrows rise involuntarily.

She asks: 'You could be that specific? Like... telling them "Turn the TV down now!"'

'No, it doesn't work like that,' Lilian says. 'I just planted the idea in their head that the TV is on loud, or perhaps it's too noisy for our neighbors. The rest is up to them. To make the connection I mean.'

The interviewer thinks for a moment.

'But how did you know which neighbor to ask?'

Lilian answers vaguely.

'Well, I didn't. I could only transmit it in vague terms. It worked. So, whoever it was, they must have been within range, I guess. They must have been close, otherwise their TV wouldn't have disturbed me in the first place, would it?'

Carmel taps onto a screen, appearing to make some notes. In truth, she is rehearsing how best to phrase her next question. Almost a minute passes before she asks: 'And is there, or rather *was there*, a limit to the range over which you could transmit?'

'I never found one,' Lilian lies. 'But it never occurred to me that I could communicate with anyone outside my immediate vicinity. Can some people do that?'

The interviewer lies in return.

'I don't know, Lilian. I'm just here gathering information. No one tells me anything! But what about you? You never tried to communicate over a distance, or felt someone doing that to you?'

'No, I never tried. As I say, it never occurred to me I could.' She pauses, then adds: 'It would explain a few things that happened to me though. Such as words or pictures appearing in my head. I assumed until now they were the result of my accident... I mean, my being brain-damaged.'

The interviewer pauses too, then says, 'I'd like to ask you that question again, Lilian, if I may. You see, it's just that some others we've interviewed have told us they communicated with you. They named you specifically, as if they knew you.'

Lilian lies again.

'I think they must be mistaken. Or else they were doing it in their own heads. Communicating, I mean. I was certainly not aware of it!'

At this stage of the interrogations, no definitive evidence has been obtained to show that any users of the Bio-AID devices communicated at will over distance. Hence, rather than pursuing her line of questioning, the interviewer changes tack.

'Have you heard from your partner, Sarah? Only I understand she left you in the lurch.'

'She certainly left me. And I've heard from her only once since.'

'It's just that she's disappeared,' Carmel says. 'We tried to trace her, but she has left the country and disappeared. I don't suppose you know anything about that?'

'I'm afraid I don't know much, except she told me she was going on a long vacation.'

Lilian is clever enough to know that her story must be consistent to be perceived as true. Thus, throughout any subsequent interviews she maintains the twin lies of being unaware of any longer-distance abilities, and a lack of communication with Sarah save for the one call to her.

Later, when asked about her knowledge of Larry's whereabouts, Lilian adds a third lie.

TWENTY-EIGHT

In spite of growing disquiet and speculation over the Presidential decree, through most of November the official line continues to be reiteration of a terrorist threat and denial of any specific information. Then, on the twentieth day of martial law, the UK and US chief government scientists admit in a joint press conference that 'some' of the claims made in the online press cannot easily be refuted.

When they clarify that the 'irrefutable' abilities they have found include intuition and thought projection tested over some distance, the nature of press coverage changes overnight. Strident headlines dominate the news '*Government confirms worst fears*'; '*Now you know your neighbor is listening*'; '*Are aliens controlling your mind?*'; and '*Terrorists taking over the White House.*'

As an active protester and an interested, articulate speaker, Peter is thrust daily into the limelight. Interviewed again and again by broadcast and online media, he explains all he knows about the devices while at the same time appealing for the release of his daughter or for information on her whereabouts. Conspiracy theories abound but Peter remains resolute under questioning, repeating only that it's 'time our Governments came clean.'

A call from Maureen to the new head of NBC, an unmarried career woman of forty-three named Miss Eleanor Dobbs, results in Peter being invited to NBC's New York studios.

'He's ready you know,' Maureen tells her. 'He just doesn't know it yet.'

Barely able to contain her excitement at meeting him, Miss Dobbs ensures she is present when Peter is interviewed in their main studio for the first time. She stands beside the automated, fixed-position camera two to watch. The interview is short and is part of the second featured story of the evening news. Her hands remain clasped together at her chest the whole time.

Always wary of big government, public sentiment in the US shifts decisively when, only a few seconds into the interview, Peter holds up a picture of his white, pretty, middle-class daughter. He tells his fellow Americans: 'The idea that my daughter is some kind of terrorist is ridiculous. Lilian was born here and has lived here in the city or in London her whole life. Her device was fitted without her knowledge by experts at New York's Presbyterian Hospital, not by some wacky Middle Eastern dictatorship.'

The human-interest angle is especially appealing to the media, who follow-up the interview by splashing pictures of Lilian alongside her father below every headline. As soon as they learn of Peter's past marriage, Margaret is paid handsomely to provide the media with more pictures, as well as background for use in derivative and follow-on stories. They are especially keen to acquire the rights to images of father and daughter playing together while Lilian was a child, and their stories frequently stress her free-thinking, lesbian credentials.

When the media learn that Peter is opening a healing practice in San Francisco, it is featured both locally and nationally. At first there is concern he may have somehow acquired an illicit Bio-AID device.

Once cleared, Peter's new-found fame as an intuitive healer means his AR buzzes continuously.

Unable to respond to the constant requests for interviews from persistent journalists or for appointments from desperate ordinary men and women, Peter soon employs a secretary to manage his diary. He first asks Angela to perform the task, but his request is declined.

'Working together and sleeping together rarely works out, in my experience,' is her only explanation.

The undertone in her voice is noticed by Peter but he chooses to ignore his intuition. He thus fails to link her sentence to his father. Unprompted, a new secretary is recommended by Maureen.

Following a brief interview, she quickly arranges a temporary 'healing room' for Peter in a serviced office a mile or so from Maureen's, south of Market. More than once, the downtown building is besieged by reporters.

By the time Peter's online fame reaches its frenetic height, his diary is constantly full, and it is three months since Lilian's first warning. Throughout this period, examples of abuse and manipulation multiply. Impending chaos is predicted by all sections of the media, travel is increasingly unpredictable, and fear and tensions frequently boil over into mutual accusations and gunfights. Crime rates as well as death rates for men and women under the age of fifty more than double.

Peter's public profile expands further when he is invited to Washington to attend a House Ethics Committee meeting. Appointed by the President and led by Senator Francis Jackson from Texas, the panel is conducting an urgent investigation into the potential use and misuse of the Bio-AID devices, as well as the related security and 'vital interests' threats they pose.

Its stated goal is to provide advice and guidance to both Houses and to the President herself. In particular, to recommend whether and how such devices should be marketed, what restrictions and safeguards should be 'built-in', and what supervision and supervisory organizations should be created to ensure their safe use. Peter is invited to represent the public interest and to act as a conduit for opinions from all non-political spectrums of American life.

࿐

The FBI report concludes there is no credible, indictable evidence of Lilian having committed any crime. It adds that evidence would be extremely difficult to obtain and impossible to prove beyond reasonable doubt. In the absence of any confession, federal prosecutors therefore advise there is no case against her to answer.

Lilian is released at the cessation of martial law in early January. The announcement is made at the White House with her father in attendance and in the full glare of publicity. Speaking to the world's press for the first time, Lilian holds her father's hand.

'I have been held against my will and interrogated for weeks, over a device that was implanted in me without my knowledge and consent. This raises questions of who authorized this fundamental breach of my rights. Without malice, but from concern that others are not treated so badly in future, I will be seeking compensation and appropriate action against all involved. At the same time, I thank my father and all those others who campaigned tirelessly for my release, and for the release of others held like me without justification or explanation.'

When asked about her experience with the devices, Lilian explains, 'Used in the right way, they are marvelous. Mine gave me insights into others' points of view, even of their deepest loves and fears. And it allowed me to share my thoughts with my father here, which has deepened forever my love and respect for him.'

A journalist asks whether there has been any regression in her condition since the device's removal.

'My memory is affected, yes. Otherwise I'm not aware of any adverse effects. And thank you for your concern.'

It is an accomplished performance from a beautiful, photogenic young woman that results in many requests for interviews. After a break of just two days, she is interviewed live on *The Tonight Show*. Watched again by her father, she receives tumultuous applause after telling the story of her ordeal.

After the show, Lilian is approached by a slim, black-haired female journalist of Sino-American descent. She introduces herself as Diana, hands over her card and requests an interview. Lilian is at first hesitant.

'Sure, give me a few more days to recover. I'll call you next week.'

Holding eye contact, Diana persists.

'Would you give me your number at least? Just so you won't forget.'

Lilian honors the request. They meet within a week. Within a month Tina is forgotten. Diana and Lilian begin an affair that both later describe to Peter as being 'totally in love'.

For a while they are separated for days at a time by the distance between Diana's home in a Washington suburb and Lilian's in New York. The day after their declaration to Peter of mutual love the couple set up their first new home together in lower Manhattan.

TWENTY-NINE

After presenting his views at the Senate committee hearing, Peter returns to San Francisco. Less than a week later, he receives a call.

'Mr Walker, my name is Dunwoody, Jennifer Dunwoody. I am Senator Jackson's executive assistant.'

Miss Dunwoody goes on to explain: 'The senator would very much like to have a private meeting with you. As I am sure you will appreciate, he is a *very* busy man. Would it be possible for you to visit the senator here in Dallas? He is happy to pay any expenses, and even to send a secured plane.'

She adds that, as chair of the proceedings, the senator cannot be seen consulting with a witness to the hearings. Peter agrees and the meeting is set for the following day.

'We will send our plane to collect you,' Miss Dunwoody says. 'It has been hardened against interference, so you will be safe. A car will collect you to take you to the airport from your home. Another will pick you up from the airport here to bring you directly to the senator's home. He lives on a ranch about ten miles north of the city.'

When Peter arrives the following day, he finds that the Senator's ranch is a huge estate of over fifty thousand acres, at the center of which sits a twelve-bedroom porticoed mansion. Painted white with a red-tiled roof, the building dominates its surroundings, which include a large garage, two barns and a number of smaller homes for staff, all screened from the main house by a line of trees.

Miss Dunwoody greets Peter at the entrance.

'How good of you to come, Mr Walker. And please, call me Jennifer. If there is anything at all I can do for you while you are here, please do not hesitate to ask.'

Jennifer shows Peter into a large library and pours him a glass of water. He sits on one of the two large couches placed at its center. She withdraws as the silver-haired, portly figure of the senator enters.

Shaking his hand with the squeeze of a strongman, the senator tells Peter to sit before asking about his journey. After these preliminaries, he explains: 'Mr Walker, I'm delighted you are here. During the hearing I was so impressed with your knowledge, I determined right away I must meet you and learn more about you and what you do.'

The senator asks a series of questions. Peter's detailed replies confirm everything the senator already knows. Confident he may trust Peter, he outlines the real reason for his invitation.

'Mr Walker, I understand you are a savant. Or is it an intuitive? I'm never quite sure of the meaning of such words. Whichever it is, I believe I have similar powers myself and I wanted to know from you whether I am imagining them or whether they are really true.'

He is stunned by Peter's answer.

'Senator, we all have my abilities. It's simply that most of us have not yet learned to access them. If you feel this way then, like me only a few months ago, they are probably ready to emerge. May I give you an example?'

'Of course, please do,' the senator replies.

'Well, I know for instance that you had an affair with your secretary a few years ago. It produces an occasional awkward moment even now, but you both like each other. That is why you kept her on your payroll and close to you. And she is devoted to you, by the way.'

The senator's jaw drops. Peter continues. 'Don't worry, no one else knows and I certainly won't tell anyone. I only say it to you as an example. You might conclude that it's only a supposition. After all, you spend a great deal of time in each other's company, so no one would be that surprised. It's human nature, to be attracted to a member of the opposite sex. Well, for many of us, at least.'

The senator only nods, believing Peter may not know the political consequences if his affair were to become public. Peter continues his explanation.

'However, that is not how I reached the conclusion. The truth is I knew the moment Jennifer greeted me at the door that she had an affair with you that lasted nearly two years. Her subconscious thoughts remain full of it.'

The senator's neck jerks a half-inch backwards in reaction to this revelation. *I thought she no longer cared about me*, he thinks.

'Oh, Jennifer cares about you, Senator,' Peter says. 'That was also clear. You see, I am able to hear – or even to *see* – the subconscious thoughts of others, you included. Hence, I knew your reaction. As well as its context.'

'That's remarkable!' the senator exclaims. 'I never quite believed all the evidence presented at the hearings until this moment. And we were denied permission to run any test. They said it was too dangerous. "Whoever does the demonstration could influence the Committee," is what we were told.'

'It is remarkable, but nonetheless true,' says Peter. 'My abilities stem from a great deal of effort, mostly from meditation. It's really an advanced kind of contemplation, what many nowadays call mindfulness, although that is in truth only the first stage of many. I believe they put me in touch not only with the subconscious minds of others, but with the *Divine* consciousness, of which we are all part.'

Creases of doubt and confusion form on the senator's forehead.

'You mean God?'

'If you like, but I try not to personalize the experience. That's a little like holding up a glass of water and comparing it to an ocean of love.'

Peter allows the senator a few moments to contemplate his words before he continues his exposition.

'Imagine for a moment that you have had more than one life. It's okay, you don't need to believe in reincarnation. This is just a mental exercise. Just imagine, if it were true, what parts of you would travel between lives?'

'I guess you mean my soul?'

'Well, yes, but the trouble with words like that is they have so much history of interpretation and re-interpretation. So they really aren't very useful.'

Peter carries on with a description.

'Let me help you. It wouldn't be any part of your physical body, would it? You might even have been a woman during a prior life.'

He coughs before continuing: 'Nor would it be your conscious memory. Otherwise we would all be able to remember our previous lives. Pretty much the only things left are our emotions and some kind of core of whatever it is we are. But we've already said that it can't be anything physical that transfers between lives. So, our "soul", as you put it, really must be some kind of distilled essence of what we are.'

One side of the senator's mouth rises, and his eyebrows knit together.

'I'm not sure I follow you at all, Peter!'

Peter's response is rapid.

'Exactly! I'm pretty sure we can never understand exactly what it consists of, until or unless we actually experience it. I call it our *Higher Self*. Other terms I have heard include *Divine Archetype,* which stems from the Eastern churches that split from Rome, largely because of our Catholic Church's mistaken insistence on dualism. What I truly know is that I can show it to you, if you wish?'

'Please, I'd be delighted,' the senator says.

Peter moves to sit adjacent to the senator.

'All I need you to do is fully relax,' Peter begins. He moves closer. 'Take a couple of deep breaths, long and slow, and let each breath flow fully out. Completely exhale.'

As soon as the senator has completed the task, Peter continues: 'Now, take hold of my hands, palm to palm. Like *this*.'

The senator does as he is asked.

'Now, close your eyes and breathe just as I showed you. Deep and long, but don't struggle at all. Just relax both shoulders, and let your lungs do their work, calmly and easily.'

Satisfied the senator is following his instructions, Peter closes his eyes. The familiar swirling patterns appear at once. Peter issues an instruction. A second later his mind, conscious and subconscious, is transported upwards, through layer upon layer of light and moments of darkness, until he reaches a pervasive white light.

Peter takes a deep breath before issuing another instruction, this time to the *Universe*, to spread light downwards to permeate every cell of the senator's physical, mental and spiritual bodies.

Peter's eyes remain closed for almost a minute while he watches the light move as commanded. It flows into the crown of the senator's head and spreads throughout all of his bodies before flowing out of his hands and feet and either circling back or dissipating.

A few seconds later, Peter opens his eyes.

'Please, keep your eyes closed a moment longer and remain relaxed, breathing deeply,' he says.

Soon, he issues his final instruction.

'Okay, Senator. You may slowly open your eyes. Take your time and try to continue breathing a little more deeply.'

Once the senator's open eyes have adjusted to the light, he exclaims, 'Peter, either my imagination was running wild or that was incredible. It felt as though something was trickling through me. Throughout my whole body, I mean. And at the same time, I felt these sensations of floating, or of being… I'm not sure how to describe it… being in the presence of greatness, I suppose.'

Nodding, Peter says, 'Good, I'm glad you felt it. Not everyone does. At least, not at first. What you felt was in effect the *Love* that pervades the *Universe*. Most feel it as a vibration; some feel its flow, others see colors. Within a day or two, maybe even today, you may find that other visions appear. Or better still, you may feel the presence of your *Higher Self.* It's always with you. Most of us feel it as a presence on our shoulder, either left or right. One way to perceive it, as I said, is as the part of you that transported to this life.'

Unbeknownst to the senator, he is grinning broadly. He asks: 'Is there anything special I should do?'

'No,' Peter says quickly. 'Simply try to remain as relaxed as you can over the next few weeks and take time to meditate. Or at least, to sit quietly, doing nothing. Avoid alcohol too, or any stimulants for that matter. They can block all this, at least temporarily. The rest of it will come to you, provided you remain open to it. If not, we can repeat this until it does.'

The senator rises and pours them both a glass of water. They take large gulps. The senator makes a joke about this being 'thirsty work'. Placing his glass down, he asks: 'So tell me, Peter, is this what all those people fitted with the device have experienced? If so, it's truly a remarkable invention.'

'I'm afraid not, Senator. You see, we are all connected to the *Divine*, whether we know it or not. The method I've just shown you is connecting us consciously to it, something that is normally reserved for our subconscious mind to do.'

Peter coughs again – a residue of the cabin air on his flight – before continuing.

'Whereas the Bio-Aid devices allow no access to the *Divine*. They simply increase brain function. The initial results are similar, but only up to a point. The bearer is able to access or 'listen to' the subconscious minds of others. This works well when people are nearby. And I am certain the telecommunications built-in to the devices allows them to access the subconscious minds of others, provided they too are on the network. The web, I mean. I suspect it also allows them to manipulate those subconscious minds, by suggestion.'

'You mean they can plant ideas into these other people's minds? That's what the FBI report stated,' the senator says.

'Yes, it seems likely. I can't think of any other explanation,' agrees Peter. 'What they do not do, is anything more. There is no connection to anything other than those minds. Nothing *Divine*, I mean. Other than in the sense that everything is Divine, of course. At least, that's true unless they were already practiced at meditation. And I've heard nothing from anyone that shows any of those people fitted with the devices were so practiced.'

The senator takes another large swig of water before summarizing his views.

'What I sense, Peter, is that these people have accessed something all of our brains are capable of doing, but which we have not so far learnt to do. It's as if our evolution has arrived early, before we are ready for it. The heart of the problem with it lies in our lack of preparedness. If everyone wears them, there is no problem. Or at least, the problems are manageable. If they do not, the risk of exploitation is obvious, even inevitable.'

Instead of answering verbally, Peter places a thought into the senator's mind.

Peter would like to stay for lunch.

The telepathic reply is instantaneous.

Oh, you must be hungry, Peter. Let me organize some lunch. There is so much still to talk over.

The senator is aware of Peter controlling this non-verbal communication. He expresses the experience thus:

'The thoughts that make up that conversation, they are yours and mine. Clearly my reply came from me, but you were controlling the process?'

'Yes, that's correct. In time you will be able to do so too. You just have to learn how.'

Peter receives a follow-on thought: *And do you think Jennifer still loves me?*

Peter answers, 'Oh! I am certain of it, Senator.'

Both men laugh, the senator loudest.

'I'm going to tell her I love her too. Just as soon as you've gone.'

Peter leaves after lunch, during which both men agree to keep in regular touch. The senator ends their meeting by firmly crushing Peter's hand and stating 'Thank you for coming to see me. You've confirmed everything I've heard from others. Somehow, from you it makes far more sense and I know its truth.'

The senator checks that all the travel arrangements for Peter's return journey have been made. Then, shaking his wilting hand again, the senator adds: 'Thank you also for the sincerity of your advice. About Jenny, I mean. I'll make certain you're appointed as some kind of paid advisor to the committee. If that's okay with you, of course.'

Peter makes no mention of another key piece of information he has picked up from the senator: his fears over what the military will do, and what the National Security Committee will in future decide. The potential for abuse of power is immense, as Peter already realizes. What neither he nor seemingly the senator are certain of, is the use their own government will make of the new Bio-Aids, or others.

As good as his word, Peter receives a letter of appointment signed by the senator less than a week later. By the next time they meet, Peter is pleased to see him moving more easily. *I must one day tell him why that is*, he thinks.

A few weeks later at Senator Jackson's sumptuous wedding reception he does so, telepathically. On hearing this the senator walks over and responds by saying, 'I have a little something to tell you too, Peter.'

Laughing aloud, he places an arm on Peter's shoulder. He takes a step back and points out two of the secret service agents who have followed Peter ever since their first meeting.

'They're for your protection, my dear friend. They were ordered to find out all about you before you were allowed anywhere near me. They must have liked you because they asked to stay on this assignment permanently. They're good men, you should thank them sometime. I'm afraid they will have to be part of your life from now on.'

Peter's lips part in awe at this casual expression of power. A slap on his back and another loud laugh are accompanied by a request, an exceptional one.

'You know Peter, the President herself is most keen to meet you. She's asked me to make the arrangements. If it's OK with you, we'll do that here in Texas. She's due tomorrow. You'll stay here overnight, of course?'

Peter answers 'Well, of course. How could I possibly refuse? No, I mean I'd be delighted. Please tell her that. I'm an admirer of hers. Truly, I am.'

'Good. Follow me a moment please, Peter. There are some other people here I'd like you to meet. One's the British ambassador. She's keen to meet you too.'

THIRTY

By the time of Peter's visit to Texas, all known Bio-AID devices have been accounted for and destroyed. The controversy does not end there. An initial moratorium is negotiated and agreed within the UN, resulting in the abrupt *Universal Declaration on the Non-Use of Biological Enhancement for Humans*. The Declaration is signed by representatives of over one hundred countries.

Anxious not to be left behind in any behind-the-scenes race for power and market share, the *Declaration* is quickly ignored by the industrial and financial powers of all the largest nations. In most cases the pace of development increases, sponsored by or with the active support of national and state governments.

As an advisor to two governments Peter becomes involved in the many-sided public and private debates: something he could never have imagined only a year or so before. He sits through a number of US Senate and UK Parliamentary hearings, where he watches discussions over amendments to the weak, existing legislation descend into lobbying and posturing.

Initial attempts to prevent or control manufacture and distribution of the devices are an utter failure. Subject to intense lobbying from interested manufacturers, most of whose ultimate control is Chinese or Russian, there is no will among mainstream politicians to slow development of the huge new market. Peter watches with despair as those fringe politicians who resist the relentless pressure quickly find themselves the subject of intense smear campaigns and are forced to resign.

After consulting with Maureen, Peter wisely decides that he may best contribute by avoiding controversy and continuing to point out to the public that the same capabilities may be accessed more reliably and without any loss of privacy, through the application of regular effort at meditation.

Ignored by the masses, Peter's message is instead accepted and supported by the alternative media, which continues to flourish. His calm certainties appeal to their readers and he finds himself becoming a celebrity in those circles. At the same time, the credibility and popularity stemming from his involvement in the original exposure of the devices, as well as his representations to Senate and other governmental institutions, prevent him from being openly pilloried in the state-sponsored mass media of both countries.

Having enlisted Maureen's help, Peter realizes that their joint powers of manifestation extend far beyond their immediate personal worlds. During an early visit to her office, Maureen explains to him how this works.

'We must visualize the world as we want to see it. Otherwise, if we focus for example on the negative news spread by the media, then that is what we will receive.'

When Peter asks for clarification, she briefly explains about vibrational energy and 'what most people call the Law of Attraction' then suggests they direct their first meditation towards the kind of city they would like to live in.

'Picture it like this, Peter. We are walking along a street. It may be sunny or raining. If it is only sunny, then picture a puddle or two to show that it has recently rained. And as you look around, is the architecture on a human scale, developed for people to enjoy being in and around? Are there trees and plants, and can you hear birds singing or see wildlife meandering among us as we walk? There must be parks and children playing, surely. And the people are smiling and happy, without hate in their hearts. This is the kind of world we should create, Peter. Don't you think?'

At first, he finds it difficult to visualize these scenes in sufficient detail. Then he realizes that even his ability to do so is under his control. So, he pictures himself visualizing with clarity. The next time he meditates, the visions that follow are clearer, their colors are brighter and their edges more precise. And their clarity continues to incrementally improve over time.

'Next time we meet,' Maureen cautions 'we must work more on the kind of *people* we want to populate this city.'

They are unable to delay the creation of a huge new market in the devices. However, through regular meditation and occasional public-speaking engagements, Peter successfully increases the world's level of skepticism, and helps to create a general concern over privacy and state-sponsored misuse. This results in much tighter controls over their physical content and thus the *political* use that is made of them, except within dictatorships.

అ

Within months, the first mass-market products are manufactured, exported in bulk and made commercially available worldwide, despite residual concerns about Chinese and other countries 'tampering'. Rarely have new products been so keenly awaited.

Popular media coverage ignores the ethical, social and evolutionary questions raised. Their articles focus instead on the many new jobs being created, both in manufacture and in related services such as training or mental health counseling. It soon becomes clear just how large the new market is. Protests and union fears about job losses in older, redundant industries like the existing mobile telecommunications networks are swiftly overridden.

Demand is so high, and business is so profitable that every hospital and doctors' surgery is soon equipped with automated means of implanting the devices. The equipment employs the latest nanorobotic techniques. As a result, the Chinese nanobiotechnology and nanorobotics industries undergo a major boom.

Fortunes are made by suppliers and speculators in every country. Within two years of launch, over fifty percent of adult human beings receive and are active users of the new devices, transforming the lives of billions. It is routinely predicted that within a single product generation the devices will be installable via a simple injection of accretive nanorobotic particles, rather than requiring surgery.

Increased intellectual capacity, improved memory recall and broader spatial awareness are immediate benefits for all. The majority of recipients learn quickly how to listen to the thoughts of others, and how to switch transmission of their own thoughts on and off. Most are swiftly capable of conceptual transmission and reception over any distance, increasing the scope and extent of shared knowledge.

While this breakneck growth is happening, Peter and Maureen focus their manifesting on redirecting the energy created into positive directions. One of the other areas they agree to visualize is an improved environment, so they spend many hours together picturing a world with far more vegetation and wildlife.

Supported by her Order, whom Peter is aware of but is yet to meet, the result is an increased general awareness of the effects of climate change. Pressure quickly builds for real, measurable action on reducing fossil fuel use, to the consternation of nations reliant upon its extraction, refining and distribution.

The need for global telecommunication networks and business travel is anyway reduced. Alongside popular pressure their decline aids a reinvigorated, worldwide push to ameliorate and reduce the drastic effects of global warming, as predicted by Peter.

'Of course,' Maureen opines one day 'you realize that if those in control of these industries ever find out it's we who are reducing their power, then…'

Her sentence remains unfinished before Peter asks: 'Do you think they can? Find out who we are, I mean. After all, there must be others like us.'

'Yes, and you know perfectly well there are others like you and me. I can feel you exploring my mind, you know. It's time I explained to you the goals of our Order. It's also time that you met them all. Believe me, they are desperate to meet you.'

Maureen goes on to explain, wordlessly, the history, extent and purpose of the Order to Peter. Although aware of its existence – he has felt its presence during more than one meditation – Peter has so far failed to understand its full, historic significance. The two are by now so well connected that, as soon as she allows him unfettered access to her mind, the entire conversation lasts less than a minute.

She returns to using the spoken word to explain.

'The elite of this world think of us as some kind of mysterious, psychic resistance to be overcome. But in reality, we just spread messages of love.'

Maureen knows that Peter has now realized that he and she share a common past. Her cryptic answer is designed to throw him off the scent, for now. She quickly changes the subject, at the same time reasserting control over her own psyche.

Peter and Maureen's efforts at visualizing the kind of people they wish to live among result for the most part in a greater sympathy for and understanding of other human beings. This is true even of people from very different racial or cultural backgrounds, especially when communicating one-on-one.

'We must focus on ensuring there is empathy,' says Maureen.

As soon as he understands her meaning, Peter finds he is more than capable of creating this.

Instead of communicating by language, most travelers and businesspeople learn to work more swiftly by using concepts and images rather than language, transmitted telepathically. A means is soon developed of interfacing these ideas directly to various AI-based systems, which in turn allow automated creation of designs and contracts. The requirement for designers, translators and lawyers is thus reduced, as is any need for learning unfamiliar languages.

The accidental but frequent sharing between businesspeople of personal images, including intimate pictures of their families or friends, has the unexpected effect of increasing empathy, exactly as Peter imagines during his meditation.

When Peter outlines his observation that political views and positions seem to be polarizing, Maureen describes it as an 'opposite and equal reaction.' She goes on to describe how fear has always held humanity back.

It won't be long now before he is more powerful than me, senses Maureen. *I must make the arrangements as soon as possible.*

Excitement and anticipation permeate every cell of her being - physical, mental and spiritual.

∞

Children are at first discouraged by regulation and convention from having the devices fitted. However, driven by ambitious parents and supported by evidence that children are being unknowingly manipulated, special infant versions are soon being installed at birth and upgraded later to full function.

Problems occur once it is generally realized that the mental and moral development of children under six is inadequate to cope with the opportunities and problems that result. Lilian's new lover Diana is one of the first to discover and publicize the problem, and its extension to older children.

Working in one of Brooklyn's less salubrious neighborhoods a few miles from their home, she interviews a classroom full of children for a breakfast show. Learning of a new game being played by boys and girls as young as four, Diana asks them to explain. The children's stories are consistent with rumors she has heard elsewhere.

'Whenever we see someone asleep in a doorway. Especially when they smell of wee. We stand a few feet away and tell them they need to pee, right away. They always stand up and pee right where they are. Sometimes they don't even have time to undo their zipper,' explains one girl with pigtails, aged nine.

Another, taller but of the same age, elaborates. 'Yes, not only that. We sometimes tell them they are burning up. Even when it's really cold, they stand up and start undressing. Sometimes we even see their bare butts! Most alleyways round here have these people, you know.'

The taller girl is followed by an eight-year-old boy, who exclaims with delight: 'And once, we even told one his ass needed a whoopin'. You should'a seen him. He was whacking away for ages, till his skin went red an' raw! We laughed for hours, didn't we boys?' Several of the boys in the class guffaw.

Diana asks: 'Do you just pick on homeless people?'

The answers are uniform: the children know these people have no money, so they will not have a device fitted. To them, anyone without a device is fair game.

'And you never pick on each other?'

'Oh no, we all have one, so there'd be no point even trying!'

All of these stories are captured on camera, which is broadcast that evening at prime time. By the time Diana returns home it is almost midnight. She is welcomed to congratulations from Lilian.

'That was fabulous! You must be the hottest journalist in the country after that report.'

Diana thanks her. Lilian offers to open a bottle of champagne, but she is told: 'Normally I'd be the first to celebrate, but I'm pooped. Perhaps tomorrow instead?'

'Okay, lover. In that case, we'll go out for the evening. There's a new restaurant opened on Seventh, then we'll go on to Marty's.'

Diana laughs and they spend the next few minutes discussing the menu, which Lilian recalls from memory. Her partner is impressed but does not realize that, supported by her Bio-Aid, her abilities are growing more rapidly than ever.

Over dinner the next evening, Lilian asks Diana for the first time to give up reporting and work for her business.

'It's our firm, after all. And look at the hours you're working as a journalist, for peanuts.'

Later that same evening, Lilian confesses to having a newer device fitted.

'It's the latest model. You should do the same, Diana. You won't believe...'

'I've already had one for weeks. I thought you knew.'

The two women laugh. When they compare dates, they realize that both upgrades were fitted on the same day. Diana exclaims: 'No wonder we didn't notice!'

Within a week Diana has agreed to join Lilian's company, with the proviso that she focusses on 'developing the legitimate side of the business.'

Even though the margins are lower, they are still substantial, so Lilian readily agrees.

'You'll be VP of marketing and PR, okay?'

Tales of more heinous child and youth crimes soon emerge, including incitement to drowning or incineration. These elevate the problem to the headline pages of all the major news websites. There is much debate, but no easy solution. Every parent who is interviewed refuses to consider removal of their children's devices: they are 'so much happier, so much more capable and independent' is a common explanation. Equally, there exists no desire to lower the age of infant liability.

After watching the initial reports from Diana and others, Peter suggests to Maureen that they visualize a world where there are no homeless people.

'Or we visualize one where the homeless people have chosen to live on the street but have enough money to buy one of these devices.'

'I guess you're right, Maureen. After all, this life is their journey and, if they want to spend it on the street there must be a reason for that. So, who are we to tell them otherwise?'

Shortly afterwards and long before any international action is agreed, the problem eases when programs are initiated by various charities to distribute to the homeless free coupons for devices and their fitting. Automated supervisory links are included, connecting the children's version to parents' or guardians' devices. Together with a new version of Bio-AIDs with improved software, these solve the problem. With a much-reduced chance of success, children forget their pastime in favor of newer, less harmful games and applications.

Legislation has again proven too slow and inadequate to deal with the issue.

'The wheels of Government are too big a problem for us to deal with. At least for now,' laugh Maureen and Peter together, before agreeing on a different subject for that day's meditation.

Both know it is their biggest task but is one that requires careful planning, as well as cooperation and concerted effort from more than the two of them.

During the transitional period there are many attempts at fraud and deception. These occur even in tightly-controlled economies, where 'screened' individuals – tested for their psychological propensity to use or abuse the devices – manage to dupe the test. Many others obtain devices through bribery or theft.

At first widespread, an initial rise in murder and suicide rates drops when the discovery is made that a general questionnaire, analyzed by a lie-detector linked to an artificial intelligence robot, can reliably reveal the truth about any attempt to influence others illegally.

The detector is created and distributed without the need for any related manifestation by Peter and Maureen. Fears persist about its true purpose, with reports from several countries of its use during interrogation and torture.

'We can't cure every evil.'

'Not yet anyway,' agree Peter and Maureen.

In many countries, use of such questionnaires for routine and random testing of users of the devices becomes the norm, in spite of persistent and vocal concerns about the privacy implications.

'There is no other choice to be made,' the President assures the American public. 'We must look after the vulnerable.'

Similar statements are made by leaders in every country, which receive general acceptance following a continuous wave of propaganda from federal or national authorities. Courts use new laws to impose significant penalties on the guilty. These include a multi-year ban on using any Bio-AID device, which proves to be the most effective deterrent. As soon as the overwhelming majority of people are using the devices, all such problems become extremely rare.

AI-based 'Guilt-Determination Systems' are soon developed and distributed. These prove far more reliable than a panel of jurors for assessing culpability. Peter recognizes the significance of this: 'We truly are now in the hands of technology, whether in our heads or in our Courts.' His prediction of man evolving to become *homo technica* has come true.

'I suppose,' Maureen tells Peter one day, '… I suppose it is time we should turn our attention to the systems of political control in this country. Otherwise we will end up no better than China.'

Peter agrees but neither can summon the will, on that day at least, to deal with all the negative energy crafted daily by the thousands of politicians, lobbyists, businessmen and hangers-on that making such a change must involve.

'It's a Pandora's Box,' says Peter. 'We'd need to be absolutely precise in what we seek to create. Or they'll manipulate it around us.

That's their expertise after all, isn't it? Turning love into partisan or internecine squabble.'

They decide to postpone that issue to another day.

Maureen has by now made the arrangements for Peter's introduction to the Order, the first step in the process of beginning the changes foretold. A specific question forms as it permeates her conscious thinking. *Perhaps political control is the singular, defining issue on which Peter must concentrate?*

She recognizes at once that this is the truth, and that the Order must help him with the task of redefining and reshaping politics and its goals, both domestically and internationally. *Somehow*, she believes, *this must involve a change in the very nature of mankind.* Later that evening her meditations range widely. By three am she is reading from a copy of Mary Magdalene's original text, searching for clear guidance.

With relevant laws being difficult to enforce internationally, cross-border incidents of manipulation remain a persistent problem, but become relatively small in scale due to the low and reducing likelihood of finding an innocent victim with any money or assets left to steal.

Most countries have applied revised immigration rules, expanded to include mandatory testing of all individuals fitted with the device. Once enacted, almost none of these laws are repealed even after their original purpose – protecting those without a Bio-Aid – has long passed. The number of international travelers has dropped dramatically, and remains low. The nature of human interaction is changed forever. There is less routine physical contact, a process already begun by the rise of the internet and social media and continued by regular manipulation of health scares.

'We really have to deal with this self-imposed isolation,' Maureen says to Peter one day, expressing her greatest concern. 'We cannot let all of mankind drift into becoming couch potatoes. It will promote indifference.'

They agree to spend daily meditation sessions in her office devoted purely to this subject.

A short while later, self-help groups begin to proliferate. Some are for those struggling to cope with the new freedoms and new responsibilities. Others concentrate their efforts on the surprisingly large numbers who struggle to distinguish physical reality from their thoughts. This condition is quickly adopted as a theme by psychologists, who claim it is an acute mental health problem that they alone are qualified to treat.

Many more groups are formed to help reduce the number of people living alone, or at least to involve them in social activities, as well as arranging for visits to those physically unable to leave their isolation through age or disability. International and cross-cultural groups are formed, overcoming state and legislative resistance to spread understanding across international boundaries.

'In time,' Peter tells Maureen one day, 'we may come to see these very human responses as our greatest achievement.'

He still has 'blind spots' she knows but, on this day and after that prescient statement, Maureen first knows for certain that his clairvoyant abilities now far exceed her own.

THIRTY-ONE

Except for the single warning from Lilian, Peter has no reason to doubt Angela's motives for becoming his lover. She has never asked about the size of his inheritance and has never sought any gifts or loan. Angela spends all her spare time with him, attending classes or sharing dinner, and his bed.

He has made a conscious effort not to use his new-found powers to exploit or control their relationship. *That way lies madness*, he tells himself. He knows that it is important to keep himself 'grounded.' That is, present in the everyday world and to not use his growing powers to change the minutiae of his life and his relationships.

Maureen has meantime assisted Angela on an almost daily basis to grow and expand. Her prime purpose is to teach her how to block any attempt to read her mind.

'If the prophecy is true, he will soon enough be able to do so at will. Nothing and no one will be able to stop him,' she explains to Angela. 'In his case however, the result of such an investigation may only be benevolent. It can be no other way. It is among the most ancient and powerful foretold.'

Maureen also knows that Peter's powers must remain focused on the big picture, on mankind's future, and not be distracted by his personal life.

Now that he is fitter and healthier, Peter has begun to believe he and Angela make a very compatible couple. Their age difference is significant, but by no means problematic. He views her as intelligent, lively, and good company. His feelings for her are lustful and loving, although he worries that his early infatuation has not grown into a fully-fledged feeling of being 'in love' with her, in its traditional, obsessive sense. Or so he tells himself.

They are contented, happy and relaxed in each other's company. However, the idea planted by Lilian has bloomed into a fully formed flower of uncertainty. Peter's initial fears over why such an attractive younger woman would wish to hook up with an older man have faded. But this new doubt is strong and resilient.

Reverberating inside his head, the repeated tolling of his daughter's words signals the eventual evolution of their contented relationship.

The real reason for the attention Angela lavishes upon you is because she has always known you will inherit Pop's wealth it peals, over and over.

He remains unwilling to use his new powers for personal gain, and he has gained the strength of will necessary for him not to do so. Peter truly has no desire to allow their relationship to die. Hence it is many weeks before a change begins. In the midst of a deep meditation, he one day finds himself asking the universe for guidance.

'Tell me or show me a sign of what I must do.'

The following day, Peter is standing alone in his kitchen when he answers a call by glancing down at the AR on his wrist. A young woman's voice speaks.

'Mr Walker, is that you? I have a call for you, from Mr Bradley Williams III. Please wait one moment.'

There is no opportunity to decline; the young lady clicks the call directly through to Williams, who begins speaking at once.

'Mr Walker? Thank you for taking my call. It has been a few months now. I was wondering, have you thought over our offer to introduce you to some financial advisors? It's just that your father – who was a dear personal friend – asked me to ensure you invest your money wisely.'

Peter has given the subject barely a moment's thought. 'Err… um… well, to be honest, I haven't,' he says.

'Well, your money is on deposit at your bank, I understand, but that will hardly earn you a good return. I was wondering, would you like me to arrange a couple of meetings for you here? I'd be happy to do so, and to take you for lunch afterwards.'

Peter agrees. Williams explains that his secretary will be in contact to confirm dates and times.

'Well, goodbye then and please, call me Bradley,' he says. 'I'll look forward to meeting you again very soon.'

Williams adds a coda.

'Oh, and Mr Walker. In case you were wondering, nothing ever came of the complaint being brought by that young woman.'

Confused for a moment, Peter is unsure whether the comment is directed to him. He asks: 'I'm sorry? I don't…'

Williams explains.

'Oh, of course. You had such a lot on your mind, I did not wish to bother you about it before. We went ahead with the reading of the

Will because we could see the lady had no grounds. She is a most persistent young woman though.'

Intrigued, Peter asks: 'She has a claim on my father's estate?'

'Indeed. Based upon her assertion that she was living with him. That turned out to be a lie, of course. She was in fact living with another man, a few miles away. Her brother, I believe.'

Pop never mentioned to Peter any special woman, certainly not one who lived with him. He tells the lawyer: 'Oh! I never heard of any particular woman, although I was living five thousand miles away during his last years.'

Williams continues: 'Your father was a very popular man, Mr Walker. But we researched her claim and found it to be untrue. She lives in the city. Angela something.'

Frozen at the mention of her name, Peter's legs soon melt and give way. He grips the cool edge of a ceramic sink, before reaching over to rest on a chair. Their final exchange passes in a blur.

He drifts on unsteady legs into the lounge, where he stares out of the window barely aware of the view beyond. Mixed with emotions of hurt, betrayal and desire, questions about Angela's motives are entangled and inseparable, impossible to resolve.

After an hour, his mind clears to the point where he can rationalize. He finds a notebook and writes:

Angela's motive for being with me is money, not passion -
Her relationship with Pop was almost certainly physical -
She cared for him during his last months   +
Her desire for me is likely faked   ?
She has been very helpful to me   +

As soon as he writes the second question mark, Peter decides he must drive to Angela's apartment to confront her. A cold fog has been stationary over the city all day. He speaks to his AR.

'Tell the car to warm up. I'll be there in a moment.'

The last sentence is superfluous; the car's default setting will keep it warm for an hour.

Once inside the car, Peter barks Angela's address, which he knows despite never having been there before. As the car whirrs away, he leans back into a seat, closes his eyes and reflects.

Angela has known all along about Pop's money, so she is indeed a gold-digger, as Lilian warned. She may have actually been his lover, only taking up with me as a fallback. Whatever happens, I don't want to know anything more about her relationship with him. It's too hurtful. Worst of all she has been seeking recompense from his will, behind my back! That's plain deceitful. On the other hand, she has always been kind and caring to me, if only out of self-interest. That's the question I need an answer to, her motive. And from her mouth, not from within my own head.

A few minutes later, Peter hammers on her front door. It is opened moments later by Angela. Stood behind her is a female client of about her own age, readying to depart.

'Oh Peter, what a lovely sur… but, what's wrong?'

Angela stands aside to let her client pass by. Peter does the same then tells her, 'We need to speak.'

Angela grabs hold of his hand to lead Peter inside. He withdraws his hand but follows behind. As soon as they enter her small lounge, Peter begins.

'Angela, what precisely did you know about my father's estate?'

Wrinkles spread across Angela's forehead. Her mouth opens and closes, but she says nothing. Her head moves from side to side as Peter continues, 'You knew he was wealthy, didn't you?'

Angela averts her eyes, looking down to the carpet for a moment.

'I knew he was comfortably off. That much was obvious from his lifestyle. Not that he was flash, I mean. He was always generous.'

Angela's eyes rise to meet Peter's before she adds, 'That's all!'

While Peter mulls over what to ask next, Angela repeats her assertion.

'That's all, Peter! But why do you ask?'

Peter ignores her question.

'Did you think I would never find out about your claim? You know the one: based on the fact that you lived with him!'

Angela's face reddens – Peter is unsure whether with anger or embarrassment. She shouts.

'All right! Yes, I made a claim. And so what?! I deserve the money! I wasn't after it all, just some. And your father promised to look after me when he was gone. He promised…'

In a calmer voice, she continues, 'Who do you think looked after your father when he was ill? I shopped for him; cleaned for him. I even helped him out of bed sometimes. You never saw him, how bad he was, or how ill he was at the end.'

Peter's anger and hurt are clear to her when he says, 'Oh, I'm sure you helped him out of bed all right!'

'And so what if I did? He was a wonderful man.'

Angela puts her hands to her face and sinks to the floor. She begins to cry. Sobbing, she tells her story.

'I loved him, but not in that way. He was kind and caring. It just seemed a natural thing to do, to stay over. He never made a pass or anything. It's totally different with you. It started out because I was lonely, and I wanted to keep some kind of connection with Jeff. I never expected to fall in love with you!'

Peter is surprised; Angela has never used that phrase before. Unsure what words will fall from his mouth, he begins to speak.

'I don't know how you can tell me that, Angela. You slept in my father's house and now you love me. Well, whatever the truth of it all, it's over between us.'

Angela looks up. 'No! Why?'

His answer is coolly spoken, if only partially truthful.

'Because you lied to me, Angela. I'm not sure I can trust you anymore.'

Angela silently mouths, 'No' as Peter looks at her.

He turns around and makes for the door. Grabbing and turning its handle, he glances over his shoulder and says, 'I'll send you some money. As a thank you for looking after Pop. Goodbye!'

The door is slammed shut behind Peter, narrowly missing his trailing heel. He does not look back.

Later the same day, he makes a payment of a quarter of a million dollars to Angela's account. He calls a locksmith and has all the locks to his apartment changed. He then tells its control system that Angela no longer has access.

One hour later, he calls Margaret to tell her that he has come into some money. A sum far greater than she ever imagined possible, Margaret quickly agrees to accept an increased payment of one million pounds as a final divorce settlement.

By evening and over a glass of red wine, Peter decides he needs a break from San Francisco, and to put some distance between Angela and him. Within a further hour he is packed and ready to depart for the airport. He takes one last, long look around to memorize every detail, not knowing when he will return. Then he catches the overnight flight to Washington.

A week later he flies on to London.

THIRTY-TWO

Peter pays extra to check in early to a hotel overlooking the river, close to the Embankment and Charing Cross. Overlooking the South Bank, his room's terrace affords one of his favorite views of the city, to the right towards Westminster and eastwards to the left past an avenue of trees towards St Paul's Cathedral. He imbibes the sounds and smells, reflecting all the while on his change of fortune since he left Janet's tiny, terraced house.

After a shower and a brief nap, he spends the next few hours wandering the streets. He ambles in and out of shops with no real aim or purpose other than to pass the time. By late afternoon he is sitting in an open-air café in St James's Park, listening with closed eyes to twittering birds, a busker and the excited chatter of tourists.

Resting his buttocks on the hard back of a bench, Peter raises his eyes to the clear skies above and breathes a deep sigh, loud enough to be audible to passers-by. As his breath subsides, Peter is left with an empty feeling at the base of his stomach. With a start, he realizes that all he craves – all he needs – he already has.

Unconditional love is a remarkable gift, he decides, *and one that should be cherished.*

Peter's chest no longer wheezes when he breathes, nor does his belly protrude between the buttons of his shirt. These are all gifts from Angela, whom he is tempted for a second to call. Not to admonish, but to forgive her and to thank her. For a moment he feels utterly alone. Not lonely, but calm and confident. For the first time he can remember, he feels at ease being on his own.

Peter rises from the bench and begins to walk. Stopping to admire flowers or to watch the splashing ducks, he completes one circuit of the lake at a leisurely pace. He watches tourists giggling or laughing or taking photographs, then admires the concentrated efforts of ducks, playing or scrapping over morsels of food.

Leaving the path to walk across the grass, Peter meanders through rows of deck chairs towards Piccadilly. As he walks, he is drawn towards a large oak tree, standing fifty yards or more from its nearest neighbor, but one of many dotted around the park. The tree is in full leaf and adorned with tiny white flowers.

When Peter enters the shade of its branches, he stops. For a moment perplexed, he stands completely still and silent. The hustle and bustle of nearby tourists and the sounds of rush-hour traffic die away.

Peter and the tree are left alone. He sees the tree in sharp focus, while all around him blurs. Peter closes his eyes and is at once aware of the secret energy of this ancient tree. Within a split-second, he receives a powerful burst of information, directly into his subconscious. The transmission includes a welcome, an invitation to talk, and an expression of pleasure at the presence of an enlightened one.

This is a rare treat, says the tree. The words appear as concepts, fed directly into Peter's mind in the same manner as those from his daughter only weeks before. Peter is by now more than capable of managing their conversation himself. However, just as it was that first time with Lilian, their communication is controlled by the tree, and the source of Peter's reply is his own subconscious.

Please he says, *may I come closer and talk awhile?*

The tree welcomes Peter, telling him to stand a yard away from its trunk and to extend an arm so the palm of his hand touches bark.

It's the easiest way to communicate, the oak explains.

Their entire conversation has so far taken less than a second. Peter walks a few steps forward and does as asked.

As soon as his hands touch the trunk, Peter again closes his eyes. Patterns swirl in the darkness behind his eyelids. They have great depth, extending for tens of yards through the darkness. He feels a surge of energy from the heart of the tree, entering his body through hands, feet, belly and the crown of his head. Bathing in a *Divine* force, he cannot help but smile as he knowingly shares a direct experience of the *Universal* energy that permeates all.

A vision of a single tree enters his mind, a brave and twisted pine standing alone on a vast plain surrounded by distant blue mountains and clear skies. He is reminded by the oak of a passage from the center pages of the journal.

Weve reached a huge grass plain they call Powder Valley. Smack in the middle is a single tree, felled but with leaves still on. It must of bin cut down only a day before. I want to cry out loud. It feels like the whole land for miles around is cryin out for its loss. As if its very heart lies broken.

Peter has read the passage before but is no longer perplexed by its meaning. The tree is a metaphor for all trees and all vegetation, even for the whole of planet Earth.

We are one, the same and indivisible, it wordlessly tells him, *you and me and the whole Earth. We are here to grow and to prosper, our lives intertwined and interdependent, developing our souls and curating this planet for all beings. We are its beating heart. We grow together, or together we wither and die.*

The tree also shares some of its history, sometimes as a plant, more often as animal or human, and more than once as a visitor to a different planet.

Peter has no idea how long their conversation lasts but later decides it must have been less than a minute. By its end, he feels buoyant; younger and lighter, as if lifted from all cares. He and the tree say their goodbyes, directly to each other's subconscious. Both know they are now linked, friends for all time and through every one of their lives past, present or future, no matter what form they take.

The mighty oak is the first tree with whom Peter communicates 'and one of the wisest,' Peter later decides. Within a matter of days, the surprise of talking with vegetation has become a distant memory. Peter speaks routinely to many more, bushes and plants as well as trees.

Peter learns of the past and future lives of each one, of how they are all linked to the Earth and through the Earth to each other, and their various reasons for taking such a long rest and meditation. Some prefer not to be disturbed but most are welcoming, delighted to meet him and to share their knowledge.

By the end of his first week in London, Peter no longer marvels at each new revelation; he is entirely at ease with his expanding intellectual and spiritual knowledge, and his feeling of being one and indivisible with all around.

Notions of the interconnection of all matter, and of the vast sweep of *Time* and the concurrence of all *Universal* events, Peter comprehends with a depth of understanding far beyond mere reasoning.

It's as if I have woken from a long dream, he reflects one evening, lying on his hotel bed. A moment later he adds, aloud: 'What a magical place is this earth!'

Leaning over, Peter retrieves the journal from beside his bed. He caresses its leaves with the tips of his fingers before letting his middle finger fall between two pages. He levers open the cover and begins to read.

I've learned lots about folks and a little about myself. Our journey, my own and that of those people I have met seems to have only just begun. Mine would take me in a holy new direction.

He places the journal onto the bed, then walks over to the desk. From its drawer, he takes a sheet of headed notepaper and begins to write.

We all start our journeys with a mixture of hope and ambition. Some of us lose sight of those qualities as we travel; in others it strengthens. For all of us the journey is a discovery, not least about ourselves and who we really are.

He rises and places his sheet inside the journal.

Satisfied he has at least begun his own contribution to its knowledge, Peter places the journal down and returns to the bed. He stretches out on his back with the journal closed across his chest. By the time Peter wakes, it is some hours later. Outside, darkness is descending.

Peter rises, returns the AR to his wrist and dictates a message of forgiveness to Angela. 'It's time,' he says aloud.

'Angela, my darling. Thank you for all you have done for me. I know I owe you a great debt. I have loved you and I still love you, and I am sorry if I have hurt you. At present all I know is that I need time alone while I work out who I am and what I want to do and be. I hope you understand. My very best wishes to you, Peter.'
The spoken message is delivered within a few seconds.

He orders room-service food, which arrives and is consumed as soon as he is dressed. A few minutes before nine, he departs from the hotel by Robo-taxi. A half-hour later he arrives at the little terraced house in a rain-soaked, chilly London suburb that months before had been for a while both his temporary home and his salvation.

With some trepidation, Peter rings the new doorbell, which seems not to work. He raps loudly on the door, which is answered a few seconds later by Janet, whose love and devotion Peter has at last realized has been a constant presence. Before Janet can say anything, he asks: 'Janet, will you ever forgive me? You have been a wonderful friend to me. And I have given nothing in return, except to ignore you for months and months. So much has happened, I can't…'

Janet interrupts, in a raised voice.

'Oh, don't be silly, Mr Walker! It's so lovely to see you again and looking so well. You'll have to forgive me being dressed like this. I was just about to go to bed. But please, do come in! I want to know all that you've been up to.'

Peter leans forward and places his arms around her.

'Janet! What a wonder you are! I can't tell you how much I've missed you.'

They hold each other close for a long while Peter kisses her forehead more than once before Janet releases her embrace. They enter the house. Peter closes the front door then joins Janet in the kitchen.

While the kettle boils, Peter begins his tale. He tells of his time staying in the apartment, of how he met Angela, of how she helped him become fit and healthy, of how they became lovers, and of how he became a healer.

'And you've become famous, Mr Walker,' Janet smiles. 'I saw you on television a few weeks ago. You were being interviewed about those bio-things. How smart you looked.'

Peter smiles too.

'Yes, it's funny how things turn out. And aside from my temporary fame, I also make a living. Not that I need one anymore!'

Janet looks at him quizzically.

'I miss Pop a great deal, Janet,' Peter explains. 'As I'm sure you know. I make a great deal of money now acting as an advisor, but his legacy has anyway made me a rich man; very rich. I had no idea he was so wealthy. None!'

'Oh, I'm so glad!' Janet is delighted. 'And after all you've been through too.'

Tea is served.

'Decaffeinated,' Janet announces. 'I hope you don't mind. It's just that it's so late, and...'

Peter interrupts: 'That's fine, Janet. Absolutely fine.'

A few seconds later, he apologizes again.

'I'm so sorry, Janet. I should have realized. This is very late for me to call. It's just that... well, I wanted to see you straight away. It's been such a long time and I know I owe you so much. It's wonderful to see you again, wonderful!'

'You'll stay the night, I hope?'

'Of course,' Peter says, 'and thank you. Thank you, Janet, for everything.'

The pair enter the lounge, where they sit and talk for another hour. Peter tells her of all his experiences; Janet tells of how she eventually found a job as a secretary.

'One of those virtual ones, Mr Walker. You know, where there's no office and everything's done on the phone.'

Raising her arm, Janet pulls back her sleeve to reveal an AR.

'Well, one of these anyway,' she laughs.

Peter tells her: 'Janet, I'd like you to come and work for me. I've been asked to speak at some engagements here, and I'm opening an advisory and healing practice in London too. I aim to live both in San Francisco and here. I'm going to buy a house somewhere, a small one, for whenever I'm here.'

'But you're always welcome to stay with me, Mr Walker,' says Janet. 'Even though you no longer need to.'

Peter is pleased by her offer but is insistent.

'That is so kind. Of course, I shall visit you often, but I cannot impose on you like that. I'll find a house nearby, one where I can have an office too. We'll see each other every day, when I'm in London at least. None of this virtual rubbish. It'll be just like old times except this time I'll be making money instead of giving it away. And I'll pay you properly too. Whatever you earn now plus a deal more!'

Janet is delighted with the offer. There is a moment's silence while they stare into each other's eyes. Broad smiles crease both their faces. Peter is the first to break the spell.

'There's one more thing, Janet. I'd like to give you some money. Enough so you don't have to work. If you don't want to, that is.'

'Oh no, Mr Walker. I couldn't take that,' she protests.

'Janet, I insist. That way if I ever take you for granted again, you can just resign!'

Janet laughs, forgiving with her love as always. That is her destiny.

'Oh, well, in that case…'

Peter joins in the laughter. Both continue, loud and long.

Early the following morning, Janet hands in her notice. Peter arrives as promised at nine-thirty AM. They spend an hour online, searching for suitable premises in the area. By eleven they leave together, walking with linked arms towards the first of their appointments. Peter is daydreaming aloud.

'A house big enough for a waiting room, my office and interview room, plenty of space for you, and a large bedroom for me upstairs, Janet. That's what I want.'

By three in the afternoon, both are tired. They stop at a café for lunch. Over their bowls of pasta and salad, Janet tells him: 'Those horrible people who stole your company went bankrupt, by the way.

Apparently, they tried to do the same to someone else, but the gentleman took them to court and won. They had to pay millions in compensation, and pretty much lost everything. That fat man from Stevenage had to sell his country house.'

To Janet's surprise, Peter's reply is magnanimous.

'Well, I don't wish them ill. It's all worked out for me and you in the end. But maybe it shows there is justice in the world after all.'

Before his office is open and a week before he returns to San Francisco, Peter holds the first of many healing sessions in England at the home of his old friend Ceiridh. Knowing from all the publicity that he is now a healer, she has contacted him and asked for his help.

&

'Tell me first then, all about your childhood, your early childhood,' requests Peter.

Ceiridh replies with a question 'You mean around the age of seven?'

Peter nods. Yes,' he affirms. 'It's clearly a crucial time in your life.'

'Well, I had a really happy time as a young child. We moved around a lot, of course. My father was in the military. He specialized in guarding embassies and consulates, especially in the Middle East.'

Ceiridh can still feel a residual warmth from the hands he has just removed. She coughs and looks across at Peter, whose eyes are fixed on hers.

Peter tells her: 'Please, take a sip of water. It's easier for me when you are well-hydrated.'

Her tale begins. 'He left when I was seven. There were rows before, of course. But I never paid them much attention. I was too busy playing with all the other children. Our schools were good, the teachers were kind, and I had lots of friends, who all lived close-by on the same army base.'

Another sip of water is taken before she continues.

'After that, we had to return to England. It was cold. It rained all the time. I'd never experienced that before: I thought the sun always shone. I had no friends. And the girls in my school all hated me. They were jealous, of course, especially of all my travels and the stories I could tell. I was miserable.'

Her gaze returns to meet Peter's. Ceiridh forces a smile and jokes: 'I'm afraid it's all been downhill since then.'

Peter listens for a further ten minutes, to explanations of how her mother failed to cope with being alone, how her stepfather was a bully, how neither were able to show her any affection, and of occasional, awkward visits from her father.

'No more than once or twice a year.'

He has only been active as a healer for a few weeks but already Peter knows that nearly all his clients' problems stem from unresolved issues in their childhood, mainly from a lack of affection. Other issues are inherited, passed on genetically, or are the residue from adult experiences, often through some form of domestic abuse. The more difficult, hidden ones are from previous lives. *They're always the most interesting, of course,* he muses before asking her to tell him why she moved to Devon.

'I always loved the place, and we used to holiday near Exeter every year. It just felt like somewhere I would belong. And I wanted to get away, to spend some time alone. I suppose I was grieving. Not for my mother, she's still alive. For my failed marriage, I mean.'

Ceiridh has been staring at the floor while speaking. She looks up, seeking guidance on whether to continue. Listening to the sound of her words rather than their meaning, Peter nods and asks her to finish her tale. The exposition of her husband's infidelities takes another five minutes to complete.

'I was heartbroken,' she concludes.

'OK, Ceiridh. Let's just sit back and relax for a minute or two. I was sorry to hear about your marriage breaking up. As you know, your husband was a friend of mine too. Still is, although I haven't seen him for some time. He's never once spoken to me of the reasons why he left, and I've never asked.'

Peter takes a deep breath before continuing.

'You told me when we started that you weren't sure why you contacted me. But it seems to me you are very clear. You want to know how to be happy again, isn't that true?'

'Oh, yes! More than anything, Peter.'

'It's very common for children from broken homes to feel unloved, and for them to then be unable to show affection to their own partners or children. You're a counsellor in your spare time, so I'm sure you must know that already.'

'Yes,' she confirms 'but I made a special effort. I really did. Not that you'd ever know. My daughter never speaks to me now.'

Her eyes widen, pleading for help. A tear begins to form. The confident sound of Peter's voice ensures it does not fall.

'Well, we can change all that. But you have to trust me. All I need you to do is to relax. It will help if you hold my hands too, if that is okay?'

Ceiridh affirms her acceptance then follows his instructions to release her shoulders and to allow her belly to do the work of inflating her lungs. Once her eyes have closed, he takes hold of her hands and lowers both of his own eyelids.

Within an instant, Peter is in a deep meditation. From within his meditation, he removes in turn each one of her complex web of negative and limiting beliefs and replaces them with the single belief that she is entitled to be happy. He observes the healing with his eyes closed while his instructions are followed. Once these changes are completed, he implants the experience of two feelings: one of happiness and the other of how to be joyful.

After he finishes, Peter takes one last detailed survey of her aura. *I know her,* he realizes. *I don't know why I never realized before. That is the real reason why she is here.* Told to open her eyes, Ceiridh blinks during the few moments it takes for them to adjust to the light.

'How do you feel?' asks Peter.

'Uhmmm, I don't know. Lighter somehow. Unburdened may be a better description.'

'All that negative stuff will clarify and work its way out over the next day or two. It's already happened, it happens straightaway. It just takes our body and mind a few days to accept that it's gone. Drink plenty of water, it always helps the adjustment.'

Taking the hint, Ceiridh raises the glass to her lips and sips again at the water. As soon as the glass is placed back onto the table, Peter tells her: 'I saw something else, just now. About your distant past. Would you like to know more?'

'Ooh, yes! What is it?'

'You and I knew each other in a past life.'

While her eyebrows rise, Peter adds: 'You were a soldier. A warrior is probably a better description. We both were. You were a man. At the time, I mean,' he explains.

The next half hour passes by in a flash as Peter tells his engrossed client all that he remembers about their past life. He cautions her: 'Some of what I tell you may already have bubbled to the surface in your own memory, so to speak. I think it's the real reason why you contacted me.'

A sharp intake of breath precedes Ceiridh's next statement. 'Well, that's true. As it happens, Peter, I have had some very strange dreams lately. Now that you've told me I was a man once, they kind of make more sense.'

Her explanation takes several minutes, during which Peter recognizes some of the places mentioned. He spends some time explaining the law of attraction, and how it brings together those who have shared experiences through multiple lives.

Both are keen to renew their acquaintance and to share more of their memories. However, Peter has another errand to run in a different part of the city. He apologizes and says, 'Let's meet again soon and discuss that some more. Meantime, your emotional pain should lessen. If you feel strange or maybe a little tearful, just run with it.'

Ceiridh nods an understanding and stands, ready to leave. Peter explains: 'I'm going to be away for a few weeks. In the meantime, could I suggest, if I may, that you carry on practicing a simple meditation – like the one I've just showed you, nothing more – and see what feelings or visions arise? You'll straightaway recognize any past-life experiences for what they are.'

They agree to meet again when he next returns to London.

THIRTY-THREE

'**I miss you** and you are the one woman on this planet that I want to be with. Will you take me back – not just as the great friend you have been to me, but as a lover?'

Standing on the edge of her doorstep with his heels pressed into the pavement, Peter's speech takes longer to complete than he anticipated. Passing cars and an overhead airplane draw away her eyes, diverting Angela's attention when he needs it most. Clear skies and a rising sun then greet a stare that lifts over rooftops and distant hills.

When her eyes return to his, Peter reaches forward and places his hands onto her waist. An involuntary shiver and the retreat of her shoulders tell Peter he has far to go if he is to achieve his goal. Her expression remains frosty.

Peter fears the worst. Gentle hands remove his but continue to hold a delicate grip on each palm. Their joined arms form a V that both connects and separates the former lovers. Peter tries to keep his eyes in contact with hers, but he glances towards the ground. His head lowers. He senses that defeat is imminent. It is not at all as he expected.

Angela's face broadens into a forced smile. Her shoulders lower and relax. Her head moves forward. Anticipating a delicate but hesitant first kiss, Peter's momentary hope is dashed when Angela's face moves past his hopeful lips. Brushing his cheek with her mouth, a kiss is planted next to an ear. Her next words puncture every bubble of hope.

'I'm sorry, Peter. And thank you for coming to see me. You're such a sweet man, but I'm afraid I've found someone else.'

A deflated Peter blusters, 'Wh... what? You mean, you're with another man?'

Releasing his hands, Angela announces, 'I'm sorry, Peter. I should probably have replied to your message. I thought you were done with me. That one message you sent read like a man suffering regrets, but no more. I never expected you to come back here.'

A shock passes through Peter's body. His feet tremble and dance. His mouth opens, then closes. He has no words more to say. Peter has ignored the growing feeling of trepidation all day, during his flight and his journey to her door. He now realizes too late the mistake he has made. His obsession with Angela and with her youthful beauty has led him to ignore all the signals coming from his intuition.

'I should know better,' he intones, muttering.

Peter's doleful thought is interrupted.

'Oh, Peter! We had a lovely time. Please keep in touch with me, won't you? We could do lunch, or maybe go to a class together. If you're staying here in the city, that is?'

Devoid of emotion, her words' empty comfort show Peter with cruel clarity that his love for Angela is misplaced.

Peter is still laboring under the standing instruction from his Higher Self that he must not use his powers to gain unfair advantage in his personal relationships. He thus reacts like a youthful Englishman. He feels only a cool detachment. His bonds to her are released so he is polite and affects a newly acquired disinterest.

'Yes. Yes of course, Angela! Let's do that some time. I'll be in touch over the next week or two. Perhaps we could dine at our little bistro again. It would be like old times.'

Their verbal conversation lasts a few sentences more before ending with farewells and good wishes. Both know that their words are empty assurances. The same thought occurs to both simultaneously *Having no arrangement to meet we will not speak to each other in a meaningful way again.* Neither says a word to alter that path.

They part, both expecting to see each other only at occasional classes or social gatherings, if ever. There they will hear of each other's passions and exploits with a wistful, declining concern. As he trudges away from Angela's home, Peter feels saddened, but he is also aware of a new assuredness, a confidence that stems from knowing how far he has grown. His thoughts meander while his car drives him homewards.

Only a year or so ago, I lived in misery with a woman who gave me no comfort. I left her and soon found a new woman, one to obsess and fuss over. One whose wishes and direction I followed, driven not by any deep, universal love but by a desire to possess and to be possessed. Both were wholly misguided.

Behind him in the hallway of her home, Angela sinks to the ground. Placing her hands to her face, her eyes close. Her chest shudders twice then a single tear falls, followed seconds later by many more. Absorbed in self-pity, between sobs she moans: 'I know I agreed to do this but why does it always feel the same. Always!'

Staring absentmindedly out of the car windows, Peter glimpses occasional views of the Bay over the sea wall. Loud enough to prompt the voice response system of his car to interrupt him, he mutters:

267

'An avoidance of responsibility, not an acceptance of it. That's what I was doing with Angela. My obsession was leading away from my path, not along it. At least, it's been that way for the last few months.'

He ignores the car's request for more information. His thoughts continue in the same smug, dissatisfied vein until he reaches his father's apartment. Once there, he resolves

This is my home now but I'm ready to explore and travel too. I need to spread the word of what I have learnt, to share my understanding, and especially my spiritual knowledge.

With those thoughts, Peter begins a quest, one that enlarges his fame beyond acting as a healer and advisor. One that leads to him publishing his spiritual knowledge, to lecture tours, to more advisory roles and, ultimately to a meeting in Brighton.

Peter is willfully ignoring his deepest feelings, as a means of dealing with them. Only one other person, watching their interaction from afar, knows the significance of what has happened. She longs to console him but knows that she must not. He has one last lesson to learn before he becomes their Master.

One quiet, contemplative part of Peter's mind is delighted with the events that have transpired: the part that recognizes the value of limitations on our abilities, on the need for free will. It emerges within minutes of his departure from Angela. When Maureen becomes aware of this, her heart sings. It is almost too much for her to bear to separate from watching him and to return to her own body. She now knows he is fully ready.

Settled in his bed later that evening, Peter reads a passage from near the end of the journal that he cannot recall having seen before:

I left that same instant. As I strolled along the road out of Oregon City, I realized I could not leave Mona behind. I turned round and headed back. A few minutes later I saw her heading towards me. Mona ran up to me and said she was sorry, that it had all been her fault and that she wanted only to be with me. I knew that we loved each other and I knew for sure that love conkers all. We had no idea where we were going but, wherever it was we would go there together.

The passage tells Peter what he most wants to read: that Mona followed Jake after all.

Peter places down the journal, closes his eyes and pictures the scene: two young lovers, still teenagers and almost certainly chaste, holding hands, smiling and laughing; happier to be in each other's company than they have ever been. Peter reflects with sadness that he has never experienced such a love. A moment later, he sits bolt upright.

'Of course!' he shouts. 'What on earth am I doing feeling sorry for myself! The journal is telling me that she is out there. My soulmate, waiting for me to find her. All I have to do is look!'

Peter already knows there is no *single* soulmate for anyone, but many. He also knows that those who are connected in previous lives are drawn to each other throughout every one of their lives. That we follow each other around, meeting and interacting, sharing our experiences and our love.

'It's the fundamental law of attraction,' he exclaims.

Once again, Peter delights in the wonders of the *Universe*. His quest to find a soulmate for the rest of this life begins at that very

269

moment. And whenever he suffers a momentary doubt that he will find her, Peter knows he may return to the journal, which will point him the way. His way.

THIRTY-FOUR

Sevda Bashur has served in the household of her Turkish master for two years, since the day she reached the age of seventeen. She is told to call him 'My Lord Demir' and must follow any instruction given by him to the letter. Like many Kurdish women she has become an indentured servant in her own land, treated legally and physically as a slave with few rights or protections.

The Kurdish language and culture have been actively suppressed for twenty years, ever since Turkey began its long march from secularism into an isolated, aggressive, and politically conservative state dominated by its religious leaders.

As mayor of the town of Sirnak, Lord Demir allocates Kurdish slave labor to the many resource-hungry development projects underway within the region. The workers are paid little or nothing in return for a home that consists of a bed in a shared room. Many of their brethren preferred a rapid death in the concentration camps.

Along with the other twelve of his servants, Sevda is at first refused a Bio-Aid. Her master eventually relents after one of them attempts to stab him in the neck with a kitchen knife while under the influence of 'voices' in his head. As soon as psychiatric problems are ruled out as a cause, the man is first publicly flogged and then fired. Told he must neutralize the possibility of external interference, the master places an order the same day for Bio-Aids for all his staff.

271

A week later, the Turkish government announces a new, 'guaranteed-compliance' version. His order is quickly changed to the new, compliant version. As one of his favored concubines, Sevda's is the first to be fitted.

The new version means she is fed a daily diet of government propaganda, and restrictions are placed on both the number of people with whom she may communicate as well as on the information she may access. However, the system proves unable to prevent people from other countries establishing contact with her.

Exceptionally intelligent, Sevda has taught herself several languages in spite of being refused any formal education after the age of eleven. Within two days of receiving a Bio-Aid, she has downloaded all the necessary fixes to over-ride the constraints, leaving her free to communicate. Within another day she is routinely communicating with several men and women from other countries.

Sevda quickly discovers the range of lies she has been fed about distant countries and their dangers. She is especially fascinated by the culture of the USA's west coast. Within a week she is in hourly contact with a young man who lives in Sausalito, California. His name is Dane.

'Short for Danewald, apparently,' he tells her.

It does not take them long to fall in love. When he learns she is only five feet tall, Dane gives her the nickname 'Chiquita'. They are soon plotting her departure.

'Chiquita,' he tells her, 'Chiquita, my love. I've been researching the best way to get you out. It is not without danger. I've borrowed money from my uncle. I'm going to collect you myself.'

'Dane, life here is miserable. But what happens if you get caught?'

'I don't care. I want to be with you. That's not possible where you are, so you must come here. It's the only way.'

He explains the plan. By now they are in continuous contact. Their brainwaves have begun to synchronize, to the point where they can guess each other's next thought.

Three days later, Dane flies into Ankara to begin a two-week vacation that supposedly takes in multiple locations, requiring a rental car and a week at each beachside villa. His 'uncle' has briefed him on how to block any mental probes, a precaution that proves unnecessary. Within an hour of his arrival he has cleared customs and is driving towards the town of Sirnak in a rented SUV.

Together Dane and Sevda make a dangerous nighttime crossing of the border unaided then travel through the Syrian desert towards Lebanon, from where they will take a ship out of Beirut. The second border-crossing requires extra bribes but once paid, they are escorted a few miles into Lebanon by the border guards.

'It's safer this way,' they assure the young couple.

Neither of the young couple has ever before felt so frightened. Holding her lover's hand with both of her own, Sevda silently asks: 'What if they are kidnapping us?'

More experienced at using the capabilities of his Bio-Aid, Dane has been monitoring the thoughts of both driver and escort. His intuition detects no malice. He tells her: 'It's OK, Sevda. I believe these are honorable men.'

Fortunately, his intuition is accurate. The men deliver them to a bus station in the center of Qaa. One briefs them before leaving.

'In this town are mainly Catholics. But there are also many crooks as well as many Turkish and Syrian spies, so be careful and trust no one. From here you can get a bus all the way to Beirut. Go straight to the ticket office, over there. Do not stay long in the city. Make sure you catch the first boat that you can.'

Fifteen minutes later the couple board a bus. A day later they leave Beirut's ancient port, aboard a ferry bound for Cyprus and safety. By the time they leave the city they are less than a day ahead of the search team dispatched from Sirnak to find and kill them both.

Thirty-six hours after arriving at the transit port of Larnaca they land at San Francisco International Airport. As a refugee Sevda is welcomed into an increasingly liberal democracy. One with an ageing population that needs and welcomes young, intelligent and economically active young people. The couple's wedding is arranged within a week.

~

'The bride is very beautiful, don't you think?' asks Peter.

They are standing outside the church while photographs are taken. Angela stumbles over her answer.

'Yes. Yes, she is. I mean… yes, she's very beautiful. They're both very beautiful.'

Peter looks at her with mixed emotions. He is no longer angry at her refusal, but they range from sympathy and concern to love. There follows an awkward moment. It is the first time they have met since Angela turned down his request for reconciliation.

Their eyes meet. At the same instant, both of them splutter aloud and burst out laughing. In between giggles, Angela tells him: 'I was trying to be so cool!'

'Me too! Royally screwed that up, didn't we?'

Angela has rested her hand on his shoulder. They make eye contact again. This time Angela opens her arms wide and says, 'Give me a hug, Peter. Are we friends at least?'

The former couple embrace, tenderly and delicately, but they are careful that only the upper halves of their bodies touch. After a second they separate. Peter offers her a tissue. Angela wipes her eyes and blows her nose. She says, 'Look at me!' Then asks: 'Am I a mess?'

'Not in the least, Angela. You're the belle of the ball,' he assures her.

'Thank you, Peter.'

'It's good to see you again, Angela. I wanted to come to the wedding. I hope you don't mind. I like your brother Dane, his new wife too. And I admire their bravery.'

'It's fine Peter, honestly! They told me you were coming. In fact, they insisted. Not that they needed to. I know how much you've helped them.'

'It's the most romantic story. I'm not staying for the reception, but I want to wish them well, and all the best for the future.' A moment later he asks: 'You're keeping well too, I hope?'

Before Angela answers, their conversation is interrupted by the photographer. Waving his arms he is shouting.

'Everyone, everyone, together please! Thank you. Thank you!'

Peter and Angela stand next to each other for the group photo, two among fifty. Angela places her hand through the gap between Peter's arm and chest and grips onto a bicep while the entire party shout "Cheeeese".

A minute later the former couple continue their conversation.

'I'm sorry about us,' Angela tells him. Then she adds, without explanation 'But I think it's for the best. Don't you?'

Peter is about to answer when Sevda and Dane join them.

'I hope you don't mind us interrupting you, only Sevda here wants to give this to you, Angela.'

Sevda hands over the small bouquet she is carrying. Dane explains.

'In her family, it is not thrown. They traditionally give it to their favorite relative. For good luck. And for fertility!'

Angela shrieks with delight. She hugs and kisses the cheek of her new sister-in-law, shouting aloud.

'Oh, Sevda, That's so lovely! Thank you! Thank you!'

While the two new sisters talk excitedly, Peter takes hold of Dane's arm. He hands the young man an envelope that contains a sizable gift, together with a letter telling him there is no need to repay the money he borrowed.

'Please, don't open it until later.'

The two ladies have overheard. Sevda kisses Peter on the cheek and tells him they have decided to name their first-born after him.

Angela's hands rise to her mouth. Her eyes water as Dane joins his wife in hugging their 'uncle'.

The new couple ask the photographer to take their photo while they kiss Peter on each cheek. Angela is asked to join them. Knowing their history, Sevda mischievously whispers to her sister-in-law.

'One day, it will make a wonderful memento for you both.'

There is no further opportunity for Peter and Angela to hold a private conversation before everyone departs for the reception. Peter travels home, feeling both elated and dejected. When he reaches his apartment, it feels exceptionally empty, lifeless.

He changes and makes a warm drink, before relaxing on the sofa. He remains determined not to use his intuition to answer the question that occupies his mind to the exclusion of all else.

'That would be unfair,' he reminds himself.

He picks up the journal and re-reads the passage where Jake and Mona are reconciled and leave together. He is close to tears. He speculates aloud.

'Maybe I am just a romantic, after all.'

Angela spends the first half-hour of the reception hoping that Peter has changed his mind and has decided to remain. She is disappointed.

THIRTY-FIVE

Standing behind her grey-tinted desk, Maureen watches the shadow of passing clouds lighten and darken hillsides on the opposite side of the Bay. From Oakland to the Golden Gate a patchwork moves slowly over the ground: irregular areas a half-mile across glow golden or emerald green one minute, grey or dark green the next.

She knows Angela is approaching and that her student is about to turn the corner in front of the building. Her eyes are torn between the fleeting pageant flowing across the hillsides ahead of her and the graceful, floating movement of her charge. After indecision and a rapid glance downwards, they settle on distant hills. Her gaze remains there until a minute later, when Angela knocks three times on her door.

'Come in!' shouts Maureen, just loud enough to be heard.

A glass of water is placed and sipped, an update on progress is given and a brief consideration of a few personal issues is completed before the two women, younger pupil and older mentor, settle into a discussion about the main purpose of today's meeting: Peter.

Angela begins by telling the story of his visit to her home.

'When he came to see me, I did what you told me. I've never felt so awful,' she admits. 'I miss him,' she adds.

In a rare display of affection, her words prompt Maureen to take hold of her hand.

'I also met him at Sevda's wedding, you know. I wanted to throw my arms around him. I don't know why I stopped.'

'Angela,' begins Maureen, 'it's wonderful that you are feeling these emotions so powerfully. Wonderful. If you remember how you felt or rather, didn't allow yourself to feel when we first met. Your progress is remarkable.'

Unused to such compliments, Angela's eyelids flutter and her cheeks flush. *It must at least in part be because of her proximity to Peter*, thinks Maureen, but this she does not say to her student. Maureen waits a short while for Angela to calm before continuing with an instruction.

'You must concentrate on absorbing and understanding these feelings. The closer you embrace them and the more they feel a natural part of you, then the stronger and more capable you become. It is through acknowledging our weakness that we become strong. Do you understand?'

'I…I think so,' is Angela's uncertain answer.

For the first time, Maureen senses that Angela may advance significantly during this lifetime. The belief passes through her mind that *she may even become one of us, a true intuitive*. Maureen knows the significance of such moments: they are a signal of change, that the fabric of pre-determination has been shifted.

'I am so pleased,' she tells her young trainee, 'beyond pleased, actually.'

Angela takes a sip of water. The glass is replaced before Maureen gives her another instruction.

'When you feel ready and only when you feel ready, you must forgive him.'

Angela's heart leaps. She knows there is no point in pretending otherwise to her tutor. Her head nods vigorously.

After Angela's departure, Maureen turns to her computer to dictate her notes.

'*Rarely have I seen such a change in one of my students. Angela first came to Jeff with such a thick barrier and with a strong determination that the world would never again hurt her that he felt she would never be able to progress. I am now confident that within her present lifetime, Angela may after all be able to join us as one of our beloved Sisters.*'

Within a few moments of completing her assessment report Maureen leans back into her chair, closes her eyes and commences a deep meditation. It is one of the most revealing she has ever experienced. Vistas of the new world appear with a clarity and depth of detail she has never before seen. The experience leaves her rapt, and even more determined to ensure it is her future.

Almost a footnote at the end of the meditation, a realization occurs that Angela is a proxy for her. Maureen's role in this life is to prepare and nurture Peter for his role; Angela's is to continue that care, minutely and daily. As a result of their efforts as well as his own, his knowledge will grow, and Angela will remind him of how the sharing of love between two souls will expand their mutual understanding of Love.

Maureen's meditation ends with the certainty that she will be with Peter again, perhaps in her next life. A few minutes later she makes the final arrangements for his introduction to the Order. The entire Sisterhood has insisted that they all attend in person.

'There has never been a more important moment in our long history,' they tell her.

Relaxed and in love with herself once more, Maureen sleeps that night more soundly than ever before.

❧

The morning of Lilian's wedding begins with breakfast in bed and a mad rush to make sure everything is ready. Once those tasks are completed, the remainder of the morning is just the same as every other day. Seated at her computer, Lilian conducts a series of online conferences with their partners, mainly gambling companies and escort agencies.

Lilian is managing the international expansion of her 'sex and dating' website. In between her calls, she cannot resist the temptation to review their new listings and monitors their overnight creations with complete devotion. The majority of such listings are now genuine, and are based in distant countries.

Contrary to her initial fears the advent and worldwide adoption of ubiquitous Bio-Aids has encouraged and fueled a rapid expansion of her business. Easy, many-sided communication proves on its own to be an inept means of finding a suitable partner. Fed by an endless supply of women seeking meaningful relationships and by men seeking sex as well as companionship, the need for an organized relationship brokerage remains as strong as ever.

Led by Lilian's instinctive ability to manipulate the new norms of social media, rebranded and re-packaged as 'the place to find your true love' and with an ever-expanding marketing budget, growth is spectacular. Operations become worldwide and are conducted in multiple languages. Thanks to the early adoption of instantaneous translation – far earlier than their competitors – Lilian's website allows couples from different cultures to meet and converse freely. Once compatible couples are connected, they quickly learn to telepathically communicate across the globe.

Attempts within less liberal countries to suppress women's access to her websites backfire badly, with the result that the female populations of these countries become anxious to leave. Many join what becomes a worldwide phenomenon: a women's revolution.

Political change is inevitable but is resisted to a bitter end. While their hastily prepared political controls work when both people in communication are using doctored devices, they fail when either one is uncensored. Lilian employs teams of the best hackers, many of them female, to ensure her customers' access is unrestrained and continuous. The closure of borders and isolation of entire countries thus eventually prove ineffective, even within China.

Formerly repressed women soon become the most fervent supporters of Lilian's website. In huge numbers they forge links with men in more progressive countries and flee to join them, at much lower risk than hitherto. There follows the largest mass migration in history: single human beings, most commonly of different sexes, migrate to join one another across racial and cultural boundaries. Through an unforeseen means the original, equalizing promise of the Internet is finally realized. Whether by accident or the result of Peter's unseen influence, Lilian's website has become a beneficent, global, social service, as well as its original means of old-fashioned sexual exploitation.

Run by her new partner Diana, its substantial marketing department employs teams of lobbyists and expensive advertisements. Even though its exploitative operations – linked primarily to escort services – remain its largest money-spinner, her efforts ensure public perception of their business is focused on its beneficial effects. The business is soon rumored to be on track to surpass all other social media giants.

By midday, it is time to leave for the service, held open-air at the Lakeside Restaurant in Central Park. Lilian's wealth and fame are already such that one hundred invited guests are surrounded by almost a thousand onlookers, including a multitude of media trucks and camera crews, some automated.

After the service, Peter is seated next to Margaret. It is the first time they have met for months. A gentle breeze lifts the edges of their tablecloths and napkins. Their first course is crayfish. Peter coughs. He feels an immense sense of déja vu. While glancing around to ascertain why, he hears Margaret say

'…into trouble along with those people she's hanging around with?'

Even though her daughter is now successful and on track to be wealthy beyond her imaginings, Margaret is concerned by the sight of Lilian's friends guffawing and laughing. Heedless of their surroundings they are rude to waiters, bar staff and other guests. One of them deliberately knocks over an automated waiter, causing a ripple of laughter.

'Look at them, Peter. They're leeches. The most depressing collection of humanity I've ever met. Their antics disgust me.'

Peter feels a need to defend his daughter.

'They're young Margaret. They'll gain morality as they mature and have kids.'

'Will they? Are you sure? It doesn't look like it to me. They don't care about anyone or anything apart from themselves.'

Peter is uncertain of how much to tell his ex-wife. She appears to be unaware of his rumored clairvoyance.

Margaret continues: 'Most of the youngsters I've met are wonderful by comparison to these. They work actively to promote local communities, they call-out flagging or corrupt politicians, they're forever leafleting about how to counteract the extreme heat we get every summer. By contrast all Lilian's friends do is drink champagne and brag, her included.'

Their discussion is interrupted when a succession of admirers, mainly young female guests, ask for his autograph. In spite of their rudeness, Peter is magnanimous. He speaks in turn into each of their Bio-Aids. Within moments his becomes the default voice on their devices. They thank him and run excitedly back to their less-pushy friends.

'I hear you have a new girlfriend, Peter,'

Peter does not wish to lie but neither does he want to tell Margaret the truth.

'Ye -es, kind of. She's lovely. I mean she's a lovely person: caring and loving. I wanted her to come but she didn't feel it was right. This is a family occasion after all, isn't it?'

'If those words are hers then she sounds very wise,' responds Margaret. 'Mind you, I suppose she will become part of your family sooner or later, won't she?'

Margaret raises her glass of red wine towards the happy couple while Peter answers.

'Maybe Margaret, maybe. I haven't asked her.'

'Well *maybe* you should. It's what every woman wants, whatever they say. A formal declaration of eternal love.'

Peter tells her of the wedding he attended a few days before.

'Angela's brother. A delightful young man. He took a great risk by flying to Turkey to rescue his future bride. It's such a romantic story.'

Margaret stares at him for several seconds but decides to say nothing of the change in his character. Their conversation ends on friendly terms. Peter is pleased to feel that Margaret's bitterness, while still present, is diminishing. He thanks her. She has no idea why.

THIRTY-SIX

The call from Maureen is a surprise, a pleasant but very abrupt one. She asks Peter to come to see her as soon as possible. They arrange for him to visit her the following morning.

'Come at seven,' she insists. 'To my home. We can watch the sunrise together. It will make a pleasant change.'

Her call is followed by a click as she replaces the receiver on her reproduction 1980s handset. Their previous meetings have been at her office, or his. The call is unusual for another reason too: most have been arranged well in advance, or telepathically.

Alone that evening over dinner, Peter wonders why Maureen has called. He can discern no specific reason: his mind *or hers* has somehow switched off. He sleeps fitfully, worse even than during a full moon, and rises before five to exercise and meditate.

Less than two hours later he arrives at her home, a few minutes early.

'Wait one moment,' is her answer over the intercom, 'I'll buzz you in. Take the elevator and press the button marked "P".'

Seconds later the external door opens. He enters and takes the elevator to the penthouse floor. Maureen emerges smiling from her front door, the only one on that level.

'It's good to see you again, Peter. You're looking very well!'

Peter thanks her and enters her home.

'I invite very few people here,' announces Maureen. 'Not that I'm lonely. I'm in demand more than you might think. This is my sanctuary, somewhere I can switch-off. I'm sure you of all people understand the need for that.'

'Especially at the moment,' is Peter's answer. 'Like you, I don't have much time to myself. At least not during the daytime.'

'Yes. Well, let's not waste time with idle chatter shall we. This way please and do take a seat.'

The apartment is large, taking up the entire top floor of the building. The décor throughout is clean and minimalist. The main lounge takes up half the floor, so has three sides with floor to ceiling windows. Two large, original artworks are displayed on the fourth, interior wall.

At the far end of the room are two large, white sofas placed at a right angle to each other. Facing the glass corner doors, each has a clear over a low coffee table view of different parts of the Bay. The scenery is spectacular, including the Golden Gate Bridge, Sausalito and, in the distance, Oakland.

'That's quite some view,' remarks Peter.

'Yes, I suppose it is. You know, I almost don't notice it now. Except when I need to sit quietly of course. Then it's wonderful: totally relaxing. It's a little cloudy and cool this morning, otherwise I'd suggest we sit on the terrace to watch the sun rise.'

Maureen points to her right.

'We can see it through this window anyway – it faces East. It must be just appearing above the horizon. If there were no clouds, that is.'

'This view must make you feel like a Goddess, peering down at ordinary mortals below.'

Maureen ignores his joke about her abilities and serves tea. 'English breakfast, is that OK?'

Peter nods. Inside his mind, he hears the words *Let's move on now, shall we. We can continue to use our mouths to speak.* Peter nods his head once more in acknowledgement, silently replying *I prefer to actually speak when we can, don't you?*

'I'd like to ask you about who all these people are,' begins Peter.

Maureen's eyes rise from her cup. He elaborates.

'The ones behind all the wars and nonsense in the world. I sense a conspiracy behind so much of what happens. So much so, I wonder if I'm becoming paranoid!'

A brief chuckle escapes his lips.

'Peter, you know perfectly well that our world is run by an elite. They are not so well organized as you fear, but they use their wealth and power to consolidate and retain their position. It's always been so. The problem now is they have far better technology to do this, and a docile population to manipulate. In that sense these new devices truly are the 'opiate of the masses', aren't they?'

He looks down at Maureen's wrist. She does not wear a Bio-Aid, nor any jewelry. She continues her explanation.

'We send out Love. That's what we do. It's all we can do and it's all we need to do. Time alone will show us for certain whether it's enough to counter their efforts.'

'There are many more like us, aren't there'' asks Peter.

'Yes, and you will meet them within a week,' is her reply.

Maureen does not elaborate. Instead, she changes the subject. That is for another day: very soon. The arrangements are set and, under instructions from her, his secretary has ensured his diary is blocked out for the day, now less than a week away.

'I want to talk to you about Angela. More precisely, you and Angela. You are wasting your time looking elsewhere for a soulmate. I hope you don't mind my interfering. It's just that you don't know the facts. And, for whatever reason, you are preventing yourself from seeing them.'

Startled, Peter nearly chokes on his first mouthful of English Breakfast.

'I don't mind at all,' he replies, recovering his composure. 'I have deliberately refrained from using my abilities. It doesn't seem right to do so. Please, tell me what you know.'

Maureen outlines Angela's troubled past: a broken home, an abusive fiancé, failed relationships, and a miserable job.

'At which she excelled, by the way.'

Then she tells him of Angela's attempts to deal with those disadvantages, how she turned to Jeff 'Pop, as you call him', and how he cured her of much of her pain and angst.

'"Angela has faults, but she is very brave," he told me one day. He admired her a great deal. I told him it's our faults that make us interesting.'

Maureen pauses to sip her tea and to wait for Peter to lower his cup.

'She came close to having an affair with him, you know. They were lovers for nearly a year before he went into hospital. Of course, they were not *in love*. They never had sexual intercourse, it was more a question of gratitude and reciprocal care. Her life improved beyond measure while she was with him. And towards the end, she visited him practically every day.'

'I had no idea how much…'

Maureen begins to scold.

'Well, you should have. She didn't want to tell you of course but, if you had asked, she would have done so. You were so wrapped up in your own development, you barely looked into her heart.'

'It felt wrong for me to do so,' he responds.

'Yes, it is. I suppose,' admitted Maureen. *Like all rules, they need breaking now and again*, she thinks. Her thought is shared with Peter.

A long silence ensues. Both stare out of the window. Maureen closes her eyes and then opens them again, calm once more.

'I'm sorry, I don't mean to tell you off. It's understandable, and I shouldn't criticize you. After all, look at where you are now, Peter. And how far you have come in just a few months.'

He assures Maureen he is untroubled by her scolding.

'Peter, I'm just trying to tell you to look at Angela sympathetically. Jeff felt guilty about their near affair. "I should have said no to her staying over. If it wasn't for my medication, we would have become lovers. Never should I have even thought of being with her, I'm her healer," he admitted to me one day. I forgave him for thinking of her in that way, of course. Who wouldn't? He was such a wonderful man.'

There is another long silence while both sip tea and stare out of the window at the rising sun, whose lower limb is coming into view between cloud and mountain peak. Their contemplations are ended by Maureen.

'You know she may never become enlightened, don't you? At least not during this lifetime. Keen and earnest enough of course, but I'm afraid Angela may not have what it takes.'

Peter raises an eyebrow as he turns to look directly at Maureen. His brow lowers, leaving a quizzical look on his face. She explains.

'Partly it's her concentration, or lack of it. It's also a lack of discernment. She is devoted to her spiritual development and certainly enjoys the ceremonies, the get-togethers and pageants. If I can call them that - they're not very colorful, after all! Once she realizes those are for tourists and journeymen, she will progress. But that will not happen quickly.'

'I know, Maureen. I've felt that for some time.'

'I'm telling you all this now so that, when you see her, you don't waste your breath talking about the true nature of reality or some other rubbish she won't be interested in. Just tell her how you feel. She loves you, you know. She is in love with you, I mean.'

'But... she's with another man.'

Maureen turns her gaze to meet Peter's. Her next words are stern.

'Honestly, Peter. You should know better. She's hurt. What do you think she is going to do: fall into your arms the minute you run back to her? Of course, there's no other man! I know you're only a man but, for a healer with your abilities… Really!'

Peter has no idea what to say. Maureen tells him: 'Take your mind back to when you last saw her and look into her eyes.'

He does as she asks. He first closes his eyes then casts his mind back to his visit to Angela's home. A few seconds later he understands.

'Oh! The light, you mean.'

'Yes, the light. Better still, look at her now! Close your eyes again.'

Maureen closes her eyes too and transports their etheric bodies to Angela's home.

'I had no idea we could do this so easily,' is Peter's admiring but silent, telepathic comment, noted but otherwise ignored by Maureen. Her response amuses them both. *You still have some things to learn. Good!*

Within a moment of seeing Angela's aura, Peter knows just how deeply she is upset.

I had no idea, is his second silent communication, completing as Maureen returns them to her apartment.

'Well, you know now,' is Maureen's verbal riposte.

'I must go to her.'

'Yes, you must. She is a soulmate, even if she is far behind you in development.'

'How could I have missed it?'

'Did you ever truly look?'

A blank expression appears on Peter's face. Maureen recognizes it as both guilt and repentance.

'I guess not. Thank you, Maureen. In fact, what can I ever do to thank you?'

'There will be a time for that, very soon. You and I – people like us – we must help each other, whenever we can. In fact, there's something in your diary for next week. We will talk about it before then, but only after you have sorted out your personal life. Go now, you must not delay any longer!'

They smile. Both stand. As they walk to her door, she offers one last piece of advice.

'Take her on another holiday, Peter. You both need one. But after next week.'

Peter's mouth opens as if to ask a question, but Maureen holds up a finger.

'Not now.'

Maureen offers her hand, but Peter leans forward. He holds her shoulders and kisses her cheek. Maureen's face reddens. When they separate, her right hand rises involuntarily to her chest. She pushes him over the threshold and closes the door.

After it closes Maureen looks up to the ceiling. Her hand returns to her breast. Wistful, to the empty room she speaks her next words aloud.

'We were soulmates and lovers once too, you know. But not here, not on this planet.'

The import of her words reaches Peter as the elevator descends, but they are sensed only as indistinct good wishes, as they were destined to be.

Alone in her apartment Maureen smiles in anticipation, knowing they will again be soulmates and lovers, sometime in a future where they will be capable of creating and manifesting at will. In the meantime, she is delighted he has blank spots. *It makes him human* she decides.

Her final words of the morning are spoken aloud, to confirm their truth.

'You will know within days that you are our Master of the Sun. But we will not be lovers again just yet, not in this lifetime.'

THIRTY-SEVEN

Peter arrives by car and rushes to Angela's door. Once there, he stops to brush a hand across his hair and to take a deep breath. This time he has not practiced what to say.

He ignores the bell and raps the door with his knuckles.

'Why are you here?' shouts Angela from inside. 'I can see you on my screen, you know.'

'Please, Angela! I'd like to talk to you. Please!'

He is about to rap the door again when he hears its electronic bolt whirr. The door opens. Wearing pajama bottoms and a loose-fitting t-shirt, Angela is stood several feet back from the door. Its remote control is in her hand.

'What do you want?'

'Can I come in?'

Angela stares into his eyes, taking several seconds to answer. Her hands wave up and down either side of her body.

'I can't see you like this, I haven't even washed yet.'

As his eyes adjust to the reduced light in her hallway Peter can see she is wearing no make-up.

Unwashed, her house in a mess: this is not the moment of reconciliation that Angela ever pictured. A loud exhale issues from her mouth before Angela speaks again.

'Okay. You can wait in the lounge if you want. I'll be a few minutes though.'

Peter moves forwards, hoping to embrace her. Angela raises her hand to stop him. As she turns her head away, she implores: 'Please, Peter. No! Wait in there, I'll talk to you when I'm ready.'

He turns and shuts the door while Angela makes her way into the bathroom. Then he enters the lounge and sits on a small, two-seater sofa. He hears water running in the shower so settles down to wait. For the briefest moment his hand searches for a jacket pocket and his crossword book.

'I haven't needed that for some time,' he mutters.

Eyes meander around the room, which is clean but not tidy. An empty chocolate wrapper and two used mugs rest on the coffee table; an open paperback lies face-down on the floor with the remains of a chocolate biscuit crumpled adjacent. A potted fern is beginning to wilt. Doubt enters his mind.

Maybe she'll turn me down again.

Peter closes his eyes and focuses his attention onto recalling her face. He apologizes to it then visualizes golden light pouring into the crown of her head and spreading throughout her body.

I should have done this months ago, he knows, *although it wouldn't have had the same effect then.*

He smiles, knowing he has done all he is allowed and willing to do.

Emerging from the shower, Angela is wrapped in a large towel. Peter looks up, his eyes as imploring as any poodle. His face makes her smile.

'I need to put some clean clothes on. I won't be long, I promise,' is her answer.

She slips into the bedroom, closing its door behind her.

Less than two minutes later, Angela returns wearing a skirt and loose-fitting top *with no bra,* notices Peter. She sits on the single seater chair opposite. Keeping a stern look on her face, she looks across at him and says, 'You hurt me. Really hurt me. I should have told you about Jeff and his money. I know that was wrong but…'

'Please Angela,' interrupts Peter, 'I don't care about any of that. I just don't care. And it's me who should apologize to you. I'm sorry I treated you so badly. All I know is that I'm happy when I'm with you and unhappy when I'm not.'

Her face is unmoved until he tells her: 'No, that's not all. It's much more than that. *Much* more. When we first met, I was entranced. I couldn't understand why a beautiful young woman would be attracted to me. My feelings for you then were strong and lustful, but not truly *loving.* That's what they were: possessive and sexual, and grateful.'

He took a deep breath before continuing: 'It was much later, long after we'd been living together that I realized you were more than this to me. Now I know I love you. I'm in love with you. I don't need anything else. I just want you.'

Angela recognizes the sound of truth in his words: spontaneous, melodious, and flowing. A smile creases the corners of her mouth.

As she begins to move forward, Peter leaps to his feet. He steps towards her but traps his left foot inside the nearest leg of the coffee table and stumbles. Her hands reach over to prevent him from falling.

After an imbalanced moment they are standing together laughing, caressing and kissing.

'I've so missed you,' he announces.

'Me too. I'm so happy you're here! You belong with me.'

A moment later, she pulls her head backwards and asks: 'Your feelings towards me had still better be lustful though, Peter?'

'You bet they are!' he exclaims, lifting her in both arms.

THIRTY-EIGHT

At two hundred and forty feet long, ninety-six feet high, and one hundred and forty-two feet wide, the basilica of Saint Maximin is the largest Gothic edifice in Provence, France. A bastion of the Catholic church, it contains the skull of Mary Magdalene, who lived and died nearby after fleeing persecution in Jerusalem during the first century AD.

Always keen to promote reconciliation and understanding but cognizant of Mary's warning about physical buildings never usurping human hearts, Maureen recommends this church as the most fitting place to hold the ceremony to introduce Peter as their new, male head.

'Both a homage and our first step towards a reconciliation with regressive religions,' she declares to the online Members after their votes are counted and the results known, 'as well as a step towards our future with men.'

Tumultuous online applause follows. The half dozen most trusted Sisters who stand beside her congratulate Maureen on her selection.

'It is a magnificent choice,' says one, 'both historic and symbolic.'

Before concluding their meeting, Maureen reminds all present: 'Peter may be physically a man, but he embodies the *divine feminine* in remarkable degree. As foretold, his powers of foresight and depth of compassion will help to guide the whole of mankind to glory.'

One month later Peter, Angela and Maureen are invited to join President Whitmore on Air Force One for the flight to Marseilles. The president spends as much time as possible with her guests, discussing and questioning all three about their families as well as on ethical and spiritual matters. Shortly before the airplane touches down, she apologizes and tells them they will meet again inside the basilica.

'Duty calls!'

On arrival, President Whitmore is welcomed and joined by the French president, their first female leader and a hitherto unpublicised member of the growing Order. The two presidents fly together by helicopter. They spend time before the service in an hotel adjacent to the basilica, which is cordoned-off and secured during their presence by both countries' secret services.

Although streets and roads along the route are closed to other traffic, the following cavalcade takes nearly an hour to reach the small town of Saint-Maximin-la-Sainte-Baume. For security reasons local residents have been excluded from the square and a wide area surrounding the church.

When their limousine arrives at the square in front of the basilica, the entire party is directed through the main entrance. Once inside, they walk down the centre aisle past the assembled members. All heads turn to watch. Feeling very self-conscious, Angela is seated by an attendant in the front row to the left of the altar. Peter and

Maureen are led to an anteroom at its rear. While they walk, Maureen takes hold of his arm. He has never seen her so excited.

'I can't tell you how wonderful this moment is for me,' she tells him. 'I've waited my whole adult life for this day.'

They are introduced to President Leclerc, who kisses Peter on both cheeks and expresses her delight in voluble English. The party then march together into the church, where they are greeted with impromptu applause. They sit together in a row next to Angela.

Maureen has eschewed the curé's offer to use the pulpit and instead stands at the appointed time of midday on a temporary daïs placed in front to the altar. As soon as she begins to speak, Peter shifts uneasily in his seat. He leans towards Angela and says, 'There's something very wrong. I'm not sure what. Please get ready to run.'

Angela is perplexed. Her mouth opens, her eyes dart left and right. Pointing to the left of the huge organ, Peter's next sentence is more urgent.

'Through that door. Get outside as quickly as possible. Go now.'

Amid a rising hubbub of concern, he turns to both presidents to warn them too. As he speaks Peter can hear a commotion outside.

In the centre of the square there is consternation inside the main security truck. Its aerial monitoring systems are blinking red. They suddenly switch off. Standing directly outside the truck surveying the square, the French commandant is alerted. He issues orders to place the anti-missile batteries to automatic intercept. His response is too late.

Inside the church, Peter points the presidents towards the same door, then leaps to his feet and shouts: 'Please, everyone. Leave through the main doors as quickly as possible. Now! Go, now!'

Having shouted his warning, Peter rushes over to Maureen and grasps her hand. They follow the two presidents. The presidential security details assist their escape, pointing them down a corridor and out through a side-door.

Small arms fire fails to halt the drone, which explodes as it strikes the top of the western wall of the basilica, just below the roof. Debris showers the entire inside of the church. Although the main structure of the church remains intact, many are crushed by falling masonry and timbers.

The few seconds head-start they gain over the confused assembly are enough to ensure the presidents are outside the church before the drone strikes. Both are manhandled into their respective armoured limousines, so survive the attack frightened but unharmed. Behind them, Maureen, Angela and Peter are bundled into their limousine by his security detail. Seconds later it is rocked by the explosion and showered with debris. They are battered and in shock, but their injuries are slight. Standing adjacent, Peter's security team are injured by the blast but survive.

Some of those members who managed to reach the square are killed by falling masonry or injured by shattering glass, some seriously. More than half of the two thousand members are less lucky: the majority of fatalities and serious injuries are among those remaining inside.

There is initial concern about a follow-up strike, so the presidential entourage is evacuated, and the members are led away to the edge of town. A short while later the aerial monitoring system returns to normal operation, the anti-missile batteries are fully active, and there are overflights by French fighter aircraft instructed to shoot down '*tout ce qui vole.*'

The first ambulances arrive within minutes and begin to ferry the injured to hospital. In all, over two hundred members, all female, have died at the scene and another four hundred have serious injuries.

Press reports immediately assume the target was one or both of the presidents, spurring conspiracy theories of all kinds. Maureen has no doubt that the real target is their Order. Many of those killed or injured are leaders of some kind in their home countries. As soon as she and Peter are next alone, they meditate together to determine exactly who or what lies behind the attack.

'We must be careful. There will be more,' Peter tells her.

EPILOGUE

All the issues raised by Peter's tale are of course still developing, multiplying or resolving around the two of us while I sit in the restaurant with him. His bodyguards are seated two tables away.

By this time, he is acting as an advisor to both American and British governments, and is a regular writer, blogger and speaker on popular media. He has also published details of his work as a healer, although he has never revealed any details of his relationship with the Sisters of Mary Magdalene. Hence my enquiring about his route to fame, and his interest in my new work as a software designer – a task to which I would never have guessed I was suited while still an accountant.

The clarity of Peter's writings helps all of us to understand and to foresee the problems our new Bio-AIDs bring. His work also explains and demonstrates how we can acquire intuition and telepathy, through meditation rather than through technology. He helps us to better recognize false healers and prophets, as well as to uncover some of the hidden, self-interested conspiracies that too often dominate our lives. If we follow his path, they teach us too how we may all gain direct experience of the Divine, of our true nature.

Some of the technologies uncovered in this tale are still in their infancy. Nanobiotechnology, for example. Most of us believe that far more complex biological and working quantum computers will be with us within our lifetimes, perhaps during the next decade. These may well be far more capable than we are.

Artificial Intelligence (AI) is also in its infancy. As of today, there remains fundamental disagreement over what constitutes its 'intelligence', and virtually every application that we class as such could equally be described as advanced machine learning. As storage of data has reduced to negligible cost, so the uses of AI and other technologies have increased. The combination of these technologies may well decide our fate and may choose to do so quickly.

The social and societal implications of all this are barely understood, and of course include the potential for extended dictatorship and slavery or, at least a docile servitude for all mankind. Or our absorption, or extinction.

Anyone who has studied history will know that cooperation and community between individuals maximises the effects of our efforts. Equally, they will know that recent history shows us that placing primacy on communal interests rather than individual rights usually leads to manipulation, dictatorship and arbitrary execution.

Notions of individual freedom and liberal values, of collective effort and community, of control and direction have all been challenged and revised as these uses have expanded. As have our notions of morality, of humanity's place in the universe, of right and wrong. Even of our understanding of consciousness and intelligence.

There are thus likely to be consequences beyond the technological and societal. Consequences that affect what it is to be human, to be part of the *Universe* and of our home within it, and of our experience of the *Divine*.

Since my meeting with Peter and while writing this book, I have confirmed that it is possible to gain intuition as a result of devoted meditation. This and other talents are a result of training our minds. As Peter notes, they are not, as is often supposed, the preserve of mystical or spiritual experience of the kind reserved for ascetics and hermits. I confess I never quite believed it before.

I also now know that spiritual experience, by which I mean a direct connection with our source energy, goes much further than I ever thought possible. Spiritual knowledge gives us a beyond-the-universe-as-we-experience-it perspective from which to view our humanity, our place in the world, and our view of what is right and wrong. That perspective is *Love*. The eternal and single source from which we all spring and to which we return.

I am grateful for what my friendship with Peter has brought into my life. I hope that you are too.

Raymond

Printed in Great Britain
by Amazon